MAPS OF THE IMAGINATION

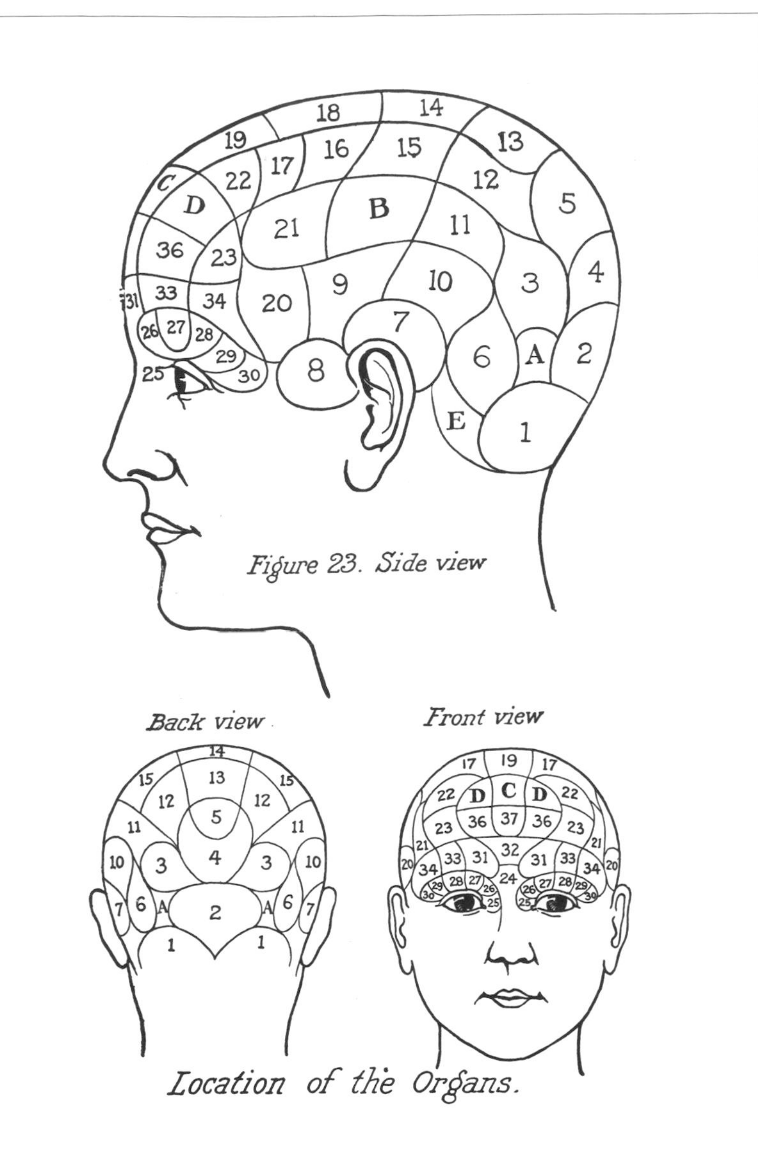

Figure 23. Side view

Location of the Organs.

MAPS OF THE IMAGINATION: THE WRITER AS CARTOGRAPHER

PETER TURCHI

TRINITY UNIVERSITY PRESS
SAN ANTONIO, TEXAS

Published by Trinity University Press
San Antonio, Texas 78212

Book and Jacket design by DJ Stout and Julie Savasky, Pentagram, Austin, Texas

Illustration credits appear on page 243

Printed in China
∞ The paper used in this publication meets the minimum requirements of the American National Standard for Information Sciences—Permanence of Paper for Printed Library Materials, ANSI Z39.48-1992.

Library of Congress Cataloging in Publication Data

Turchi, Peter, 1960–
Maps of the imagination : the writer as cartographer / Peter Turchi.
p. cm.
Includes bibliographical references.
ISBN 1-59534-005-X (hardback : alk. paper)
1. Fiction—History and criticism—Theory, etc. 2. Cartography. I. Title.
PN3331.T87 2004
809.3'92—dc22 2004008882

08 07 06 05 04 / 5 4 3 2 1

This book is for Laura and Reed,

for my mother and sister,

and for my father, who made his own way.

Tomorrow
we shall have to think up signs,
sketch a landscape, fabricate a plan
on the double page
of day and paper.
Tomorrow, we shall have to invent,
once more,
the reality of this world.

—OCTAVIO PAZ, "JANUARY FIRST"
TRANSLATED BY ELIZABETH BISHOP

A novel examines not reality but existence. And existence is not what has occurred, existence is the realm of human possibilities, everything that man can become, everything he's capable of. Novelists draw up *the map of existence* by discovering this or that human possibility.

—MILAN KUNDERA, *THE ART OF THE NOVEL*

TABLE OF CONTENTS

METAPHOR: OR, THE MAP

The writer is an explorer.

Every step is an advance into new land.

RALPH WALDO EMERSON

THE EARLIEST extant alphabetic texts, the earliest extant geographical maps, and the earliest extant map of the human brain date back to the same general period: around 3,000 B.C. While no one can say for certain when the first writing and mapping occurred, the reasons for recording who we are, where we are, what is, and what might be haven't changed much over time. The earliest maps are thought to have been created to help people find their way and to reduce their fear of the unknown. We want to know the location of what we deem life-sustaining (hunting grounds and sources of fresh water, then; now, utility lines and grocery stores) and life-threatening (another people's lands; the toxic runoff from a landfill). Now as then, we record great conflicts and meaningful discoveries.* We organize information on maps in order to see our knowledge in a new way. As a result, maps suggest explanations; and while explanations reassure us, they also inspire us to ask more questions, consider other possibilities.

To ask for a map is to say, "Tell me a story."

* Several early maps, etched into clay tablets, appear to have been made with an eye toward another essential of civilization: taxation.

WRITING IS OFTEN discussed as two separate acts — though in practice they overlap, intermingle, and impersonate each other. They differ in emphasis, but are by no means merely sequential. If we do them well, both result in discovery. One is the act of *exploration:* some combination of premeditated searching and undisciplined, perhaps only partly conscious rambling. This includes scribbling notes, considering potential scenes, lines, or images, inventing characters, even writing drafts. History tells us that exploration is assertive action in the face of uncertain assumptions, often involving false starts, missteps, and surprises — all familiar parts of the writer's work. If we persist, we discover our story (or poem, or novel) within the world of that story. The other act of writing we might call *presentation*. Applying knowledge, skill, and talent, we create a document meant to communicate with, and have an effect on, others. The purpose of a story or poem, unlike that of a diary, is not to record our experience but to create a context for, and to lead the reader on, a journey.

That is to say, at some point we turn from the role of Explorer to take on that of Guide.

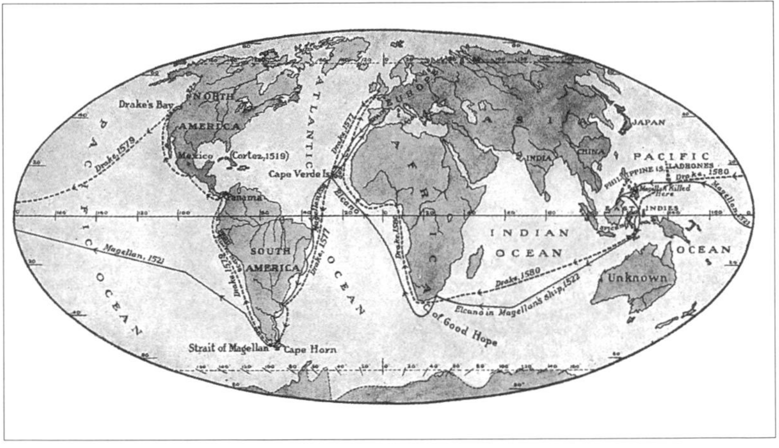

FIG. 1 **THE FIRST VOYAGES AROUND THE WORLD**

> If this book of mine fails to take a straight course, it is because I am lost in a strange region; I have no map.
>
> — GRAHAM GREENE, *THE END OF THE AFFAIR*

ARTISTIC CREATION is a voyage into the unknown. In our own eyes, we are off the map. The excitement of potential discovery is accompanied by anxiety, despair, caution, perhaps, perhaps boldness, and, always, the risk of failure. Failure can take the form of our becoming hopelessly lost, or pointlessly lost, or not finding what we came for (though that last is sometimes happily accompanied by the discovery of something we didn't anticipate, couldn't even imagine before we found it). We strike out for what we believe to be uncharted waters, only to find ourselves sailing in someone else's bathtub. Those are the days it seems there is nothing new to discover but the limitations of our own experience and understanding.

Some of the oldest stories we know, including creation myths, were attempts to make sense of the world. Those early storytellers invented answers to the mysteries all around them. Why does the rain come? Why does it stop? If a child is created by two adults, from where did the first two adults originate? What is the earth like beyond what we have seen, and beyond what the people we know have seen? What lies beyond the stars?

The stories and poems we write today rarely take on the task of explaining natural elements or the failure of crops; for those answers, we turn to science or some other form of belief. Nevertheless, in every piece we write, we contemplate a world; and as that world would not otherwise exist, we create it even as we discover it. Some imagined places are as exotic as the deserted island of Daniel Defoe's *Robinson Crusoe* and Robert Louis Stevenson's Treasure Island, Thomas More's Utopia, Jonathan Swift's Lilliput, Aldous Huxley's Brave New World, Italo Calvino's Invisible Cities, and Jorge Luis Borges's Tlön,

Uqbar, and Orbis Tertius. Some writers use settings more familiar but make those places unmistakably their own: Jane Austen's England, Nathaniel Hawthorne's New England, Charles Dickens's London, Flannery O'Connor's Georgia, Richard Russo's Maine. There is no mistaking E.B. White's New York for John Cheever's, or Joseph Heller's for Ralph Ellison's, or E.L. Doctorow's for Amiri Baraka's.

We might set out intending simply to describe what we see — to open the curtains beyond our desk and report on the landscape outside our window — but even then we describe what *we* see, the way we see it. We know the names of the trees and birds and grasses, or we don't. We're aware of the different types and formations of clouds, or we aren't. Even if we could know it all, at any given moment we would have to choose the evocative description or the scientific fact. No matter how hard we work to be "objective" or "faithful," we create. That isn't to say we get things wrong, but that, from the first word we write — even by choosing the language in which we will write, and by choosing to write rather than to paint or sing — we are defining, delineating, the world that is coming into being.

If we attempt to map the world of a story before we explore it, we are likely either to (a) prematurely limit our exploration, so as to reduce the amount of material we need to consider, or (b) explore at length but, recognizing the impossibility of taking note of everything, and having no sound basis for choosing what to include, arbitrarily omit entire realms of information. The opportunities are overwhelming.*

We face the same challenge with each new story, novel, poem, play, screenplay, or essay: given subject X, or premise Y, or image Z, there are an infinite number of directions in which the work could go. There is no reason to think one direction is inherently better, more artistically valid, than all the others. Yet we must choose—for each individual piece—just one. "The writer,"

* This explains why it can be so difficult for beginning writers to embrace thorough revision — which is to say, to fully embrace exploration. The desire to cling to that first path through the wilderness is both a celebration of initial discovery and fear of the vast unknown.

says Stephen Dobyns, "must discover his or her intention, must discover the meaning of the work. Only after that discovery can the work be properly structured, can the selection and organization of the significant moments of time take place. The writer must know what piece of information to put first and why, what to put second and why, so that the whole work is governed by intention." This is a logical and persuasive argument. We cannot create a structure without understanding its purpose, any more than we would pick up a hammer to make some undetermined building out of nails and wood. But to equate "intention" or "purpose" with meaning is to assume that a poem or story is, ultimately, a rational creation; anyone who has been transported by reading knows, however, that enchantment and beauty transcend the rational.

"Intention" is a useful term when more broadly defined. Intention might be meaning, but for another writer, or another poem or story, the intention might be to depict a particular emotional state, or to explore an ethical dilemma in its complexity, or to understand how a particular character could commit a particular act — or, for that matter, to test the limits of associative movement, or collage structure. Certainly we have some intention(s) for each piece, or we wouldn't be writing. (What explorer in our history books set sail with, as Chuck Berry would say, no particular place to go? An explorer means to explore *something*, something as specific as the Northwest Passage, or the kingdom of Prester John, or as general as the uncharted waters beyond the Azores.) The plan that guides our exploration may or may not be the structure-defining intention of the *map*, the document that leads the reader; experience reminds us that there is often a world of difference between what we hope to find, or think we might find, and what we discover. Goals of our exploration, then, include refining our intention and determining the best way to present it.

Further complicating matters is the fact that our vehicle for discovery is the work we're trying to create. While some writers are able to conduct the exploration of a new world entirely in their minds (Katherine Anne Porter is reputed to have composed and

FIG. 2

revised entire stories in her head, so that she had to type only the final version), and others might work by jotting down individual lines, sketching scenes, and collecting details in notebooks, so that writing a novel is largely a matter of compiling its parts (as it was for Angus Wilson), most of us write a draft, a draft that at some point takes what we feel to be a wrong turn or leads to a dead end. We begin again, only to find we've made a tight circle—our expedition hasn't left sight of camp. Another time, we realize we're starting from the wrong place: we can't get there—where we think we want to go—from here. (We may find *a* story, or poem, in that very first draft, but we want the story that offers us, and our readers, deeper rewards.) Eventually, we find the story not *despite* failed efforts to find the story but *through* those efforts. Without our false starts, we would have gotten nowhere at all. "Writing delivers us into discoveries of what, till we had formed some way to articulate it in language, had remained unformed, had been *unknown* to us," Reginald Gibbons says. "The articulation becomes the knowing; the knowing comes out of the process, and it refuels a further effort at articulation. A sense of ecstatic fruitfulness, of rich discoveries, of voyaging, comes to us in the exhilarating moments of being-in-our-work-in-progress."

IN THE EARLY 1960S, James Lord agreed to pose for Alberto Giacometti for one afternoon, for a sketch. The sketch became a painting, and the session went on for eighteen days. Lord kept a record of Giacometti's process, which was cyclical. Giacometti would stall, sometimes for hours, before beginning to work (some days he had to be coaxed out of a café or kept from destroying earlier drawings in his studio); when he finally sat at the canvas, he would either despair over his inability to do work of any merit or make optimistic noises; before long his tune would shift from optimism to despair, or from despair to talk of suicide. Every day, he would erase, or paint over, the previous day's work. Typically, he would continue until the studio was almost completely dark; typically, at the end of the day he would deem the work a failure.

Lord's slim book *A Giacometti Portrait* makes for perversely heartening reading. The artist tells his subject from the start that "it's impossible ever really to finish anything." By that time in his career, Giacometti had developed a notion of "finished" that assured no work could meet that standard. The reason became clear when, at the end of one day, Lord and the artist had the following conversation:

> I said, "It's difficult for me to imagine how things must appear to you."
>
> "That's exactly what I'm trying to do," he said, "to show how things appear to me."
>
> "But what," I asked, "is the relation between your vision,

the way things appear to you, and the technique that you have at your disposal to translate that vision into something which is visible to others?

"That's the whole drama," he said. "I don't have such a technique."

Having "the technique"—the means, or ability, to get from here to there — is always, and has always been, the issue. The need to find methods of expression led to speech, to drawing, to maps ("*Here's* how you get there"), and to writing. The artist is always developing and refining the techniques he uses to convey his vision, his discoveries. This ongoing development often involves the guide himself being guided; and so we have a long tradition of artists referring to divine intervention, the muses, great artists of the past, and teachers. Odysseus's long journey home, assisted by trustworthy characters, bedeviled by others, mirrors a writer's frustration and exhilaration. Every artist is in

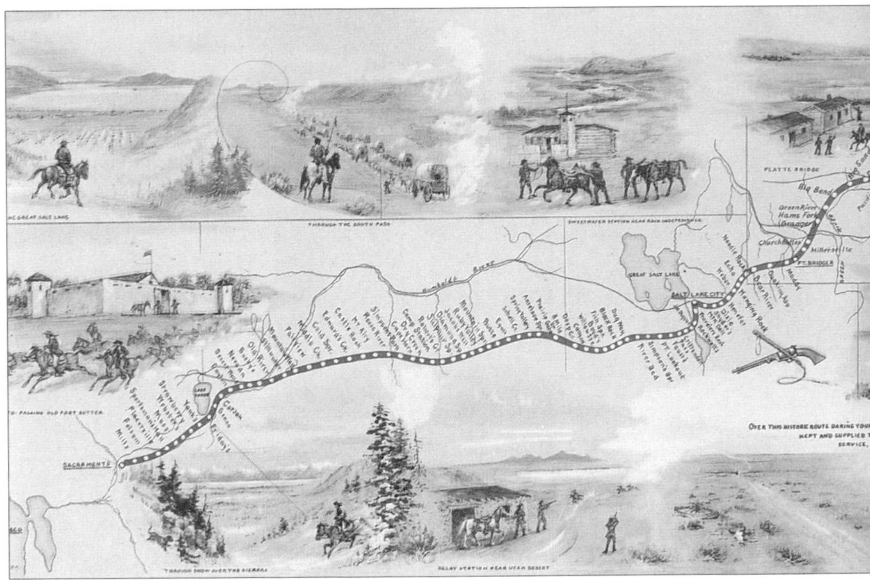

conversation with his or her own practice, peers, and predecessors. Dante the Pilgrim is led in the Earthly Paradise by Virgil:

> O light and honor of the other poets,
> may my long years of study, and that deep love
> that made me search your verses, help me now!
>
> You are my teacher, the first of all my authors,
> and you alone the one from whom I took
> the noble style that was to bring me honor.

Of course, mere imitation, mere following, won't do:

> ". . . you must journey down another road,"
> he answered, when he saw me lost in tears,
> "if ever you hope to leave this wilderness."

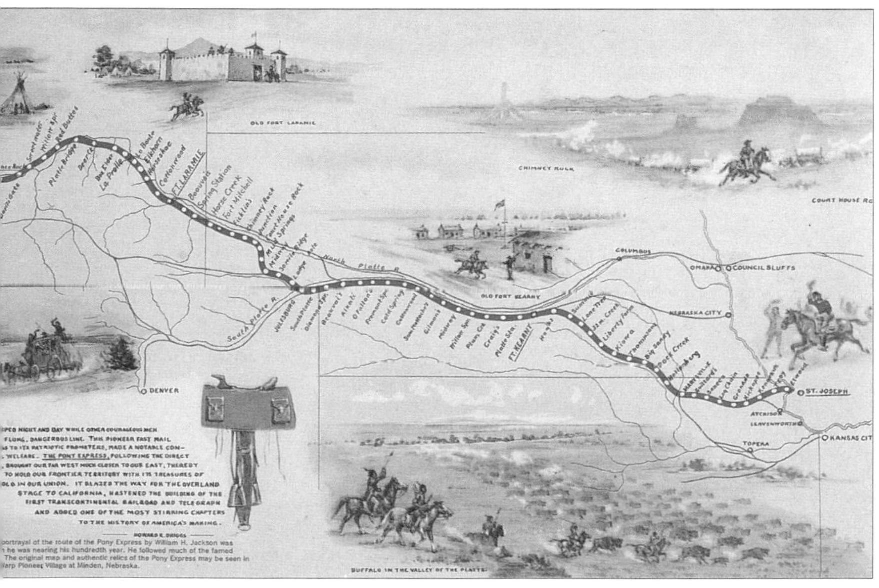

FIG. 3 **A PONY EXPRESS ROUTE MAP**

"You must" is the guide's imperative. Some advice comes in the form of stern instruction: *This is how you do it.* Nevertheless, the impulse to make and offer rules is often a generous one. Trailblazers across land are concerned less with personal glory — they are, typically, anonymous — than with the safe and efficient travel of others. We appreciate not having to stumble through vast forests or search for passage across every river; but the blazed trail quickly becomes a well-worn path, one from which most of the sights have already been seen. The writer as explorer naturally wants to see what's over the next rise, what happens to the creek when it goes under that shelf of rock. We want to be guided, but only when we *want* to be guided.

Even more than other writers themselves, their work is our guide; seen that way, the books on our shelves are volumes of an enormous atlas. Particular landscapes and routes through them are illustrated in exacting detail. Countless poems, stories, and novels have been based on or influenced by Homer's *Odyssey*, including works by writers who, like Dante, never had the opportunity to read it. That epic poem has been an extraordinarily useful guide.* Yet in the *Odyssey*, our hero often receives partial assistance: Get back on your boat, steer over there, but beware that singing; come ashore, you're welcome here, but *hands off the cattle, or else*. This is the sort of guidance we can expect from other writers and their work. Precisely what to make of it, and how to make the best of it, is left to us.

GIACOMETTI'S RESPONSE to the challenge of representation was to make evident in the "final" work its unfinished quality. In the portrait of James Lord, the subject's entire body and the background are hastily sketched in; Giacometti devoted the eighteen

* Despite Homer's apparently poor knowledge of the actual geography he described. (An entire subcategory of literary scholarship is built around investigating whether the settings of various works are "real": in Asheville, North Carolina, people meet every year to identify the "actual" settings, characters, and items of clothing worn in Thomas Wolfe's novels; in Hannibal, Missouri, Mark Twain's house is identified as Tom Sawyer's, the house beside it, Becky Thatcher's; a cramped store in London claims to be the "real" Old Curiosity Shop. Writers, and serious readers, know that's the least interesting kind of correlation between life and art.)

days almost exclusively to painting, and eliminating, and repainting Lord's head. The artist explained:

> Sometimes it's very tempting to be satisfied with what's easy, particularly if people tell you it's good. . . . What's essential is to work without any preconception whatever, without knowing in advance what the picture is going to look like. . . . It is very, very important to avoid all preconception, to try to see only what exists . . . to translate one's sensation.

Here the plan for discovery is deceptively simple: "to see only what exists." The intention is "to translate one's sensation" via visual representation.

To believe that nothing can be finished leads to moments of despair — we're taught to gain pleasure from completion — but also to obsessive devotion, as only work we believe to be of tremendous potential value is worth pursuing to the end of our days. How do we resolve the conflict between shapeliness, or control, and our sense that we are never entirely in control, in that we can never entirely close the gap between the work we envision and the work we create? Tony Hoagland writes that "control exacts a cost too: It is often achieved at the expense of discovery and spontaneity." He writes in praise of "insubordinations," against the dominance of "repression as a useful agent in creative shaping." The call is not to let anything go, but to allow for passionate excess, and the irrational, and useless beauty. The conflict is, ultimately, between unruly nature and civilization's desire for order, utility, and meaning-making. Do we admire the Navajo basket, not only beautifully designed but also so tightly woven that it can hold water? Or do we prefer nonfunctional pottery, the howls of the Beats, the delirium of Dada, the splatters of Pollock? Do we have to choose? (A glance toward the dance floor: The Talking Heads sang "Stop Making Sense" to a perfectly rhythmic beat.) Can't we admire both stay-at-home Emily Dickinson and wide-ranging Walt Whitman? Wise Dr.

Chekhov and self-destructive Stephen Crane? Flaubert's meticulously considered *Madame Bovary* and Mark Twain's uncivilized *Adventures of Huckleberry Finn*, with its ill-fitting final quarter, the raft run aground? The wild-eyed riffs of *Moby-Dick* and the canny constructions of Borges? We can, and will — so long as, whatever its temperament, every map, every story or poem, persuades us of its purpose and justifies its methods.

When Giacometti finally agreed to stop and allow the portrait of James Lord to be sent off for exhibition, he provided the end-of-the-artist's-workday view:

> He took the painting from the easel and stood it at the back of the studio, then went out into the passageway to look at it from a distance.
>
> "Well," he said, "we've gone far. We could have gone further still, but we have gone far. It's only the beginning of what it could be. But that's something, anyway."

Sam Hamill writes of the poet Bashō, "His journey is a pilgrimage; it is a journey into the interior of the self as much as a travelogue, a vision quest that concludes in insight. But there is no conclusion. The journey itself is home." We recognize the sentiment: it isn't where you go, it's the getting there. But tell that to Odysseus. As readers, we know that if a work's conclusion is disappointing, if we aren't satisfied with where it has taken us, the guide has let us down. A map may be beautiful, but if it doesn't tell us what we want to know, or clearly illustrate what it means to tell us, it's merely a decoration. The writer's obligation is to make rewarding both the reader's journey *and* his destination. Each completed work is a benchmark, an indication of how far we've come. If we've done our work well, we can be pleased with it; if we're serious about the pursuit of our art, we are, nevertheless, unsatisfied.

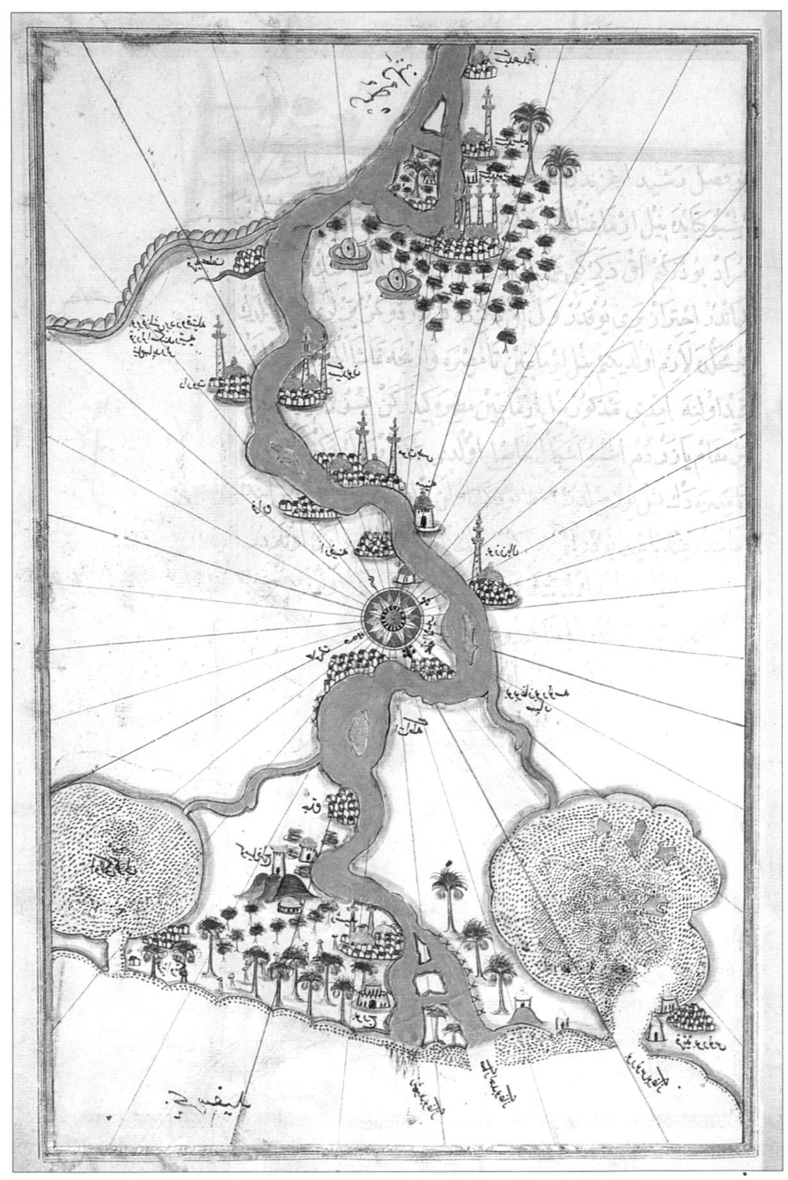

FIG. 4 **A MAP OF THE NILE DELTA BY OTTOMAN NAVAL COMMANDER AND CARTOGRAPHER PIRI REIS (1465 – 1554)**

Writing offers the Scylla and Charybdis of Authority and Humility. It requires us to assume authority over our creations, to assert our knowledge and talent; yet it also requires humility, a recognition that there is always more to learn. Danger looms at either extreme. While it may be good for the soul, living in a constant state of humility can lead to a refusal to take responsibility for the work or to pursue fully one's ambitions. Constantly asserting authority can lead to being far too sure of oneself, to the detriment of true discovery. Our task is not to avoid the two entirely, but to steer between them, making the most of the currents they create.

At some point in the lifelong journey, the traveler recognizes he has something to offer others. Having mapped the Mississippi River and its environs, Mark Twain found himself prepared to tell the world about a place it had never seen the way he had seen it. Having been asked for directions, Nick Carraway realizes, "I was lonely no longer. I was a guide, a pathfinder, an original settler." Every writer, especially every writer who teaches, is asked for directions; and to the extent that he offers them, he takes on the role of guide in another way, outside of his work.

I have no training in geography or cartography; mine is strictly an amateur's enthusiasm. Like many others in many fields, I have found mapping to be a potent metaphor. My interest is not, particularly, in writing that addresses mapping and geography in its content. Neither is it to offer instruction, at least not in the spirit of Circe when she tells Odysseus:

> I will set you a course and chart each seamark,
> so neither on sea nor land will some new trap
> ensnare you in trouble, make you suffer more.

Any number of others are both able and willing to set courses and chart seamarks. But while some writers may appreciate lists and categories, catalogs of options and examples, others resist the prescriptive, inclined toward analogy rather than explication, exceptions rather than rules. For those of us in the latter group, metaphor is as comfortable as a sweatshirt: sufficiently defined to serve as clothing, but loose enough to allow freedom of movement. We appreciate the limits to Circe's guidance: "once your crew has rowed you past the Sirens, a choice of route is yours."

The chapters that follow contemplate issues relevant to many kinds of writing: selection and omission; conventions (adherence to and departure from); inclusion and order; shape, or matters of form; and the balance of intuition and intention. The structure of each chapter is more or less associative. At times the leap from figure to ground is left to the reader, while at other times the connection is more clearly drawn. The writing addressed is, most often, fiction, though there are also discussions of poetry and film (as well as glancing references to visual arts, cartoons, board games, and haircuts). The first-person plural pronoun is used throughout to refer to writers, and at times to readers, with the assumption that all writers are readers.

ROUGHLY TWO THOUSAND years before Columbus, another explorer braved the ocean to establish colonies and trading posts. Heading out through the Straits of Gibraltar in sixty ships, King Hanno of Carthage saw islands within islands, an active volcano, crocodiles, hippopotami, and gorillas. The record of his voyage is the earliest known first-hand report of travel along the west coast of Africa. Hanno's "Periplus," or story of the navigation of a coastline, is both vividly detailed and tantalizing in its brevity. Just eighteen lines long in surviving translations, it provides an invaluable record even as it continues to inspire speculation.

This periplus, a record of a different sort of circumnavigation, is offered as a companion on the long journey through uncharted waters, with the hope that it will inspire the reader, once ashore, to pursue tempting trails left unexplored.

A WIDE LANDSCAPE OF SNOWS

It was the whiteness of the whale that above all things appalled me. . . . Is it that by its indefiniteness it shadows forth the heartless voids and immensities of the universe, and thus stabs us from behind with the thought of annihilation, when beholding the white depths of the milky way? Or is it, that as in essence whiteness is not so much a color as the visible absence of color, and at the same time the concrete of all colors; is it for these reasons that there is such a dumb blankness, full of meaning, in a wide landscape of snows?

HERMAN MELVILLE, *MOBY-DICK; OR, THE WHALE*

WE START with a blank: a world of possibility.

We desire to make a mark. To the extent that we want that mark to be original, meaningful, or admirable, the "dumb blankness"—or rather, our ambition to improve upon it—can be intimidating. The familiar image of an exasperated figure sitting at a typewriter, balled-up sheets of paper (spoiled blanks) in and around the trash can, is a depiction of the internal struggle every writer knows. Yet despite the hours we spend staring at the blank page or the blank screen, we can be so intent on what isn't there, and on what we want to be there, that we might overlook the many uses of what *is* there.

Tens of thousands of years ago, before the first trails were etched into mud with the point of a stick, before the first pictures were scratched onto stone, and long before the first graphic depiction of places on anything like paper, there must have been something we might call premapping: the desire, and so the attempt, to locate oneself. Just as a dog will make its way through the woods drinking out of the same hollows and puddles season after season, early man must have found himself choosing one path (around the bog, rather than through it) over another. And as some paths became preferable, some places desirable, others avoidable, a kind of mental mapping occurred.

Mental maps are made by bees doing their figure-eight dances to point their pals to the pollen, by dogs wandering far from and then returning to the suburban yards meant to confine them, and by you and me as we decide the most efficient way to cross town during rush hour. Our mental maps are often not terribly accurate, based as they are on our own selective experience, our knowledge and ignorance, and the information and misinformation we gain from others; nevertheless, these are the maps we depend on every day. The most efficient way across the city may not be the shortest; we might prefer what we believe to be a more scenic route, or a more familiar route, to the fastest. Our *sense* of a place is in many ways more important than objective fact. The impressions we carry of the house we grew up in and the places where we played as children are more important to us than any mathematical measurements of them.

The Earth itself was never blank. In places (the oceans, deserts of sand, deserts of ice) it may have seemed so, but in many more it was, if anything, dauntingly full—of trees, shrubs, cactus, volcanoes, boulders, rapids, chasms, and mountains. As soon as man began to discover those things and to think and then communicate about them, those geographical features existed, both for each individual and for that person's community, culture, or tribe, under an increasingly dense overlay of story. The earliest identifiable maps in many cultures, including those of Native Americans, Inuits, and Aboriginal Australians, were created and passed on orally. For Native Americans, myths, legends, and personal history were vitally connected to natural features of the earth, and for Australian Aboriginals, the land was traversed by song-lines, or paths of spiritual energy. In *Moby-Dick*, Ishmael tells us Ahab is headed for a "particular set time and place" he calls the "Season-on-the-Line": "There it was, too, that most of the deadly encounters with the white whale had taken place; there the waves were storied with his deeds."

The blank page, then, is only *a* beginning, as opposed to *the* beginning.

Even after we mark the page, there are blanks beyond the borders of what we create, and blanks within what we create. Maps are defined by what they include but are often more revealing in what they exclude. Aboriginal Australians and people of the Middle East, among many others, mapped locally. They did not attempt to map the entire world or even the places where they knew others lived. They were placing themselves. A map of bicycle trails in DuPage County, Illinois, is clearly not obliged to include roads, or train tracks, or bus stops; in fact, to include those things might make it difficult to read the information a bicyclist most needs. But won't cyclists want to know where they will cross roads, and how large or busy those roads

FIG. 5 (FOLLOWING SPREAD) **AN AZTEC MAP OF THE HACIENDA DE SANTA IÑES, MEXICO, MADE IN 1569. FOOTPRINTS INDICATE ROADS; PLANTS AND SHEEP REPRESENT CROPS AND LIVESTOCK** mojones

dos mill pasos

En la ciudad de mex.co veynte y seis dias de mayo de
[illegible] y sesenta y nueve años ante el yll.e s.r doctor
de [illegible] del consejo de su mag.d [illegible] fiscal de
[illegible] juan antonio [illegible] yndios [illegible]
[illegible] que la diferencia [illegible] entre ellos [illegible]
[illegible] juan antonio [illegible]
[illegible] de sus estancias e que dello hiziese esta pintura [illegible]
[illegible] que estan juntas [illegible]
[illegible] e que la [illegible]
[illegible] hasta [illegible] colorada [illegible]
[illegible] a la [illegible] los dichos yndios e que la [illegible]
[illegible] para la labor de los dichos y
estando [illegible] el fruto [illegible] por pasto comun y
[illegible] partes [illegible]
[illegible]
[illegible] audiencia [illegible] poder [illegible]
[illegible] de agua

Es la de los yndios

La Visitacion

San Fran.co

ay dos leguas corr a [illegible] de tuetepeque
y de distancia mil e seiscientas
y quarenta braças

Corrales

[illegible] oydores de la audiencia Real
[illegible] ynterprete de ella e presen[illegible]
[illegible] juez tioquautitlan dixeron
[illegible] todos los dichos yndios que
[illegible] de la transacion
[illegible] estan concertados y [illegible]
[illegible] de mudemaça [illegible]
[illegible] de tierras
[illegible] que de por terminos de la dicha
[illegible] vna tasillas
[illegible] de la vi[illegible] llamada hacia vnas
[illegible] dicho [illegible] vna [illegible] dhusana [illegible]
[illegible] lo mando se[illegible] dar [illegible]
[illegible] por [illegible] de [illegible]
[illegible] ella [illegible] con comision
[illegible] paso ante mi [illegible]
secretario [illegible]

tuetepeque
Sta m^a [illegible]

are? Won't some cyclists want to know the nearest commuter train stations, parking lots, and restaurants? Whether dogs are allowed on the trails? Horses? And what does the map do about those trails that, inconveniently, wander beyond the county line, and back? A map of bicycle trails in DuPage County that includes nothing except those trails in that politically defined area might not be as useful as we had hoped.

He had brought a large map representing the sea,
Without the least vestige of land:
And the crew were much pleased when they found it to be
A map they could all understand.

"What's the good of Mercator's North Pole and Equators,
Tropics, Zones, and Meridian Lines?"
So the Bellman would cry: and the crew would reply,
"They are all just conventional signs!

Other maps are such shapes, with their islands and capes,
But we've got our brave Captain to thank"
(So the crew would protest) "that he's brought us the best
A perfect and absolute blank!"

— FROM "THE HUNTING OF THE SNARK," BY LEWIS CARROLL

BLANKS WITHIN THE borders of maps can represent many things, among them the deliberately withheld. While some explorers persuaded Native Americans to draw maps on paper, those documents were not always reliable—due not to the cartographer's ignorance, but to his distrust. The sorts of things worth mapping (hunting grounds, sacred sites) were too important to be passed on to a mere curious stranger. (Europeans, though frustrated, may have understood this reluctance; their ships' logs and chartbooks were often weighted or kept in metal boxes so that, if a ship were overtaken, information regarding trade routes, winds and currents, and details of coastlines and harbors could be thrown overboard, and so kept safe from the enemy.)* The oral "maps" of Australian Aboriginals, like the stick-and-shell navigational charts made by Marshall and Caroline Islanders, were encoded, as they contained privileged information. For that matter, a landlubber would be hard pressed to make much sense of the information contained on a modern navigational chart of the Chesapeake Bay. To learn how to read any map is to be indoctrinated into that mapmaker's culture.

Blanks can also represent what is known, but deemed unimportant in a particular context, for a particular map. While it's useful to know where public libraries are located, and while some bicyclists no doubt make use of public libraries, we wouldn't expect to find libraries on that map of county bike trails. More ominously, Native American tribal areas were not included on early European maps of the Americas, giving readers of those maps the impression no one lived there — at least, no one of consequence. No landowners. These are the kinds of blanks that fire Marlow's imagination in Conrad's *Heart of Darkness* — the blanks that certain minds found to be a call for colonialism and conquest:

> Now when I was a little chap I had a passion for maps. I would look for hours at South America, or Africa, or Australia, and lose myself in all the glories of exploration. At that time there were many blank spaces on the earth.

These days we believe we're well aware of the dangers of the imperial mindset, but many would argue that the urge to fill blank spaces is fundamental to the quest for knowledge. A tolerance of blank spaces could be a sign that our aggressive ten-

* Mappable information is suppressed even today, for a variety of reasons often political, military, or financial. An article in the *Nation* about cigarette smuggling says of Portette, "The bawdy port is what one anthropologist who studied the region calls a 'phantom town'—it's not included on maps of the country and has had, until recently, few connections to the official structures of the Colombian government."

dencies are under control, but it might also be an indication of insufficient curiosity, or evidence of intense self-interest. The National Parks program is an effort to preserve a kind of blank, to keep land of natural or historic interest from being "developed" or "filled in." These are blanks we're not only willing but eager to maintain. Canadians argue that most U. S. citizens are appallingly ignorant of their northern neighbor, unable to name even half the provinces; that ignorance is another sort of blank, the product of geography, politics, economy, and national identity.

I love white space, love the telling omission . . .

. . . and find oddly depressing that which seems to have left out nothing.

— LOUISE GLÜCK

SOME OF THE most famous blanks on maps were filled with drawings — of sea serpents, dragons, griffins, hippogriffs, and freakishly exotic people. This was less a matter of encoding than a matter of decoration, but in some cases those drawings represented an earlier day's urban myths — the tales sailors and explorers told one another and the people back home. Far from being viewed as worthless, such maps were prized; for a very long

FIG. 6

time, decorative or fanciful maps were at least as numerous as what we might call "practical" maps. In the Middle Ages, when Christian mapmakers drew up *mappaemundi* locating heaven and hell, they were, according to historian Alfred W. Crosby, making "a nonquantificational, nongeometrical attempt to supply information about what was near and what was far — and what was important and what unimportant. It is more like an expressionist portrait than an identification photo. It was for sinners, not navigators." George H. T. Kimble adds, "The great majority of these *mappaemundi* are to be regarded as works of art and not of information. . . . [Their authors] would have branded any man a fool who might have supposed that he could determine the distance from London to Jerusalem by putting a ruler across a map." Geographic features, peoples, and nations were omitted; in their place were spiritual landmarks.

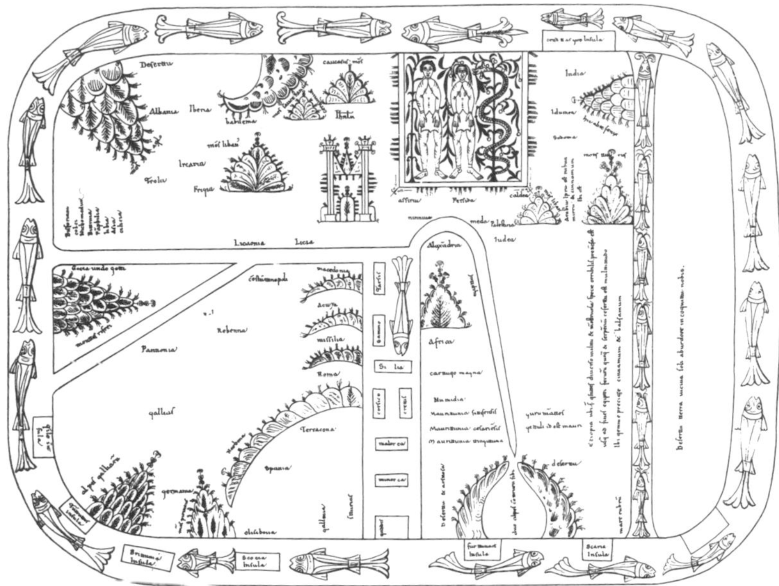

FIG. 7 A TWELFTH-CENTURY MAP MADE BY THE SPANISH MONK BEATUS OF VALCAVADO TO ILLUSTRATE HIS *COMMENTARY ON THE APOCALYPSE*. EUROPE IS AT THE LOWER LEFT; THE GARDEN OF EDEN, INCLUDING ADAM AND EVE, IS AT THE TOP

The believers who valued such maps included a great number of pilgrims, who found they needed a different sort of document to lead them on their physical journeys. Their pilgrimages, along with the need for accurate navigational charts, instigated a return to practical mapping that eventually led eighteenth-century French cartographer Jean Baptiste Bourguignon d'Anville to take a radical stance, renouncing decorations, and leaving blanks in their stead: "To destroy false notions, without even going any further, is one of the ways to advance knowledge." Some of his countrymen began to call themselves "scientific cartographers." As one introductory text puts it, "fanciful fripperies" were abandoned in the interest of stern science. (That phrase "fanciful fripperies" recalls Mark Twain's attack on James Fenimore Cooper's romantic novels. Realism, Twain argued, is superior because its world is more nearly our own.) Thanks to Jean Baptiste Bourguignon d'Anville and his colleagues, a blank on a map became a symbol of rigorous standards; the presence of absences lent authority to all on the map that was unblank.

The logical end to such a scientific approach would be a comprehensive map of a verified world. In *A Universal History of Infamy*, Jorge Luis Borges describes such a map:

> In that Empire, the craft of Cartography attained such Perfection that the Map of a Single province covered the space of an entire City, and the Map of the Empire itself an entire Province. In the course of Time, these extensive maps were found somehow wanting, and so the College of Cartographers evolved a Map of the Empire that was of the same Scale as the Empire and that coincided with it point for point.

But even that map includes only surfaces; there would be no indication of the layers of rock under the soil, or the soil under water. It would not include the migratory paths of birds or the echo of boys' voices. As Denis Wood notes in his provocative book *The Power of Maps*, to argue that sounds and smells are difficult to map, that a map is primarily visual, only underscores our acceptance of the conventions of maps — among them that maps are fixed in time and include only features considered relatively permanent.*

In the novel *A Mapmaker's Dream*, James Cowan imagines the attempt of Fra Mauro, an actual fifteenth-century cartographer, to draw what he hopes will be a definitive map of the world, based not only on existing maps but on the stories of travelers from around the world. He learns that there are an infinite number of

* Of course, our sense of what is permanent is constantly changing. In the nineteenth century, maps often indicated watering holes for horses. Today we define our location relative to roads, despite the fact that we see them being rerouted every day. It wasn't so long ago that roads and trails, packed dirt paths from one place to another, seemed arbitrary, not nearly as permanent as waterfalls or boulders. Where I live, deeds still turn up, occasionally, defining the boundaries of a family's land in terms of natural features — a creek, a live oak. Constant as they once seemed, the creek dried up a generation ago, and the oak has long since turned to fireplace ash.

ways to depict reality. As the magnitude of this realization settles in, he writes, "My map absorbs me with what it does not reveal." Later, despite or because of his efforts to be comprehensive, he tells us, "I am left with a sense of existing in an unfathomable void, surrounded by blankness."

Whatever a map's attitude toward blanks within its borders, virtually everything is left off of a map—and must be for a map to be useful. "No map can show everything," Denis Wood argues. "Could it, it would no more than reproduce the world, which, without the map, we already have. It is only its selection from the world's overwhelming richness that justifies the map."

> Had you followed Captain Ahab down into his cabin . . . you would have seen him go to a locker in the transom, and bringing out a large wrinkled roll of yellowish sea charts, spread them before him on his screwed-down table. Then seating himself before it, you would have seen him intently study the various lines and shadings which there met his eye; and with slow but steady pencil trace additional courses over spaces that before were blank. . . .
>
> While thus employed, the heavy pewter lamp suspended in chains over his head, continually rocked with the motion of the ship, and for ever threw shifting gleams and shadows of lines upon his wrinkled brow, till it almost seemed that while he himself was marking out lines and courses on the wrinkled charts, some invisible pencil was also tracing lines and courses upon the deeply marked chart of his forehead.

IN *MOBY-DICK*, the whale is a blank on which Ahab writes his own story; Ahab's quest for the whale is the blank upon which Ishmael writes his.

FIG. 8 (PREVIOUS SPREAD) **FRA MAURO'S *MAPPAMUNDI*, 1459. MAURO'S MAP, ORIENTED WITH SOUTH AT THE TOP, AND DENSE WITH DRAWINGS AND TEXT, REPRESENTS THE TRANSITION FROM MEDIEVAL MAPPING, WHICH PRESENTED AS MUCH CHRISTIAN DOGMA AS GEOGRAPHY, TO THE SCIENTIFIC MAPPING OF THE AGE OF DISCOVERY**

The blank of the unwritten is the challenge we've chosen to face. We face it because, like explorers of the physical world, we want to know more about where — and why, and how —we live. We face it because we are, in some way, both inspired by and unsatisfied by what we know and what we've read. "Everything I have written up to now is trifling," Anton Chekhov told a friend, well into his career, "compared to that which I would like to write. I am displeased and bored with everything now being written, while everything in my head interests, moves, and excites me." Blanks of the unwritten include stories and poems we never commit to paper or are reluctant to write (too autobiographical; too distant from our own experience; too much like other pieces we've written; too unlike what we think of as "our" writing; etc.) and pieces we abandon midprocess, but also characters who fail to materialize, emotions that go unevoked, significant actions allowed to play out offstage — all the omissions of work we think of as unfinished, or insufficiently developed. When we drafted, a timid voice said, "Don't go there."

In a letter to F. Scott Fitzgerald, Thomas Wolfe characterized writers as "putter-inners" like himself (who legendarily sent his editor Maxwell Perkins trunks of manuscript pages) or "leaver-outers" like Fitzgerald, whose *The Great Gatsby* is a brilliant example of selection and compression, creating the illusion that much more is shown than we actually see. As Wolfe argued, however, those categories — like all categories, like all tautologies — are oversimplified:

> Now you have your way of doing something and I have mine, there are a lot of ways, but you are honestly mistaken in thinking that there is a "way." I suppose I would agree with you in what you say about "the novel of selected incident" so far as it means anything. I say so far as it means anything because every novel, of course, is a novel of selected incident. You couldn't write about the inside of a telephone booth without selecting . . . a great writer is not only a leaver-outer but also a putter-inner.

The need for selection means that every story contains, and is surrounded by, blank spaces, some more significant than others. When we create a fictional world, our decisions include geography, or setting, but also where and when a narrative begins and ends, who it involves and who it doesn't, which actions and conversations are deemed worthy of inclusion and which aren't. In a surprising number of novels, the characters are effectively jobless; they have been granted psychic vacations from work by the author.

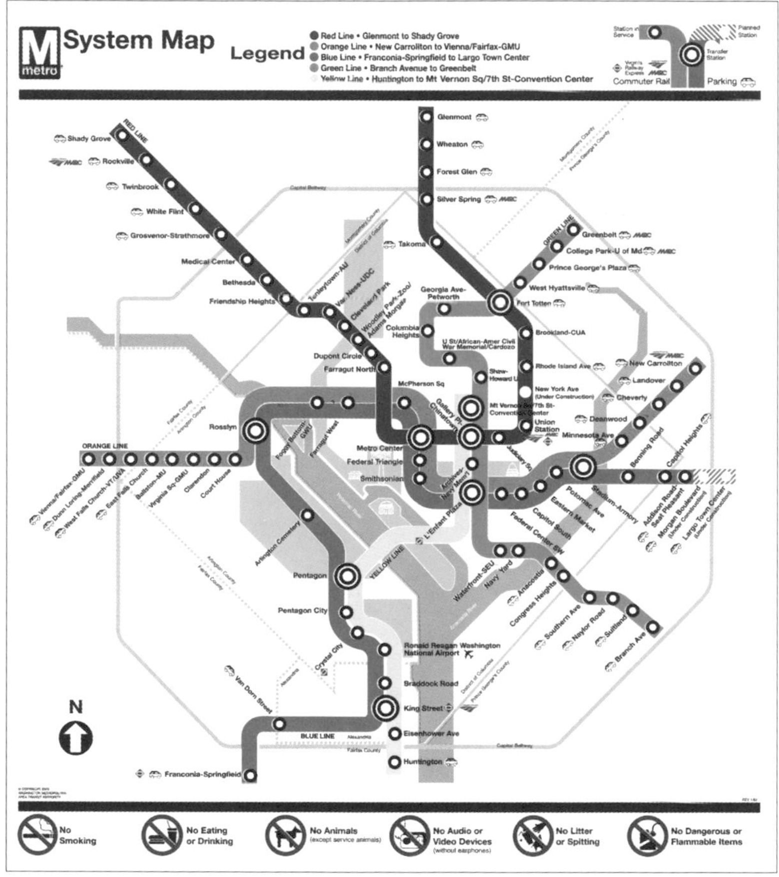

FIG. 9 THE WASHINGTON, D.C., METRORAIL SYSTEM MAP: A WAY FINDER

Their occupations might be named, but they have no employers, no colleagues, no pressing work-related obligations; which is to say, they live in a world very different from that of most readers. (Long ago, bent over one of the blue-spined books I read the moment they entered the house, I noted that the Hardy boys, unfettered by schoolwork, lived in an endless teenage vacation.) In other novels, characters have no parents, no aunts or uncles, no grandparents; they celebrate no birthdays, anniversaries, or holidays. While we are often invited to watch characters copulate, we less often watch them defecate (an observation, not a complaint), and relatively few if any words are devoted to the nearly half of each day they spend sleeping and eating, dressing and undressing, trimming their nails, paying their bills. All of which is to say, even epic novels are silent about much in their characters' lives. Short stories and poems are, correspondingly, surrounded by even more blank space.

Readers may not think of those absences. We read an entire novel in which no historical or national events are mentioned, and (if the illusion succeeds) we accept the omissions. In this country, particularly in the past few decades, many writers have examined the domestic world to the exclusion of social and political issues. In "Stalking the Billion-footed Beast," Tom Wolfe argues that the only hope for the future of the American novel is a Zolaesque naturalism in which the novelist becomes reporter—a technique well illustrated, he asserts, by his own *Bonfire of the Vanities*. But no matter how much we attempt to record, every novel has its absences. As in a magic trick, the reader's attention must be deftly steered, the reader persuaded the world of the story is full, or complete, despite all that's missing. When the illusion is unsuccessful, the reader is aware of the absence, distracted by what he wants to know.

One of the great breakthroughs of urban mapping was the work of Henry Beck, who in 1933 invented the Way Finder for the London Underground. Until then, the map of the underground was "accurate"—it preserved the direction and distance of the

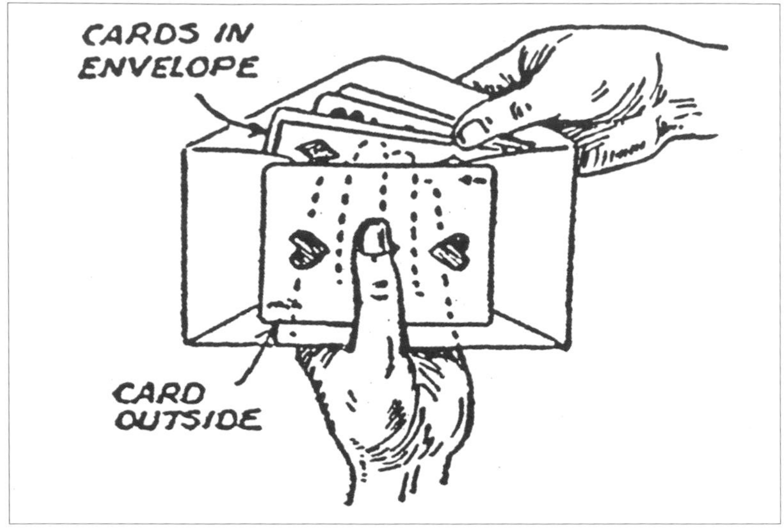

FIG. 10 DISINFORMATION DESIGN: AN ILLUSION REVEALED, IN AN ILLUSTRATION DEPICTING TEN LAYERS OF DEPTH

train lines, listing the stops and intermediate neighborhoods. The problem was, the density of information made it almost impossible to read. Beck understood that what riders wanted to know was which trains stopped where, in what order. He color coded the lines and drew them at neat angles, ignoring precise distances and directions, omitting virtually everything except for the names of the stations. The Way Finder, which has been adopted by transportation systems around the world, is a demonstration of the usefulness of leaving maps blank, as well as evidence that the most accurate map, and the most detailed map, is not necessarily the best map.

As writers, no matter whether our tendency is toward expansion or compression, we must gauge what to leave blank, and why. We need to be sure to choose our blanks, rather than simply omit parts of the fictional world that seem too large or complicated or bothersome to include. In realistic fiction, we need to be particularly wary of unintentional voids in our characters' perceptions and thoughts. It is easier to write about a simpler world, one in which characters don't think about, don't imagine, everything we think about and imagine. The trouble is, unless we're writing the book for a Broadway musical, such a world is distractingly, disappointingly artificial. The challenge is to create a fictional world that is realistically complex. Then we need to create such a persuasive whole that the reader isn't distracted by the necessary absences. In *Visual Explanations: Images and Quantities, Evidence and Narrative,* Edward R. Tufte discusses what he calls "disinformation design," and notes, "Magicians are preoccupied with . . . viewing angles, which make the difference between a successful deception and a disastrous exposure." We might resist thinking of our work as deception, but to the extent that we ask our readers to believe in people, places, and events called into being by inky squiggles on paper, we aspire to a kind of magic.

> All earthly experience is partial. Not simply because it is subjective, but because that which we do not know, of the universe, of mortality, is so much more vast than that which we do know. What is unfinished or has been destroyed participates in these mysteries. The problem is to make a whole that does not forfeit this power.
>
> — LOUISE GLÜCK

SAPPHO'S POEMS, or what we refer to as her poems, are, with few exceptions, fragments, and so both full of and surrounded by blanks. In Mary Barnard's translations, we're given the perfectly clear and plausibly complete—

> Am I still sad
> because of my
> lost maidenhead?

—as well as fragments that take on power from their very fragmentation, a combination of clarity, complete phrase or statement, and mystery—

> Believe me, I
> prayed that that
> night might be
> doubled for us

and

> My girlhood then
> was in full bloom
> and you–

—fragments that all but force us to imagine the larger context, to make and then test assumptions. We can imagine countless frames; what we have is not a path from here to there, not a beginning, middle, and ending, but a single point from someplace along the route. So we imagine each fragment as a beginning, and then as an ending, and as some part of the middle; we look for hints of emotion, we consider voice, we create narratives. While a poetic fragment may not carry its complete genetic code, these bits of Sappho's work engage us on their own and at the same time inspire us to consider, if not fill in, the blanks around them.

Guy Davenport takes a different approach to the translations, using brackets to indicate both the placement and approximate sizes of the missing lines and parts of lines.

> [   ] slick with slime [   ]
> [   ] Polyanaktidas to satiety [   ]
> [   ] shoots forward [   ]
> Playing such music upon these strings
> Wearing a phallus of leather [   ]
> Such a thing as this [   ] enviously

[ ] twirls quivering masterfully
[ ] and has for odor
[ ] hollow [ ]
[ ]
[ ] mysteries, orgies

Davenport's translations allow us something like the view of the archaeologist holding the shreds of papyrus in his hand. This explicit depiction of the blanks gives the reader a sense of the form of the original poem, more sharply defines what is missing and what might have been, and, therefore, changes entirely our understanding of the surviving pieces of each poem, the unblank. As those scientific cartographers insisted, a fuller understanding of what we don't know is itself new knowledge, and redefines what we know. Omissions, intended or unintended, provoke the imagination. In her translations of what she calls "Fragments of

FIG. 11 THE ROOM IN CHARLES RITCHIE'S *DRAPED CHAIR* IS CLOAKED IN DARKNESS . . .

FIG. 12 . . . WHILE IN THIS PAGE FROM RITCHIE'S JOURNAL, THE WARM, GLOWING LIGHT IN THE BARN IS BLANK PAPER

Sappho," Anne Carson steers a middle course: instead of printing the poems as if there were no omissions, or indicating the precise size and place of the omissions, she provides a single bracket "to give an impression of missing matter. Brackets are exciting," she says. "Even though you are approaching Sappho in translation, that is no reason you should miss the drama of trying to read a papyrus torn in half or riddled with holes or smaller than a postage stamp—brackets imply a free space of imaginal adventure."* Provoking "imaginal adventure" is one of the crucial functions of blanks in complete work as well.

> I always try to write on the principle of the iceberg. There is seven-eighths of it underwater for every part that shows. . . .
>
> If a writer of prose knows enough about what he is writing about he may omit things that he knows and the reader, if the writer is writing truly enough, will have a feeling of those things as strongly as though the writer had stated them. . . .

* Carson notes that on papyrus rolls text appears with no word divisions, punctuation marks, or lineation. The first job of the reader, then, is to insert blank spaces in order to make sense of what's written. She also discusses other silences around Sappho's work, including tantalizing allusions to poems that are today unknown. "At the inside edge where her words go missing," Carson writes, "a sort of antipoem . . . condenses everything you ever wanted her to write."

> [But] if a writer omits something because he does not know it then there is a hole in the story.
>
> — ERNEST HEMINGWAY

IN STORIES and novels, white space is commonly used to separate sections. Sometimes the effect is dramatic emphasis, as in a cutaway from an impending or just-completed action. The inevitable event, or its immediate aftermath, is left for us to imagine. Elsewhere, blanks might indicate a shift in setting, as in this example from Kate Chopin's "The Storm" —

—or a shift in setting, point of view character, and time, as in this space late in Robert Coover's "The Babysitter":

Of course, to put it that way exposes the error: it isn't the blank itself that does the work but the material on either side, charged objects creating an electrostatic field. Without anything around or within them, blanks are nothing. Those blank books displayed beside cash registers *(The Wit and Wisdom of George W. Bush, What Men Know about What Women Want)* are lame gags, the title providing the set-up, the empty pages the punch-line. There isn't enough energy about them to light any but the dimmest bulb. (The exception may be a diary: a book whose empty pages promise that a record of our days is worth keeping.) Silences *can* effectively underscore punch lines, as demonstrated by the comedian Steven Wright, whose routine consists of pacing the stage, delivering terse, practiced observations, and pausing

*For an extended discussion, see Antonya Nelson's "'Mom's on the Roof': The Usefulness of Jokes in Shaping Short Stories" in *Bringing the Devil to His Knees: The Craft of Fiction and the Writing Life.*

("I had a friend who was a clown. When he died, all his friends went to the funeral in one car"; "You can't have everything. Where would you put it?").* The length of the pause — each statement's punctuation—is critical. Wright's stage presence is unusual in that he doesn't laugh or smile, doesn't work to engage the audience in a traditional manner. He maintains a blank expression. Groucho Marx once said, "Comedy is not so much what you do as what you don't do." Long after movies became "talkies," Harpo, who erased his features with a fright wig and a baggy raincoat, continued to play the Marx Brother who didn't speak.

> These scratchings all night,
> These inquiries because you are not there, have
> become, simply, you, white paper
> Desiring the darkening effects of ink.
>
> — LARRY LEVIS, "CONEY ISLAND BABY"

JOHN CAGE'S *4'33"* is a musical composition consisting entirely of rests. To know it exists, so to imagine hearing it, is almost enough. Some who have heard it performed say the power is in the context—the concert venue, the other listeners, the pianist sitting at the piano on stage, the pieces played before and after—and in the concertgoer's expectations. Similarly, the edges of Robert Rauschenberg's white canvases assert that what is enclosed is created by the artist or selected by him. We can inspect the white for evidence of blemish or texture; or we might imagine defacing it, or filling it in, and in that act of imagining see it as tabula rasa, the blank slate of opportunity. Just as Hemingway distinguished between omitted material that strengthens a work and omission that leaves "a hole in the writing," there is a world of difference between the piano sonata I haven't written (and will never write) and Cage's composition. Compare

> The man and woman eat quietly.

to

> A man says, "But I love you."
> The woman seated across from him does not answer.
> The man and woman continue eating, quietly.

In the second passage, the couple's silence is redefined. To be confronted with "nothing" in a carefully prepared context makes us newly aware of our assumptions and expectations—and, in Cage's example, of ambient sounds; in Rauschenberg's, of everything around the canvas. The silent composition and the white canvas are not nothing, any more than Harpo Marx's silence or a black hole in space is nothing; they are potent blanks.

More conventional music offers readily apparent illustrations of both the need for and the usefulness of blank spaces. When we hum the opening of Beethoven's Fifth Symphony, or the curiously universal theme to *The Pink Panther,* we honor the rests—the silences. Those pauses are a crucial component of rhythm.* In prose, this same service is provided by punctuation, by paragraphs (which, conventionally, begin with a space), and by the whiteness within chapters as well as at the beginning and end of each chapter. Like rests in music, punctuation and periods and paragraph and chapter endings mimic pauses for breath, and provide opportunities for the reader to stop and reflect.

If the balance of detail and blankness, suggestion and opportunity, fires the imagination, the art of writing short stories is, in part, the art of selecting what little the reader needs to know. Kate Chopin's "The Storm" is highly selective, leaps through white space, and propels us into the world of the unspoken.

The story begins with a man and his son at the store. Chopin

* Silences also allow resonance. In a profile of the songwriter Paul Simon, Alec Wilkinson observed that "As a tour progresses, musicians . . . tend to play more. A lot of what Simon hoped to do in rehearsals was strip away parts. 'There's always a lot of clutter,' he said. 'After a while, it gets a little rococo.'" He tells the musicians, "You don't have to play the whole phrase. Leave out notes. It's that thing of tricking the ear into hearing what's not there. . . . Drop two notes now and then. Play the shadow of it."

announces her metaphor in the second sentence, as Bobinôt, the father, "called the child's attention to certain somber clouds that were rolling with sinister intention from the west, accompanied by a sullen, threatening roar." The author can afford to be explicit, because she's setting us up for a sucker punch. (Good writers trust good readers enough to be able to fool them this way.) The storm breaks out; they decide to wait until it passes before walking home. Bobinôt is afraid of his wife's temper, so he buys her a can of shrimps while they wait.

Then there is white space.

In the next section, Calixta, the wife and mother, is "sewing furiously," oblivious to the weather. When she realizes why it's suddenly so dark she hurries out to get the laundry, only to find Alcée, whom "she had not seen . . . very often since her marriage, and never alone." Alcée, eager to be of service, grabs her husband's trousers. The storm arrives, beating violently at the house; Calixta is in a panic. There follows a bit of overheated prose ("face . . . warm and steaming," "lips . . . red and moist," "bosom . . . full, firm"), the result of which is "they did not heed the crashing torrents, and the roar of the elements made her laugh." The prose mirrors their passionate spasms for a few sentences, until "the growl of the thunder was distant and passing away." Realizing Bobinôt and their son will soon be home, Calixta sends Alcée off, both of them aglow. From their perspective we see "the rain was over; and the sun was turning the glistening green world into a palace of gems." (This second section of the story, by far the longest, runs, in my anthologized version, just over two pages.)

Section 3 finds Bobinôt and Bibi, the boy, "trudging home," then pausing at the cistern to remove "the signs of their tramp over heavy roads and through wet fields." No palace of gems here. Bobinôt is "prepared for the worst," but Calixta rushes to greet them, kissing first her son, then her generous husband. At dinner, "they laughed much and . . . loud." Their voices can be heard, we're told, all the way to Alcée's.

The story uses the next white space to take us there: In section

4, a single paragraph, Alcée writes to his wife, who is in Biloxi with their babies, and tells her "not to hurry back[;] . . . though he missed them, he was willing to bear the separation a while longer."

And then again: In the fifth and concluding section, a paragraph plus one sentence, we travel with the mail to Alcée's wife. She is charmed by his letter, and relieved at the invitation to extend "the pleasant liberty of her maiden days." The final sentence tells us, "So the storm passed and every one was happy."

The story is under four pages long—a study in omission and selectivity. Like a game of crack the whip, it flings its omniscience far from its narrative center, in part to support Chopin's final assertion, removing the burden of proof from the narrator. "The Storm" is a provocative demonstration of Chekhov's suggestion that a writer's job is to pose questions. And what is the art of posing questions? Not simply to leave the reader in a void, but to place the reader in a carefully shaped, well-defined void. Chopin seems to be ending with an answer—"every one was happy"—but she wrote that sentence knowing the reader would immediately fill the white space beneath it with the question: *Every one was happy?* Even today, over a century later, readers are challenged to believe that a woman can violate the bonds of her marriage, gain momentary pleasure, choose not to destroy her marriage, and not be destroyed. We are shown a map of the world that includes none of the well-charted moral repercussions that loom so large in the products of popular culture. While the conclusion Chopin describes may be uncommon, it is well within the realm of human possibilities; and so, with a few quick strokes, she has made our map of existence more complete.

And since we're on the topic of silences: The question Chopin posed was sufficiently radical that, despite having finished *The Awakening* earlier the same year, she didn't feel she could publish "The Storm."

In many stories, including Chopin's, we can imagine an elliptical space being replaced by a transitional sentence or phrase:

"Meanwhile, back at the house . . ." As readers grew accustomed to that use of blanks, writers grew more daring, placing apparently unrelated passages one after the other without explanation but separated by space. In these instances, the blank says, "That bit is over; now, something different," and implies, "but of course, there's a reason for following the one with the other." In this way, fiction writers have borrowed a tool from poets: the associative leap. One famous example of such a leap comes at the end of James Wright's "Lying in a Hammock at William Duffy's Farm in Pine Island, Minnesota." Hammocks, like front-porch rockers, are sentimental icons, and the speaker of Wright's poem, as he describes his surroundings (a bronze butterfly, distant cowbells), lulls us into the belief that we're reading a hammocky idyll. But the thirteen-line poem ends with these three:

> I lean back, as the evening darkens and comes on.
> A chicken hawk floats over, looking for home.
> I have wasted my life.

The last line appears to be a non sequitur; but because it is the last line of a poem (as opposed to one line from the endless chatter issuing from a stranger at a bus stop), we accept that it is not only a part of the work's intention, and shape, but a crucial part; and, operating under that assumption, we look for, and find, the relationship between the body of the poem and its unexpected conclusion. That is to say, we immediately reread, looking for what has gone unsaid before the final line.

Larry Levis's poetry is a poetry of associations; in his later work, we seem to be following a wandering of the mind, only to learn, again and again, that the apparent wandering is in fact disciplined, ordered, and revelatory. "Slow Child with a Book of Birds" begins,

> The snow that has no name is just
> This snow, falling so thick it seems
> To pause a moment in midair.

When I had stared long enough at it, the word
That held it showed me only a swirling without
A name, a piece of untalkative sky intact
Above a row of houses, & blankness filling
The frames of every doorway, a white
That made the dark around it visible.
Yesterday, the slow child on the bus, talkative
Amidst the fully evolved quiet of those
Around us muffled in their parkas, was showing me
A Snowy Egret in the book he carried.

The space between stanzas says, "Now, for something different." We leave behind the speaker's meditation on snow and shift to a scene on a bus. The space serves as a kind of transition, but we can't yet provide words for that transition; we don't know the relationship between the meditation and the scene. The first word of the second stanza provides a temporal bridge, and the Snowy Egret is a link to the subject of the speaker's reflection, signaling the beginning of a series of related images. The white and the dark, the blankness filling the doorways, and the snow with no name all serve to prepare us for what can't be put into words, for what will remain unknown; and, at the same time, they prepare us for a journey of discovery.

Like all blanks, associative leaps through space need to be created. We must understand what makes electricity arc through the air. A conscientious reader confronted with a string of unrelated passages separated by blanks will, for a while, dutifully attempt to form bridges from one passage to the next, to discover the writer's logic or pattern, the work's intended accumulation. If no such thing is discernable, however, the reader will eventually, understandably, move on to something else. Such is the risk of communicating through silence. The rewards include the powerful bolt of understanding a leap can create, an understanding that reaches the reader beyond words, beyond rational explanation, and so is more intensely felt.

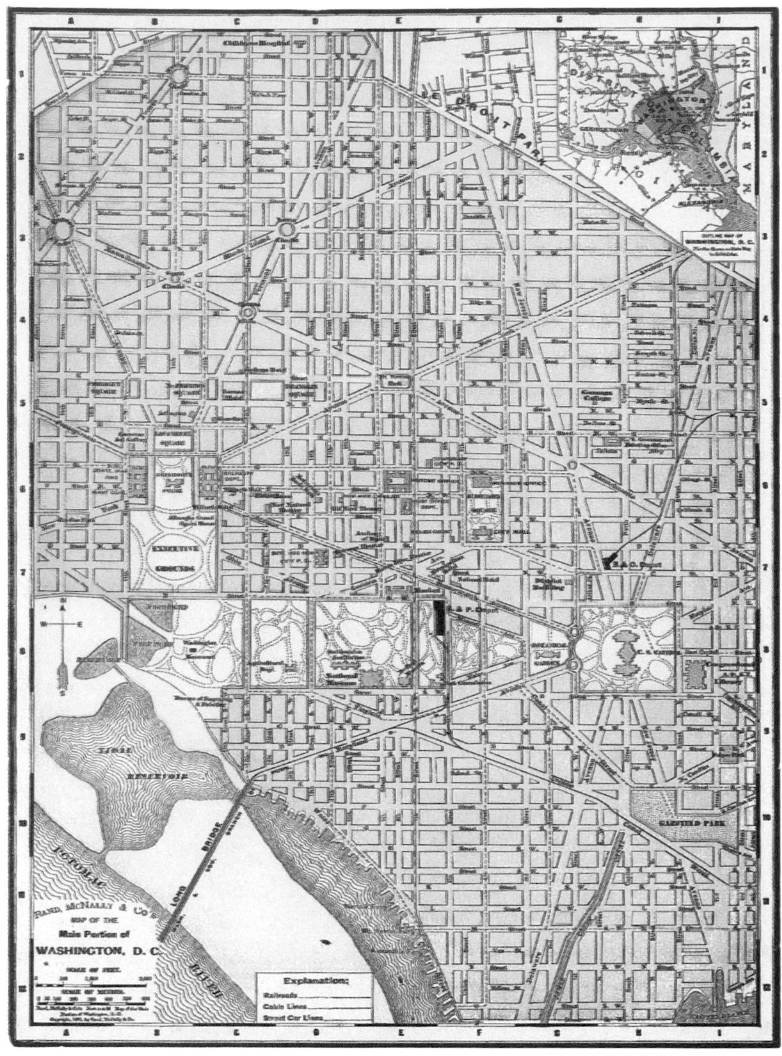

FIG. 13 **THIS 1895 MAP OF WASHINGTON, D.C., IS BUSY WITH STREETS, BUT SPARSELY AND CURIOUSLY SKETCHED WITH BUILDINGS. THE "PRESIDENT'S HOUSE" IS AN OBVIOUS CANDIDATE FOR IDENTIFICATION, AS IS THE U.S. CAPITOL, BUT "METZEROTTS MUSIC HALL"? AND WHO, WE MIGHT WONDER, GAVE THE COCHRAN HOTEL SUCH CLOUT? THE SAME PERSON WHO FELT COMPELLED TO LABEL THE "HOUSE WHERE LINCOLN DIED"?**

I remember
staring straight ahead
into the world my father saw;
I was learning
to absorb its emptiness,
the heavy snow
not falling, whirling around us.

— FROM "SNOW," BY LOUISE GLÜCK

CRITICAL CARTOGRAPHER J. B. Harley distinguished between mere blanks and what he called "silences," or "the intentional or unintentional suppression of knowledge in maps." In his essay "Silences and Secrecy," he suggests, "Silence and utterance are not alternatives but constituent parts of map language, each necessary for the understanding of the other." Significant silences in fiction are easy to find, once we listen for them. Some are as central as the withholding of the name of the narrator in Ralph Ellison's *Invisible Man*, the unmentionable and so unmentioned abortions in Ernest Hemingway's "Hills Like White Elephants" and J. D. Salinger's "The Laughing Man," and the mystery of what happens in the Marabar Caves in E. M. Forster's *Passage to India*. Most if not all of Hemingway's fiction involves the relationship of (male) characters' actions to a moral code that is largely unspoken but constantly alluded to. In "The Short Happy Life of Frances Macomber," after Frances kills a buffalo, Wilson, the hunting guide, quotes Shakespeare, then thinks, "He was very embarrassed, having brought out this thing he had lived by."* When Macomber babbles on in his excitement, Wilson is forced to articulate part of the code: "You're not supposed to mention it. . . . Doesn't do to talk too much about all this. Talk the whole thing away." Too much talking is, for Wilson, a kind of blasphemy.

David Malouf's *Remembering Babylon* tells the story of Gemmy Fairley, a British cabin boy who is taken in by Australian

* "By my troth, I care not; a man can die but once; we owe God a death and let it go which way it will, he that dies this year is quit for the next."

Aborigines and, after sixteen years, rejoins European settlers. In the opening scene, Gemmy, who has nearly forgotten how to speak English, says, "Do not shoot. . . . I am a B-b-british object." Later in the first chapter, we hear him name body parts, to prove his ability to speak the language, however haltingly. Throughout the rest of the book's two hundred pages, we often see Gemmy, and hear his thoughts, as translated by the omniscient narrator, but we never again hear his voice. This silence, which Malouf sustains without contrivance, underscores Gemmy's status in his new community: he is never fully trusted, and none of the other characters feel they know him. As beneficiaries of the narrative, we feel we know him best; but then, between the nineteenth and twentieth chapters, he disappears, his fate uncertain. Although Gemmy is the novel's central character, he is a ghostly presence.

More recently, Mark Costello's *Big If* offers examples of the suppression of knowledge on several levels. The novel is, in part, about the insatiable desire for security, or certainty. Most of the book focuses on Secret Service agents responsible for protecting the life of the vice president of the United States. Costello's book is dense with the sorts of details crucial to the success of security: details about streets, crowds, cars, bicycles, radios, helicopters, scuba divers, strangers pressing close, and the curious dance of agents literally pressed up against the man they are protecting, dictating his movements left and right, forward and back, ever ready to step in front of him or to throw him down and lay their bodies across his. Almost entirely absent from the book, and from the agents' thoughts, is the vice president himself, the person and politician. The vice president could be anyone; their job would be the same. The vice president is at the center of Costello's novel the way a hole is in the center of a donut.

The prose of the characters and of the narration captures the abbreviations and acronyms of government and military work (IAB and DEA, GS-9s and DAs) and of computer software companies (bots and AI, MIPs and IPOs) and extends it into the lives of the characters (the Plaz, the pike, the 2-3), to the point that everyone seems to be speaking in shorthand. Explanations are removed, words are removed, parts of words are removed; omissions give the language of the book, and so the world of its characters, mystery, density, and authority.

The dramatic climax of the novel comes when a man makes an attempt to kill the vice president—or appears to. In fact, his gun is empty, and it becomes clear that the man, a recently fired software designer, was committing suicide by Secret Service. A note of explanation is found tucked into his shirt pocket, shredded by one of the government's snipers' bullets. An agent reads the fragments, uncertain if the parts are even in the right order:

> "To Whom It May Concern . . .
> . . . no choice but to . . .
> . . . test against . . .
> . . . so that my message could be . . .
> . . . I am not a 'crazy' . . .
> . . . shuttle . . .
> . . . O-ring . . .
> . . . engineer . . .
> . . . my mother and my sister Ruth . . .
> Remember me.
> Vaughn Naubek"
>
> The aides and campaign handlers kept up their bright banter on the village green, but the agents in their midst were frozen, blank-faced, listening. The meaning of the empty gun was plain enough.

The man's last utterance is destroyed when he is destroyed. There isn't enough left for us to deduce his meaning with any certainty, and the character has been peripheral — we've seen him earlier in the novel, but we can only guess the reasons for his despair. We know him the way we know the quiet neighbor down the street who, one night, shows up on the news. The omissions remind us that, even if we had the note, we'd still be far from understanding the man.

ON THE MOST fundamental level, all fiction rests on the unwritten statement, "This is fiction." The reader is, traditionally, asked to ignore that knowledge, but the reader needs to have it, nevertheless; otherwise, everything that follows would be an act of miscommunication.* First-person fictional narratives, and especially unreliable or ironic first-person narratives, depend on our understanding of a particular type of silence. When Huckleberry Finn decides to help Jim gain his freedom and says, "All right, then, I'll go to hell," we understand that what Huck is doing is in fact virtuous, and more truly "Christian" than what he has been taught. Mark Twain's judgment of Huck's action is communicated loud and clear—and yet silently.

You'll recall the opening of Edgar Allan Poe's "The Tell-Tale Heart":

> TRUE! nervous, very, very dreadfully nervous I had been and am; but why WILL you say that I am mad? The disease had sharpened my senses, not destroyed, not dulled them. Above all was the sense of hearing acute. I heard all things in the heaven and in the earth. I heard many things in hell. How then am I mad? Hearken! and observe how healthily, how calmly, I can tell you the whole story.

The story is in the form of a monologue by a man who says he has heard "all things in the heaven and in the earth." While we distrust the narrator, not for a moment do we distrust the author. From the beginning, there is a distinction between what the narrator asserts and what we believe; our recognition and acceptance of that distinction is a silent but essential bond between reader and writer. There are no words to this effect, but the words

* In the last century and in this one, an increasing number of writers as diverse as John Barth, Tim O'Brien, and David Shields have made that very issue the subject of their work. Such writing rests heavily on our awareness that we bring different expectations and assumptions to prose that calls itself "fiction."

create the effect. Ironic distance is often a cause of exasperation for beginning writers, as they either intend irony their readers do not perceive, or they mean for their character or narrator to be taken at face value, but readers disagree with the character's pronouncements and so find themselves unwilling or unable to share the story's assumptions and judgments. Satirists make a living walking the line, as in Jonathan Swift's notoriously immodest proposal.

In the opening paragraphs of "Revelation," Flannery O'Connor tempts us to judge Mrs. Turpin as an obese southern racist and snob; by the end, she allows Mrs. Turpin a vision and, without saying so, exposes our own prejudice. O'Connor's fiction investigates, rather than dictates, the beliefs most important to her. Her stories raise questions and leave us in carefully designed voids. In "Cathedral," Raymond Carver's narrator has a vision, a vision he can't put into words beyond, "It's really something." Like many of Carver's characters, the narrator of "Cathedral" can't articulate what he feels to be transcendent insight. The

FIG. 14 **JUST AS WE RARELY CONSIDER WHAT LIES UNDERGROUND, TO A MOLE, WE MIGHT IMAGINE, THE WORLD ABOVE THE SURFACE IS A LARGE, POSSIBLY TERRIFYING BLANK**

absence of explicit, coherent expression represents the character's movement to the brink of comprehension.

In some cases we obscure the presence of a blank—draw the reader's attention away from it—only until we want to call attention to what has been missing. This is the classic strategy of a certain type of mystery, as when Sherlock Holmes supplies the swamp adder, the key to "The Adventure of the Speckled Band." A similar strategy is put to much different use in Richard Russo's story "The Mysteries of Linwood Hart." For the first two and a half pages the story appears to be about young Linwood's decision to play American Legion baseball. Those pages are about a particularly contemplative boy and his interest in the will of inanimate objects, including Wiffle balls: "Their frantic wiggle after leaping off a plastic bat suggested . . . desire, though his father, who at the moment wasn't living with Lin and his mother, explained that the symmetrical holes cut into the plastic sphere were responsible for the ball's erratic and exciting flight." The information offered parenthetically, in the middle of the sentence, changes our understanding of everything we've read up to that point, and redefines our expectations for what lies ahead. In the very next sentence, we are newly aware of an enormous omission. "Okay, but to Lin's way of thinking, the holes merely set free the inner spirit of the ball." There is no mention of Linwood's parents' separation, but now everything he thinks resonates off the one subject he *doesn't* allow himself to think about; the reader is on high alert as the boy continues pondering repressed inner spirits.

Such skillful writers decide precisely when and how to draw the reader's attention to their omissions, as when a magician "clumsily" reveals the secret to his trick, so that the revelation of the "secret" reorients his audience. A blank that recalibrates the reader's viewing angle occurs in *Lolita* when Humbert Humbert stops short of describing a sexual act ("I will not bore my learned readers with a detailed account"). Humbert's refusal to provide the lurid details works both as a joke and as a reminder of the difference between the book we're reading and the imitation-Victorian pornography some readers might (and did) mistake it to be. In every narrative, by providing certain details and omitting others, we are signaling to the reader how we want her to focus her attention. Humbert's silence later in *Lolita*, when he declines to name "the name that the astute reader had guessed long ago" is a different kind of joke, and draws our attention to what we can't (yet) see. On first reading of the novel, we have no idea who has been chasing Humbert. His sense of the obviousness of the puzzle's solution reminds us that he is so deeply focused on his own world, and on his obsessively intricate narrative, that he doesn't realize when he has lost his reader's sympathy or understanding. (This is not to say that Nabokov has lost us, which would be another matter entirely.) Humbert's allusion to the name he imagines we've guessed also serves as a reminder that he knows more than he's telling — which is to say, Nabokov's gesture expands the world of the story. Authoritative nods to all that goes unsaid help to create the illusion that the reader is seeing only a glimpse of a much larger fictional world.

The very short lyric, and the short short story, products of selection and intense compression, have something of the power and effect of the fragment, making use, as they do, of the evocative powers of allusion and elision. Any given novel or story is both selective and shaped. It asserts itself as whole and at the same time claims to be a portion of something potentially larger. In that sense, all fiction and poetry draws on the power of elision. In the past century, however, an increasing amount of fiction (such as Michael Ondaatje's *The Collected Works of Billy the Kid*), poetry (Brenda Hillman's *Loose Sugar*), and nonfiction (D. J. Waldie's *Holy Land*) has drawn on the power of fragmentation. Just as a visitor to Rome can't help but stop and imagine what the Forum looked like at various earlier times, and a viewer of the Elgin marbles is led to an appreciation of the

Parthenon as it once was, the reader of fragmented work is encouraged, and in some cases required, to fill in the blanks—to take part in that act Carson calls "imaginal adventure."

While such work reflects our current world and culture, its techniques have long precedent. J. Isaacs identifies as one of the sources of imagist poetry the Japanese form known as the "stop-short," referred to as such "because the words stopped and the meaning went on." In the Busōn haiku

Apprentice's holiday:
hops over kite string
keeps going

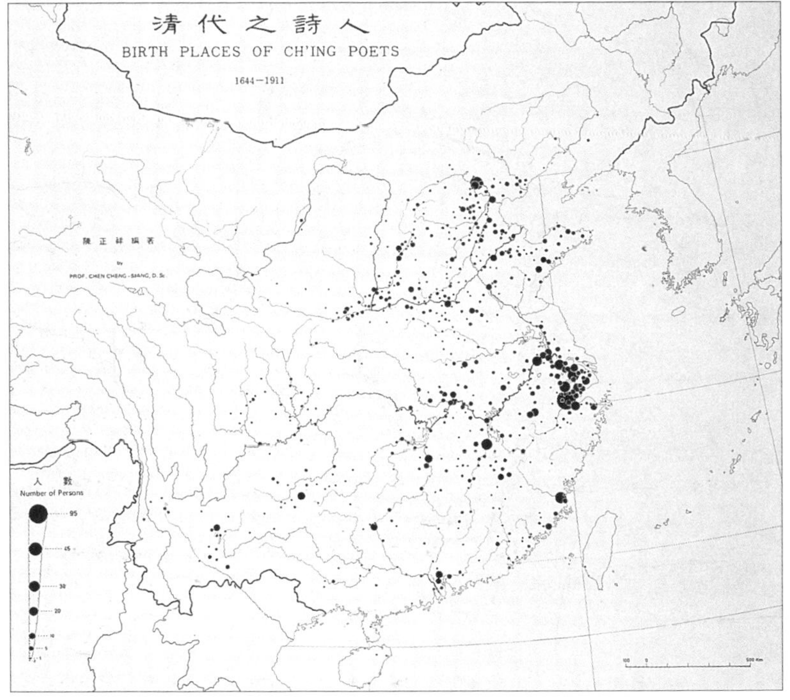

FIG. 15

the apprentice himself appears through optical illusion, the possessive noun and the verbs implying his presence. The kite itself is invisible — never seen, never noted — yet it is absolutely present. The kite is a powerful blank; the kite *string* is held taut by the unseen.

Haiku, the most famously concise poetic form, traditionally begins with a theme related to one of the seasons, then adds a penetrating image. Like aboriginal songlines, traditional haiku were deeply codified — to try to appreciate their original intent, modern readers need the equivalent of a map's legend, an explanation of the code. Many of the seasonal references (deep autumn, snowfall) were stock and alluded to a larger body of poems with which the reader was presumed to be familiar. The seasonal reference served as the poem's orientation, as in these by Bashō:

Deep autumn—
my neighbor,
 how does he live, I wonder?

It's not like anything
they compare it to —
 the summer moon.

Sick on a journey,
my dreams wander
 the withered fields.*

Haiku are not fragments, but they function like a shard of glass reflecting the moonlight—the detail Chekhov suggested a fellow writer use in place of a long description of night in the woods. For all its hundreds of pages, an evocative novel works the same way.

* Bashō—who was, with Wordsworth, one of the great walking poets—returns to the notions of journey and place. His last "travel book," *Back Roads to Far Towns*, is a collection of prose poems and haiku documenting a nine-month, 1,500-mile trek through Japan's northern mountains, begun when he was forty-six. Not surprisingly, the book conjures a great deal more than it states. The calligrapher who copied out the text includes a brief epilogue in which he describes his first reading of the work: "Once had my raincoat on, eager to go on a like journey, and then again content to sit imagining those rare sights."

> Reality is a very subjective affair. I can only define it as a kind of gradual accumulation of information; and as specialization. You can know more and more about one thing but you can never know everything about one thing: it's hopeless. So that we live surrounded by more or less ghostly objects.
>
> — VLADIMIR NABOKOV

LOLITA DEPICTS the way our interactions with the world are often based on illusion, and on both our willful and unintentional reliance on hazy perceptions. The opening passage about her nicknames notwithstanding, the reader is encouraged to forget — as Humbert tries to forget—the twelve-year-old Delores. Only Humbert calls her Lolita; the girl called Lolita is his creation, one who stands in the place of Dolores Haze, a girl whose thoughts and words we hear only through the powerfully distorting filter of Humbert's obsession. The novel is a love song to that obsession, that object of desire named Lolita; Delores Haze is all but silenced. Humbert recognizes this. He feels, after a night in the Enchanted Hunters hotel, that he is "sitting with the small ghost of somebody [he] had just killed." At the end of the novel, when she is married and pregnant, when Humbert cannot so easily project upon her his vision of a nymphet, he sees—so we see—Delores (now Dolly Schiller) more nearly as she is. The novel expresses, among other things, the tension arising from Humbert's inability to erase Delores Haze from the image he means to present the reader of the ideal nymphet. But again: while Humbert fails at his stated purpose of "fix[ing] once for all the perilous magic of nymphets," his failure is not Nabokov's failure. Nabokov's novel depends on Humbert's lapses, and on our catching glimpses, beyond the nymphet Lolita, of the girl Delores.

Humbert wants to live in a fantasy world, one in which Delores Haze is completely erased by—or, better yet, transformed by the power of his desire *into*—Lolita. But as much as he wills it, he cannot fully inhabit that world; he can only enter it, briefly, alone. It is a world of his imagination.

A reader enters the world of a poem or story, realistic or otherwise, willing, at least for a short time, to believe it and to accept its terms. An enormous amount of popular art, or entertainment, asks us to inhabit its world in order to escape from our own. More ambitious art invites us to inhabit its world but also to see around it and beyond it — to see our own world through it. It draws the imagination outward.

James Wood writes that the best fiction "appears to discover facts by giving us the impression that our reading of the text completes the bottom half of a discovery whose plaintive stalk the writer has merely uncovered. Fiction should seem to offer itself to the reader's completion, not to the writer's. . . . Perhaps this illusion of discovery, the uncovering of a world which is related to, but not continuous with, the known world, is fiction's greatest beauty." Chekhov is a master of this counterpressure, or resonance of the seen off the unseen. At the end of the short story "Anyuta," he allows us to overhear someone shouting "Grigory! The samovar!" The speaker and the man he addresses are unknown to us. The line has no bearing on plot or character. Rather, in a single stroke, it moves us back from the scene of a medical student and his poor mistress, returning them to their context, reminding us that what we've witnessed is an all-too-typical moment. Chekhov says none of this, but with a single gesture he sketches a frame around his story, and so changes our perspective on it.

We're left with essential questions: How do we know when we've left too much in? Taken too much out? Is less always more? Is a story really like an iceberg?

Wolfe, the notorious putter-inner, is right. We can't help but select, can't help but omit. It's possible to fail on both sides: by telling too much (giving pages of detail, description, and event that detract because they fail to develop and direct, cluttering

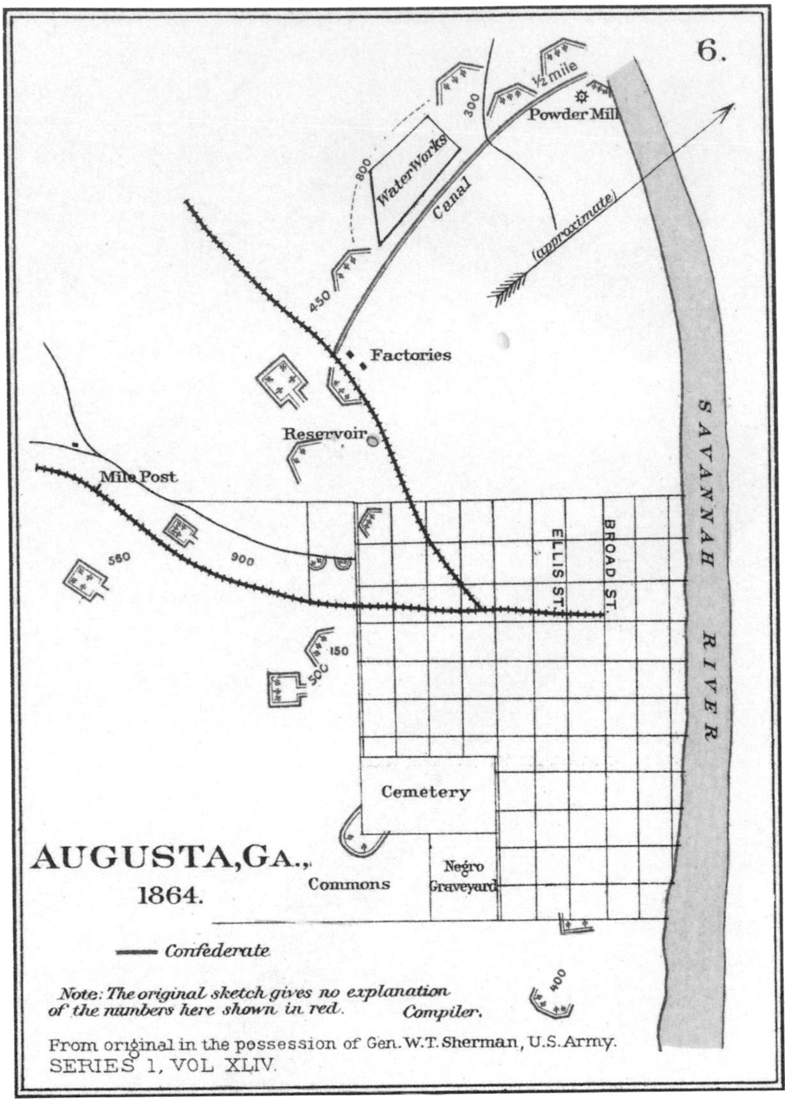

FIG. 16 THIS MAP OF AUGUSTA CARRIED BY GEN. WILLIAM TECUMSEH SHERMAN DURING HIS NOTORIOUS "MARCH TO THE SEA" IN 1864 DEPICTS TRAIN LINES, WATERWAYS, CONFEDERATE POSITIONS, AND CEMETERIES, BUT VIRTUALLY NO EVIDENCE OF CIVILIAN LIFE—NOT EVEN OF THE HOME OF THE YOUNG WOMAN HE LOVED AND HAD VOWED TO PROTECT

the story) and by not telling enough (by failing to fully enter a scene or a character's point of view, by failing to explore beyond our early impulse). While the narrative poets can teach valuable lessons about compression, there is no superior virtue in the ability to tell a story in few words. Proust, Dickens, and Melville aren't merely long-winded predecessors to Carver, Donald Barthelme, and Lydia Davis. Just as we still have need for atlases and street maps, some fictional worlds are the richer for their densely populated cities, their large vistas.

But there is also beauty in the telling detail, the provocative glimpse, the perfectly framed snapshot. The question of what to include, how much to include, can only be answered with regard to what, precisely, we mean to create. A story isn't as utilitarian as a map of bicycle paths, but like that map, it is defined by its purpose. To serve its purpose, a story might very well be stripped down to a few spare glittering parts; alternately, it might require, or benefit from, apparently useless observations, conversations, and excursions. Perhaps the only answer is that we can't know what needs to be in, what needs to be out, until we know what it is that we're making, toward what end.

And so every story is an iceberg. Or an ice sculpture. Sculpture, after all, is the art of cutting away, of finding David in a block of marble, or one of all the possible Davids. Even a child eyeing a pumpkin in October knows that most of the work ahead will be deciding what to remove.

LITERARY FICTION is sometimes said to offer the reader a window into other worlds. It has alternately been described as a mirror reflecting our world back to us. In *Duck Soup*, Groucho Marx walks in front of what appears to be a mirror. But there is no glass; instead, standing on the other side of an imaginary line, is Harpo, dressed in identical costume. As Groucho moves, Harpo moves. One is the "real" man, the other reflecting him.

FIG. 17 **GROUCHO EYES HARPO, SPEECHLESS**

At first, Groucho seems to think he's looking in a mirror, seeing himself, and Harpo tries to maintain that illusion (though he doesn't necessarily imitate the man; as the scene goes on, he finds clever ways to cheat). But Groucho knows the mirror is broken, knows he's looking at an illusion, and decides to put it to a series of tests. The space between the man and his "image," where glass once was, becomes highly charged. The viewer sits forward, waiting to see what will be revealed.

We could say Groucho is the reader and Harpo the story, or an active fictional reflection—which is to say, no mere reflection but a distinct world of possibility, one that can reflect, exaggerate, or contradict; one that can stay on its side of an imaginary line, accepting a formal distance, or step directly into our lives. The mirror, or barrier, is a joint construction of the imagination, one dependent on the willed suspension of disbelief.

Or Groucho is the reader, Harpo the writer. As writers, we can't speak directly to each individual reader, but through our actions—through our writing—we can deceive, puzzle, and enlighten. Perhaps the ultimate blank is the space between reader and writer — or, more accurately, the space between the story we create and send out to the world and the story each reader perceives. The work leaves our hands; after the reader reads, it leaves hers. She returns our book to the shelf newly aware of what had been blank space, emptiness, a previously unremarkable desert in her imaginative landscape. With our invisible pencil, we have added a line to her chart of the world.

PROJECTIONS AND CONVENTIONS

These men are forced into their strange fancies by attempting to measure the whole universe by means of their tiny scale.

GALILEO GALILEI

TO THE BEST of our knowledge, every culture has engaged in some sort of mapping. The question has never been whether to make maps, but what to select for inclusion and how to represent it, given that any map is, as Mark Monmonier says, "but one of an indefinitely large number of maps that might be produced from the same data."

Cartographers must continually confront the fact that there is no such thing as objective presentation. All maps are like the Way Finder in that, in the name of usefulness, they must assume a bias. The first lie of a map—also the first lie of fiction—is that it is the truth. And a great deal of a map's, or story's, or poem's authority results from its ability to *convince* us of its authority. While we expect realistic writing to be accurate when it refers to the world we know, in fiction and poetry, authority has relatively little to do with objective reportage, or simply getting facts right.

As early as the year 130, Claudius Ptolemy noted that, "when the Earth is delineated on a sphere, it has a shape like its own,

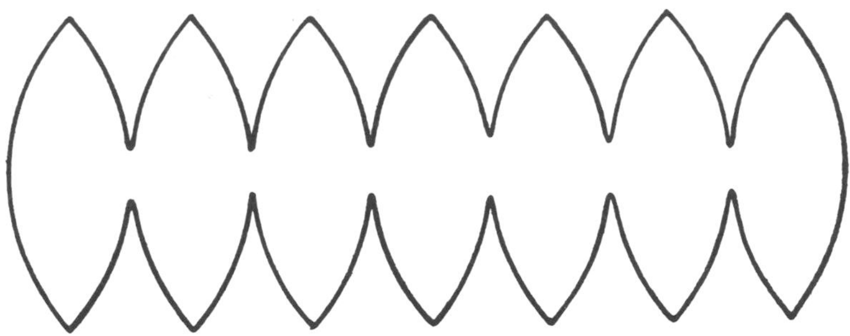

FIG. 18 **THE ORANGE PEEL PROBLEM**

[without] need of altering," but to transfer that sphere to a sheet of paper requires "a certain adjustment." (Introductory texts refer to this as "The Orange Peel Problem." If you were to remove the entire peel from an orange in a single piece — and so, by analogy, remove the surface of Earth — there would be no way to lay it flat without cutting it in several places and/or pressing and pulling it.) To that end, Ptolemy devised the first scientific cartographic projection, one that was influential over a span of 1,400 years.* In 1569 Gerardus Mercator created a map using "a new proportion and a new arrangement of the meridians with reference to the parallels."† Mercator's projection dominated popular cartography to the end of the twentieth century—to the extent that most of us grew up seeing a German globe-maker's view of the world. He would have been as surprised as anyone; he thought he was solving a problem for sailors. Mercator described his 1569 map as a "New and Improved Description of the Lands of the World, Adapted and Intended for the Use of Navigators." His projection was tremendously important because it was so practical, so useful—for a particular purpose. It allowed sailors to lay a ruler on the map and plan a

* A projection is simply a mathematical formula used to project points from a sphere (such as Earth) onto a sheet of paper. As there is no way to do so with uniform accuracy—just as there is no way to get that orange peel to lie flat without stretching it—cartographic projections are sometimes referred to as "distortion formulas." Every flat map includes some distortion of shape, area, or length.

† Born Gerard Kremer, at eighteen he took for himself a Latinized name for merchant, one with allusions to a type of roving bookseller.

straight-line course for their destination. Despite its being used for centuries to teach schoolchildren geography, it is a particularly misleading projection for that purpose. On Mercator's map, distortion increases as one moves farther from the equator (and the most important sailing routes of the sixteenth century) so that Greenland appears to be the size of South America—though in fact South America is nine times larger.

Visual artists face an equivalent of the cartographic paradox: a painter attempts to render a three- (or four-) dimensional world in two dimensions. This can only be accomplished through techniques that are never entirely satisfactory. "A two-dimensional painting," James Lord writes,

> is obliged to make a correspondingly greater concession to the conventions of illusion. And one of the most rigidly established of those conventions has been that a representational image, however remote from actual reality, must nevertheless in its own terms appear complete and homogeneous. Like so many other visual habits, however, and like so many conventions, this attitude constitutes a limitation. What is important is the acuity of the artist's vision and the degree of realization of that vision, nothing more.

"Conventions of illusion" date back at least as far as the first cave paintings, and every artist since has worked with the prevailing conventions, or against them.* One of the most celebrated examples of a new vision in the arts is the French impressionists' struggle for acceptance. The early impressionists broke with "official" art in part by mixing paint on the palette rather than dropping pure color on the canvas. Their paintings were rejected for decades not only by the Salon, and by many of Europe's leading museums, but also by the public; yet today museums are forced to turn thousands of people away from major impressionist exhibits. Winslow Homer, who began his career as a highly suc-

* The sources of such conventions and their universality are worth more consideration than I'll give them here. The petroglyphs on rock walls along the San Juan River in New Mexico are surprisingly similar in representational style to those on rock walls in Africa.

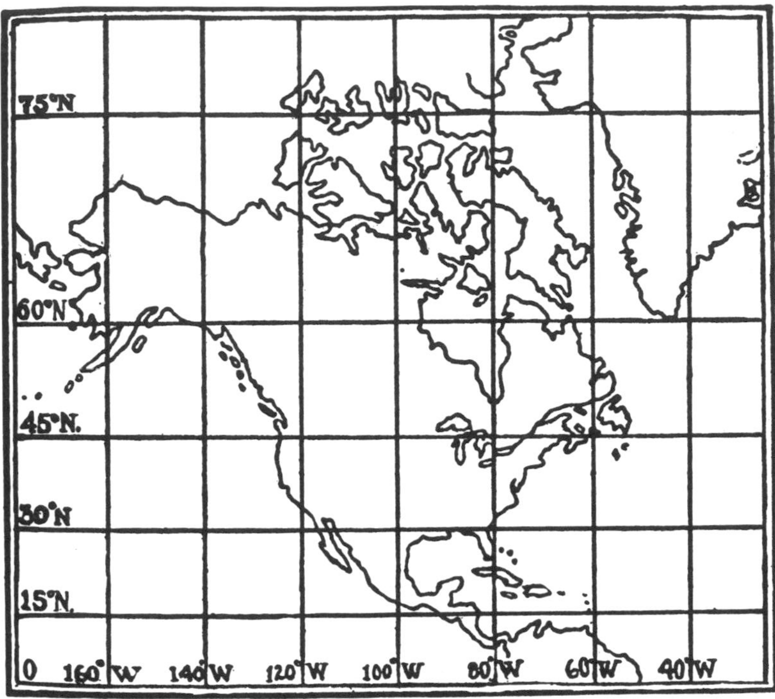

FIG. 19 MERCATOR'S PROJECTION COMPLETED

cessful illustrator for *Harper's Weekly*, traveled to France in 1866 and returned a changed painter. He began to experiment not only with color and light but with subject; his depiction of women at the seashore (preposterously overdressed, by today's conventions) was considered immoral. But that wasn't all the critics said. They found his use of color "absurd"; one landscape's background was described as "a bank of frozen oatmeal." Another viewer felt the figures were painted "in reckless disregard of all truth—in defiance of all law." His sketches were called "grotesque," the work of "a man's shutting his eyes and rubbing all his pencils and pigments at once over a canvas in a conglomerate frenzy." One reviewer wrote, in response to an 1869 exhibition, "How an artist of acknowledged worth in a certain field of art could permit this horror to leave his studio is simply incomprehensible to us. . . . [It] suggests unhappy accident on canvas." Today, reproductions of those same paintings commonly appear on greeting cards. But the point isn't that the critics of the day were wrong; it's that art can change not only what we see but how we see.

Breaks from tradition, resulting in work that seems (and is) rebellious but which, in time, *becomes* the tradition, are not the exception but the rule. "What happens when a new work of art is created," T. S. Eliot wrote in "Tradition and the Individual Talent,"

> is something that happens simultaneously to all the works of art which preceded it. The existing monuments form an ideal order among themselves, which is modified by the introduction of the new (the really new) work of art among them. The existing order is complete before the new work arrives; for order to persist after the supervention of novelty, the *whole* existing order must be, if ever so slightly, altered.

Our view of the world changes in many ways, for many reasons. Hundreds of cartographic projections have been devised, and while many are closely enough related to be categorized by type, over one hundred are currently in use. Each projection is a tool. Some are better at preserving size, some at preserving shape, some are more accurate over east-west distances while others are preferred for north-south spans.* But minimizing distortion is not the only criterion by which mapmakers decide which projection to use. The ultimate challenge to the dominance of Mercator's vision, according to Susan Schulten, was World War II.

> At three pivotal moments in the war—after the German invasion of Poland, the bombing of Pearl Harbor, and the assault on Normandy—Americans bought in a matter of hours what in peacetime would have been a year's supply of maps and

* The Mercator projection is drawn to no single scale, so does not allow the viewer to calculate distances easily, and results in infinitely large poles; Ptolemy's projection preserved areas (so land masses that are the same size appear to be the same size) but not shapes; the Peters projection preserves size in the equatorial regions with considerable distortion of shapes; and so on.

> atlases. The countless maps Americans bought showed them a world that would have been utterly unfamiliar a decade earlier. Gone was Mercator's ordered plane, which had comfortably distanced Americans from Europe and Asia. The global nature of the war, together with the advent of aviation, completely reconfigured the look and shape of the world on a map. Americans now pored over maps that represented the world as a sphere, or that placed the North Pole at the center, projections and perspectives that would otherwise have been familiar only to cartographers. These new maps emphasized America's *proximity* to Europe and Asia over the North Pole and across the oceans, shaking the nation's well-developed sense of isolation.

Early in 1942 President Roosevelt urged people to have a map nearby for his next fireside chat, but they probably needed no presidential dictate. The American people wanted urgently to see the world as it had been redefined. Nearly sixty years later, when the towers of the World Trade Center were destroyed, millions of people suddenly wanted to know better the precise geography of lower Manhattan, including the identification of nearby buildings, historic sites, and bridges. (At the same time, New York City's Department of Design and Construction called upon one of the original designers of the buildings' foundations for accurate information on the locations of walls, passages, floors, and water, sewer, electrical, telephone, gas, subway, and train lines under the ruined plaza. No single drawing contained that information; the best resource was one man's mental map.) Soon after, newspapers began printing maps illustrating the topography of Afghanistan and its neighbors, the location of military bases and suspected terrorist strongholds. How we see depends, in part, on what we want to see.

> We are creatures of habit; given a blank we can't help trying to fill it in along lines of customary seeing or saying. But the best poetic lines undermine those habits, break the pre- off the -dictable, unsettle the suburbs of your routine sentiments, and rattle the tracks of your trains of thought.
>
> — HEATHER McHUGH

A MAP OF New York state. A map of New York City. A map of central Manhattan. A map of Central Park. A map of the Central Park Zoo. A map of the Central Park Zoo's tropical rainforest. A map showing footpaths through the zoo's rainforest; another showing bird nests; another showing where visitors tend to spend the most time; another showing how the mist sprayed from the ceiling disperses through the exhibit and the effect on temperature over time.

There is no end to the information we can use. A "good" map provides the information we need for a particular purpose — or the information the mapmaker wants us to have.* To guide us, a map's designers must consider more than content and projection; any single map involves hundreds of decisions about presentation. There is the issue of color (which ones to use, and how); there is the size of the map, which will affect its scale and depends on whether it will be used by armchair explorers or campers, which helps to determine the amount of information included, which involves consideration of font sizes and types. Will the names of towns be in uppercase letters? Will they always be above, or below, or to one side of the dots (or squares, or iconic skyscrapers) representing the places they name? What should be done when two places are so close together that their names don't fit? Which features should be

* Maps have long been used as the tools of government and business to encourage settlement and commerce, often distorting, or conveniently omitting some of the facts. Even when their justifications seem benign, such documents reveal their providers' concerns. Recently, the map distributed to visitors of the Arizona-Sonora Desert Museum depicted exhibits that didn't exist — exhibits under construction. This relieved docents of the need to explain the work going on, implicitly encouraged visitors to return when the work was complete, and, perhaps, encouraged donations.

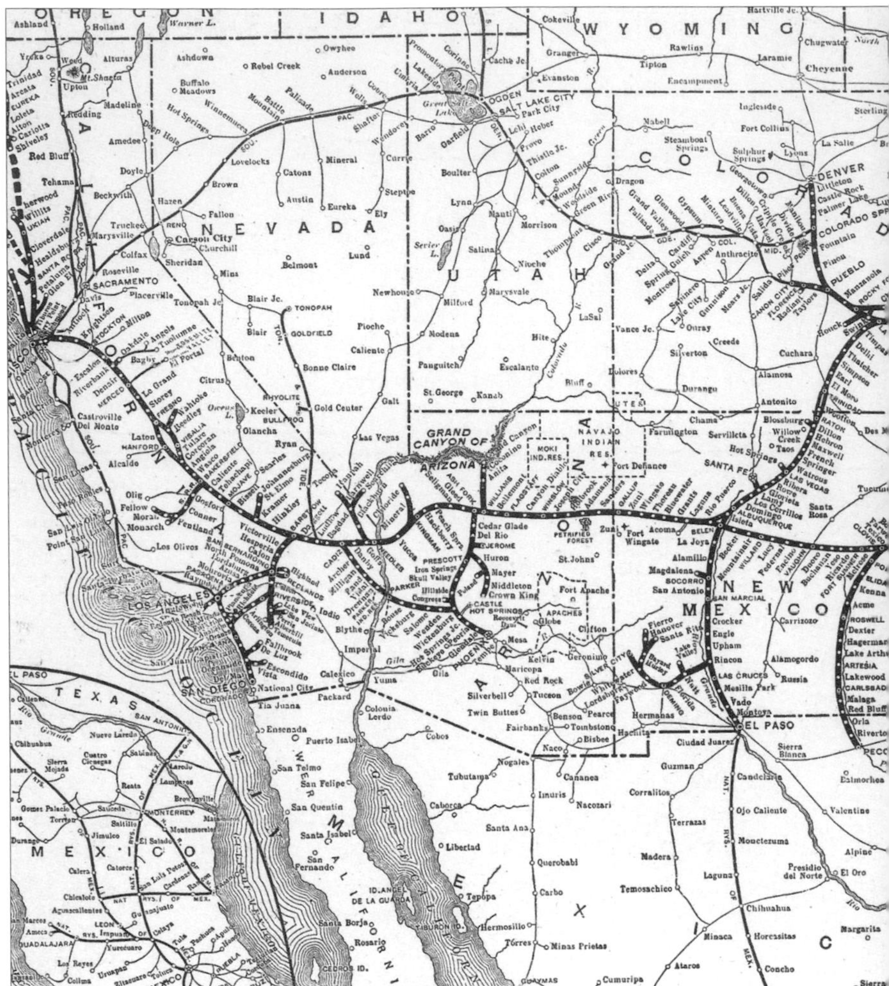
IDAHO
WYOMING
NEVADA
UTAH
COLORADO
CALIFORNIA
ARIZONA
NEW MEXICO
TEXAS
MEXICO
PACIFIC
GRAND CANYON OF ARIZONA
Cheyenne
Laramie
Rawlins
OGDEN
SALT LAKE CITY
DENVER
COLORADO SPRINGS
PUEBLO
SACRAMENTO
Carson City
TONOPAH
GOLDFIELD
Las Vegas
LOS ANGELES
SAN DIEGO
Yuma
PHOENIX
Tucson
SANTA FE
ALBUQUERQUE
EL PASO
Ciudad Juarez
Chihuahua
MONTERREY
MEXICO

FIG. 20 A 1915 MAP OF THE ATCHISON, TOPEKA, AND SANTA FE RAILROAD CHANGES SCALE AND SUFFERS TYPOGRAPHICAL DENSITY IN ITS EAGERNESS TO IDENTIFY EVERY CITY, TOWN, AND OUTPOST THE SYSTEM SERVES

included both graphically and by name? These decisions are crucial to a map's effectiveness.

Most often, what we ask of a map is to help us to get from here to there; and most of the maps we use mean to be transparently useful. To do this, they adhere to prevailing conventions so they can be "read," and used, immediately, with no special instruction or training. These include the maps we get at rental-car counters showing us how to return to the airport, maps of hiking trails handed out at national forests, and the color-coded maps of amusement parks.

The conventions of such maps are familiar: some variation on the compass rose, for orientation (or, in the case of an amusement park, the clear location of the entrance, usually at bottom center); a dark line indicating the trail, or trails; an indication of the map's scale (likely to be absent from the map of the amusement park, whose owners prefer we not know the wearying distance from the go-carts to the roller coaster); and a legend explaining the map's symbols (major highways, secondary roads; marked trails, unmarked trails; restaurants, first-aid stations). These maps want to guide us as efficiently as, say, a pulp romance novel or next summer's action-adventure movies. They want nothing to impede our journey. If they do their job well, they don't cause us a moment's inappropriate thought.

Readers don't turn to literature for an effortless, thoughtless journey; but as writers we want to guide, to the extent possible, their thoughtful reading of what we write. Usually we want their focus to be on content rather than on our decisions about presentation. We compel readers to look in the direction we want them to look, to see what we want them to see, the way we want them to see it.

Edward R. Tufte demonstrates the crucial relationship of presentation to understanding by considering two famous events in which certain facts were readily available but their meaning unclear. In the mid-nineteenth century, some people believed cholera spread through polluted water, but others believed it was airborne, and still others felt it rose from the ground in ceme-

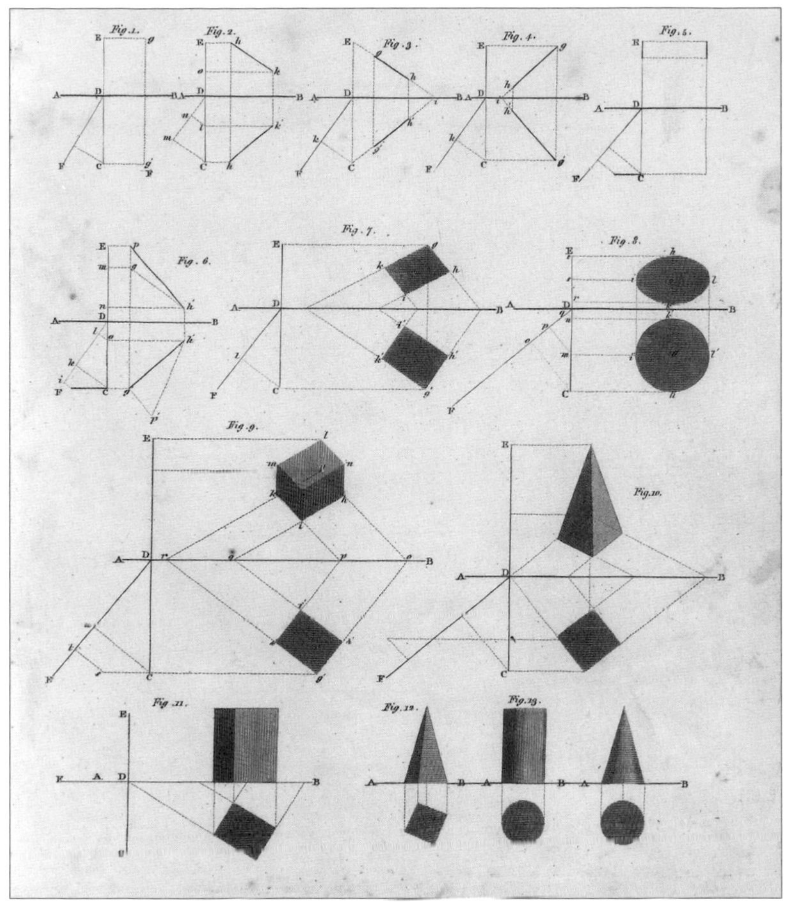

FIG. 21

teries, from the bodies of plague victims. In 1854 in London, John Snow suspected — correctly, as it turned out — that the then-current outbreak was spread through water at a polluted well. He plotted the addresses of plague victims on a map. The greatest number lived near the Broad Street pump, but there were curious exceptions: large groups who lived or worked in the same area yet were unaffected, and individuals from seemingly remote areas who had died. To test his theory, Snow investigated the apparent exceptions, and discovered highly plausible explanations.*

Confident in his conclusion, Snow set about carefully plotting the evidence. He de-emphasized sequence, or time, and instead emphasized location (the residences of the deceased) in relation to thirteen community well pumps, including the Broad Street pump, thus illustrating cause and effect. He represented the number and location of victims by dark-gray bars on what is called a dot map. Map in hand, he approached the local authorities and persuaded them to remove the pump handle, thus bringing an end to the epidemic—and even more importantly, helping to solve the mystery of the origin of the disease. Snow's thematic map was persuasive evidence largely because of its choices in presentation.†

That textbook example, like all persuasive arguments, might seem commonsensical; but as Mark Twain wrote, common sense is a curious name for something so rare. Tufte's contrasting illustration is the explosion of the space shuttle *Challenger* in January 1986. As the world now knows, the shuttle exploded due to the failure of two quarter-inch-thick rubber O-rings. The world was slower to learn that engineers at Morton Thiokol had recommended the shuttle not be launched precisely because they knew the rubber O-rings were likely to lose their resiliency in cold temperatures. The politics of the tale are dismally predictable, but the relevant point here is that Morton Thiokol's engineers made their initial recommendation based on "a history of O-ring damage during previous cool-weather launches of the shuttle, the physics of resiliency (which declines exponentially with cooling), and experimental data." They knew, or strongly suspected, what was going to happen; and yet, armed with conclusive evidence, the engineers failed to persuade NASA to postpone the launch. Their failure was not entirely due to political

* Among other things, he discovered a workhouse in the area had its own pump, which explained why the inmates were unaffected. Also spared were the workers of a brewery, both because it had its own well and because, according to the proprietor, "The men [were] allowed a certain quantity of malt liquor . . . [and did not] drink water at all."

† By redrawing that map in various ways, Mark Monmonier has illustrated that different, and perfectly plausible, presentations of the same evidence could have led to different conclusions or been inconclusive.

pressure. To support their recomm[illegible] thirteen separate charts, many of them dense with difficult-to-read information. Not one of the charts depicted a simple correlation between temperature and the resiliency of O-rings in test launches. So while the critical evidence was contained in the charts the engineers prepared—hurriedly—the night before the explosion, the presentation obscured the logical conclusion.

The relationship of presentation to a poem's or story's ultimate effect(s) explains why we might be persuaded to accept, even enjoy, lush descriptions in one piece but not in another, even if they are produced by the same writer. No individual word, phrase, sentence, detail, exchange of dialogue, or event is right or wrong, better or worse, on its own; context, or the entire piece of writing, defined by its intentions, is everything. Jorge Luis Borges makes the point in his "Pierre Menard, Author of *Don Quixote*," in which the title character sets out to write *Don Quixote*—identical, word by word, to Cervantes's book—two centuries later. By changing nothing other than the time in which it is written, Borges argues, the book becomes a completely different work.

Critical cartographers Denis Wood and J. B. Harley teach us to read maps carefully, alert to their implicit assumptions and omissions. Doing so allows us to annotate a typical United States map, such as the one produced by Raven Maps & Images, newly aware of the effect of conventions so common that they have become, for many of us, transparent.

The map neatly shows us something no one has ever seen. This is true not only because a curved and irregular surface has been flattened, but because any eye far enough away to take in the entire continent would almost certainly have seen clouds, and more certainly would not have seen the political borders of states, or place names. The colors of the land have been carefully selected to create an "elevation tint scheme." This "clear" image, then, is an artistic representation of certain natural and political features. It is an intellectual construct.

FIG. 22 (FOLLOWING SPREAD) **UNITED STATES (EXCEPT ALASKA AND HAWAII)**

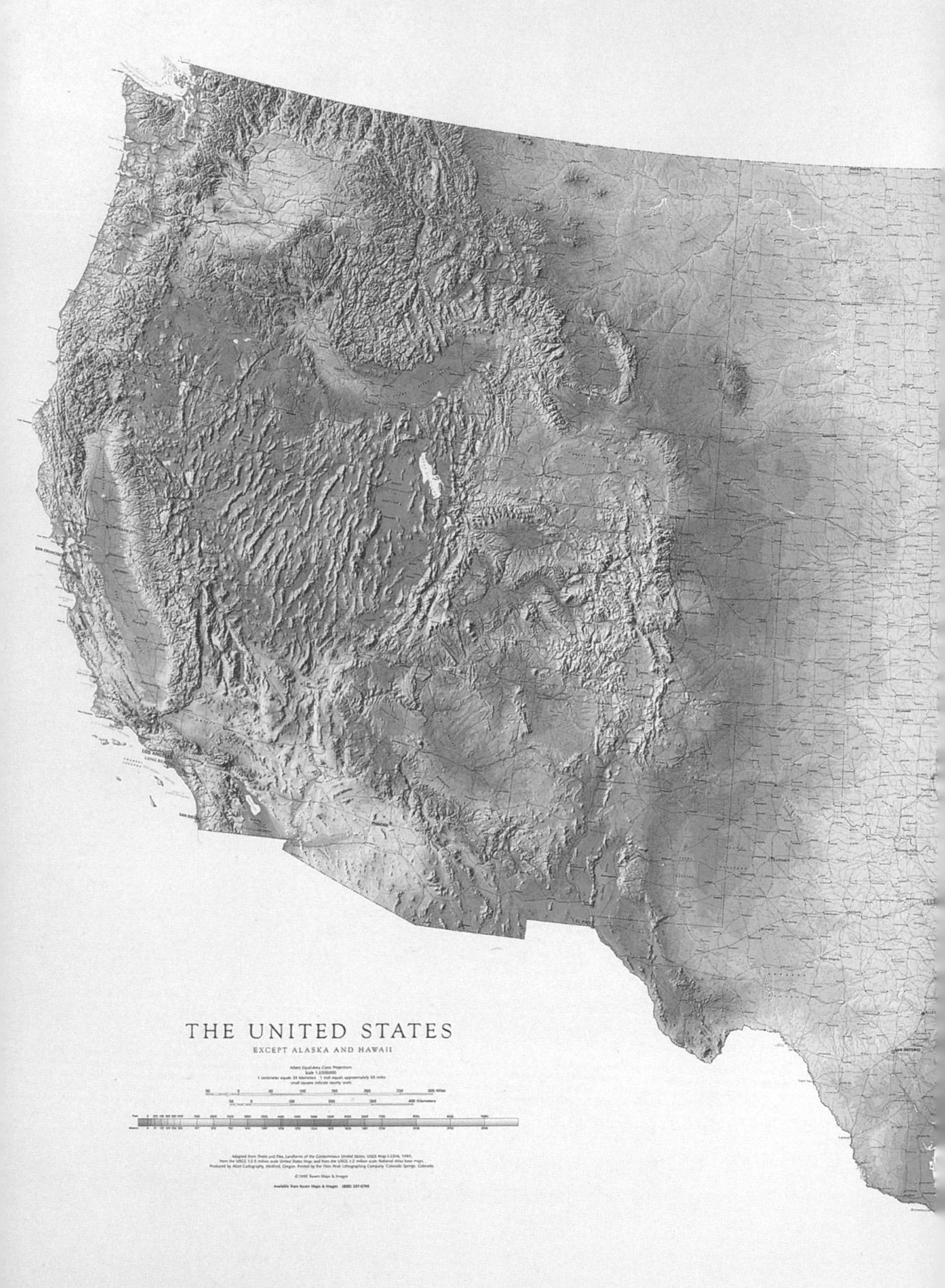
SAN FRANCISCO
LOS ANGELES
SAN DIEGO
EL PASO
SAN ANTONIO
THE UNITED STATES
EXCEPT ALASKA AND HAWAII
Albers Equal-Area Conic Projection
Miles
Kilometers

MILWAUKEE
CHICAGO
DETROIT
TOLEDO
CLEVELAND

We must recognize, too, how the unavoidable act of selectivity affects the map. Raven's map of the United States is in fact a map of the contiguous United States (and labeled as such). Alaska and Hawaii, the locations of which make them inconvenient to include on a single-scale depiction, are simply excluded. For roughly two million Americans, these are disturbing omissions. And while location has played a crucial role in determining what is included, the mapmakers have decided that proximity alone isn't enough. Mexico and Canada are not, of course, among the United States, but the presence of white spaces in their stead makes them invisible, inconsequential. Their absence on Raven's map makes this an explicitly political document, as national interests, not natural landforms, are the primary determining factor. But while the waters off the coast are, for political purposes, the nation's to protect, defend, fish, and drill, the Atlantic and Pacific Oceans and the Gulf of Mexico are neither depicted nor labeled. Land is, implicitly, more important than water.

The cartographers have chosen to include "Cultural Information," which, they say, consists of "cities, highways, airports, and other information independent from the landforms but of interest to the viewer." That assertion, and the information selected, reveals a great deal about the mapmakers' assumptions. Similarly, one of my colleagues in environmental science recently led students in a project to encourage local children to think of themselves as living not in Asheville, or in western North Carolina, but in the French Broad River watershed. He was, of course, holding a map designed to do just that. Those apparently objective maps are not so different from the cartoonish ones distributed by chambers of commerce that depict, at least as prominently as highways and national parks, the restaurants, antique shops, and retail stores that have paid for the advertising. In return for underwriting the map, those businesses are made visible, to the detriment of their invisible competitors.* Every map intends not simply to serve us but to influence us. If we fork over the money for one

* This ploy is offered as a service to the consumer by the Internet service Mapquest. A list of advertising hotel and fast-food chains allows the user to create, for instance, a map of the country according to Denny's.

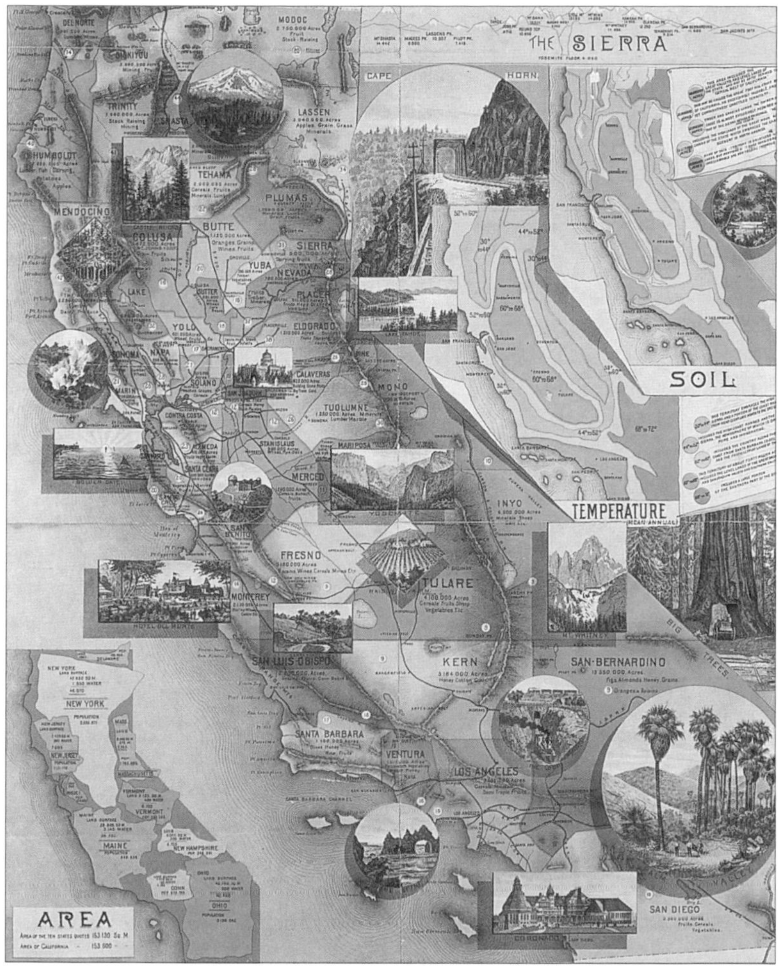

FIG. 23 **IN 1890, E. McD. JOHNSTONE MADE *THE UNIQUE MAP OF CALIFORNIA* FOR THE SOUTHERN PACIFIC RAILROAD COMPANY AND THE STATE BOARD OF TRADE OF CALIFORNIA TO LURE FARMERS AND OTHER SETTLERS TO THE LAND OF PLENTY**

of Raven's beautiful products, we're buying something quite different from the simple document we may think we want. We are, instead, buying a visual statement, a way of seeing — one that asserts tremendous authority, which few viewers are likely to question.

WORDS CAN NEVER be a simple reflection of life. Our very limited set of symbols, the letters of our alphabet, are forced to translate the unspeakable data of our senses, our thoughts, and our emotions. This is why it is important for all of us realists, damned by that word "conventional," to remember, always, that we have chosen a particular projection — one that seems to us to minimize distortion and to speak powerfully. *This is our choice*. And simply to learn how others have done it, to pick up the graph paper and begin plotting our points, limits us from the start. Realism, like every other artistic endeavor, fails when it becomes an exercise in filling in the blanks. Realism succeeds when the author remembers to question his or her assumptions. Why do we represent dialogue the way we do? Why are smells so often absent? What is the relation of chronology to the way we think? What are we doing when we imagine a character's consciousness, the flow of thoughts through her head — and then render them on the page in some particular order, in a particular syntax? How are we manipulating the data? To what ends?

The same holds true for surrealists, experimentalists, modernists, postmodernists, and romantics, hopeless or otherwise. All of our approaches are possible projections. "How to choose?" Denis Wood asks. "This is the question, for the answer determines the way the earth will look on the map. . . . The selection of a map projection is always to choose among competing interests, to take . . . a point of view."

If no map is objective, we must reconsider what we mean when we ask if a map is "accurate." Under the most rigorous examination, no map is accurate. On the other hand, you can probably

FIG. 24 THE MAP OF NORTH CAROLINA'S RIVER BASINS DISTRIBUTED BY THE STATE'S OFFICE OF ENVIRONMENTAL EDUCATION

draw on a scrap of paper what is called a sketch map sufficiently accurate to guide a new colleague from your workplace to your home. "Accuracy," then, must be judged against the map's stated purpose. In the case of a piece of writing, we can determine accuracy in light of implicit intention.

Wood argues that maps give us "a reality that exceeds our vision, our reach, the span of our days, a reality we achieve no other way. We are always mapping the invisible or the unattainable . . . the future or the past." He adds that through the map we "link all [our] elaborately constructed knowledge up with our living." Whatever our beliefs with regard to God and science, for many of us a belief in God and a belief in the combustion engine are not so far removed. Try explaining to a child why she should believe in the immaculate conception, or Moses bearing the Ten Commandments, but not in Santa Claus; in the benefits of fluoride but not in the Tooth Fairy. The most profound questions of our existence cannot be answered through a mere collection of concrete evidence; at some point, whether we are theologians or automobile mechanics, dentists or draftsmen, each of us reaches a border of the verifiable world, and every one of us leaps. A great deal of what we know, we know only through our imagination—and that knowledge is crucial to our lives.

THE CONVENTIONS of fiction are invisible to most readers. We write in sentences and paragraphs. We typically follow the standard grammatical and mechanical usage of contemporary written English; we begin sentences with uppercase letters, begin paragraphs with indentations. We name significant characters, while leaving others anonymous; we describe the physical appearance of our fictitious people; we obligingly give them some sort of trouble and bring that trouble, or some part of it, to resolution. We assume the reader will be able to distinguish between a first-person narrative relayed by a fictional character and a first-person address by the author. Such was not always the case; among discarded conventions is the quaint introductory paragraph telling the reader that he is reading a piece of fiction, or pretending that the manuscript of the story about to begin was found in a bottle, or in an old trunk.

"Sensibility is not enough if you're going to be a writer," according to V.S. Naipaul. "You need to arrive at the forms that can contain or carry your sensibility; and literary forms—whether in poetry or drama or prose fiction—are artificial, and ever changing." Some conventions of writing are momentary fads, like hairstyles or baggy shorts; others are more like social conventions, such as leaving a card when paying a visit or dressing formally to go to the theater. Just as people have done away with prefatory social remarks in e-mail messages or stepping into a private room to conduct a telephone conversation— conventions we can reclaim, if we choose—writers long ago shrugged off the rigid classical definitions of tragedy and comedy, and in his preface to

Shakespeare, Samuel Johnson relieved dramatists of the need to honor unity of time and place.

When we think of conventions of content in fiction, we might think first of genre writing. Fans of science fiction, fantasy, horror, romance, and western novels can explain in detail what the books they enjoy do and don't include — the rules those books agree to share. Fans of mysteries, among others, can identify any number of subgenres. Procedurals and whodunits and courtroom dramas all have their own established methods of operation, and anyone writing such a novel had better be aware of them. This is not to say that such novels are identical, any more than all sonnets are identical. And Louis L'Amour's westerns, not so far removed from the dime novels of a century earlier, can be found in the same bookstore as James Michener's popular historical novels, Larry McMurtry's and Cormac McCarthy's modern westerns, and Robert Coover's parody of the genre's clichés in *Ghost Town*.* These books, each insisting on its own reality, coexist; and while they may appeal to different audiences, those audiences overlap, as any one reader can and does accept different rules for each book he or she opens.

No matter whether we adhere to or dispense with convention, we are engaged in silent conversation with the reader about our choices.

It's common enough to say that good writing gives us a new perspective, whether that means taking us somewhere we've never been or, more often, showing us one of the familiar places in some new way. The question, always, is how to do it. In "The Babysitter," Robert Coover guides our attention by emphasizing sequence over characterization, setting, and other narrative elements. The story demonstrates the economy of convention by grounding us in the familiar—even in cliché and stereotype—so that it can simultaneously challenge one of the most fundamental conventions of narrative.

"The Babysitter" concerns a suburban couple going off to a

* So as to inhabit them better in his prose, Michener painted maps of the settings of his novels.

party who leave their children in the care of a teenage girl. More accurately, it offers us several stories—about the husband, the wife, the children, the babysitter, that girl's boyfriend, that boy's boy friend, and, notably, the television. The narrator shifts attention like a store security guard monitoring every camera at once; even more perplexing, when the characters begin to act, various passages begin to contradict one another. It soon becomes apparent that all of the things we're told are happening can't be happening—which is to say, they can't be happening if we insist on clinging to our worn notions of time and space. Coover even tells us the time at the beginning of some of the sections, just as if

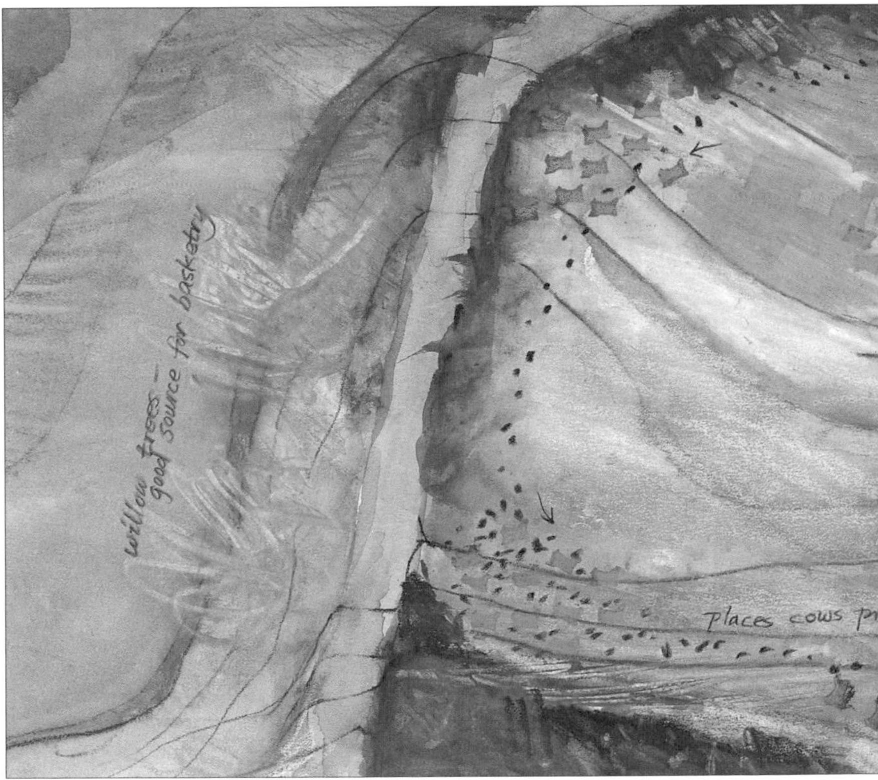

we were watching through that security camera. But our security is false; that clock is a magician's decoy.

Readers of the story may find themselves trying to identify one chain of events as the "real" one, the others "imagined" by the characters, but that exercise ends in frustration. Coover forces us to confront our desire to believe in the "real" story; he leads us to understand that there is no "real" one or, rather, that all the stories are equally real. They are all going on at once, in our mind as well as in the minds of the characters. We might think, "*This* is the real story: Reading a book, we ponder where we might find something like truth in it." Or: "When we read

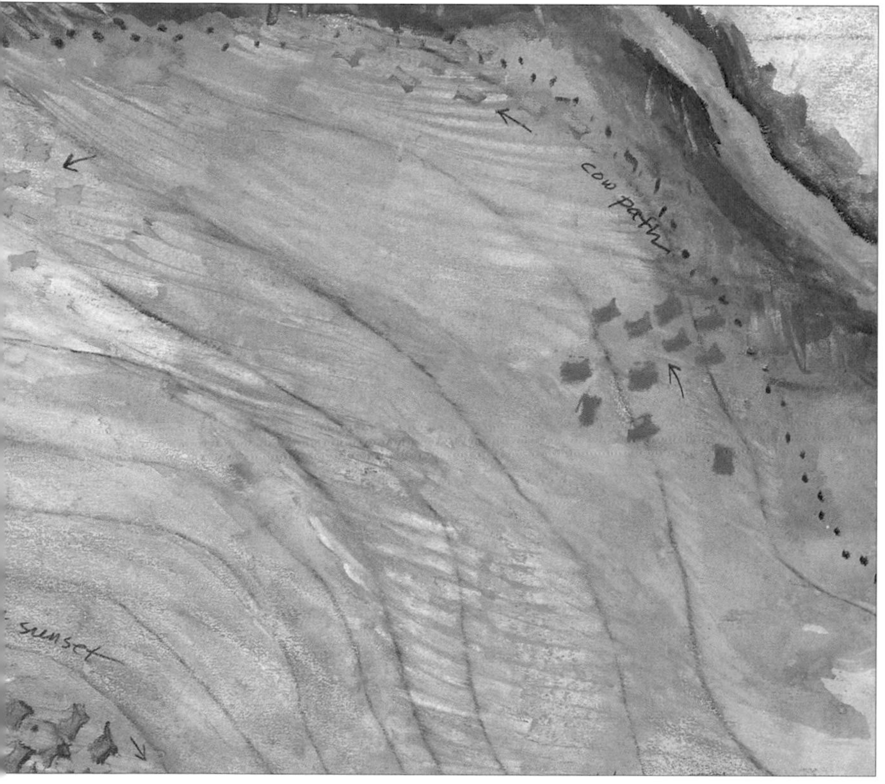

FIG. 25 **GWEN DIEHN'S *THE BOVINE WALK***

fiction, we agree to be *there*, in the world of the story; but we are always *here*." Or: "This is how it is *for the writer*. The story could be any of these things. Why pick one over another? Why not tell them all?"

Gwen Diehn, an artist and colleague of mine, spent most of a year making what she calls "artistic maps" of walks around the Warren Wilson College campus. They all depict trees and the Swannanoa River; some include contour lines, many include written descriptions. One she calls "The Bovine Walk," a map of a pasture with tiny herds of rectangular-stamped cows in the places they congregated as Gwen watched them, night after night, from her house. What her walking maps don't indicate are trails to follow. She says paths are too limiting; they take you where they want to go.

This is the mystery of meaning in art. Meaning is there, but not the way Exit 55 is *there;* meaning is there, somewhere; there to be found. But it isn't buried treasure. It's more like an energy-line apparent to a feng shui master.

Feng shui, the ancient Chinese art of divining energy in the landscape, is today being used not only in the traditional manner, to site buildings so that all who enter will benefit from the good *ch'i*, or vital energy, and not suffer from bad *ch'i*, but to situate everything from desks in office cubicles to doghouses. My colleague the mapmaker pointed out to me a land form on our campus that is considered both rare and remarkably fortuitous. Where dark, lush grass grows above an underground stream or at the site of an old riverbed, the feng shui initiate can make out a form known as the Frolicking Green Water Dragon.

Meaning in art is there all the time, or it is never there; it can be seen from a particular perspective, but only if we have been prepared to see it. It isn't that a map creates a Frolicking Green Water Dragon; the map chooses to reveal it. There is nothing in the landscape itself that would assign those words, or that image, to a characteristic of the land. To be able to imagine the dragon is not the only way to see the pasture, and unless we are culturally or spiritually predisposed toward it, there is no reason to assume it is the best way to see the pasture. I have walked by and driven past that pasture before the sawmill for years; the Frolicking Green Water Dragon was always there—or, a nonbeliever might say, it was never there, and still isn't. But now it is there for me.

I'll put it another way. Starting in England, three friends and I once resolved that each of us would make our way to Fez, in Morocco, where we would meet and buy a fez. We slept on cold cement floors, our lives were threatened; it was one of the great trips of my life. But standing in the center of the old city, preparing to negotiate with yet another merchant, we understood there was no need to buy a fez. As travelers through fiction and poetry, we need to distrust the urge to scoop up theme and meaning, as if the things we can neatly pack are necessarily the things we came for.

IMAGINARY SCROLLS

Perhaps, being lost, one should get loster.

SAUL BELLOW

ONE OF MY earliest remembered classroom humiliations — and there have been legions — occurred when an elementary school teacher asked who could point to the North. I raised my hand and, when called upon, extended my forefinger: North was Up. In every map I had ever seen, including the ones tightly rolled above the top of our fourth-grade-classroom's chalkboard, north was at the top. What I didn't know then, as even our teacher laughed, is that the practice of orienting maps to the north is a convention; orientation is entirely arbitrary. There is no "up" or "down" in space; the term "orientation" comes from the practice of locating the East, which for Europeans was the direction of the Orient, at the top of maps. The East earned its priority thanks to the Earth's rotation (the sun appears to arrive from the East) and because it was believed to be the direction of Eden, or Paradise. With the discovery of magnetic north and the invention of the compass, most maps swung around ninety degrees. Yet many Islamic maps were oriented to the south, as was Fra Mauro's world map, and today Australians happily promote a map not only oriented toward the south, giving the Southern Hemisphere the superior position, but locating their continent in the center.

FIG. 26 (FOLLOWING SPREAD) **UPSIDE-DOWN WORLD**

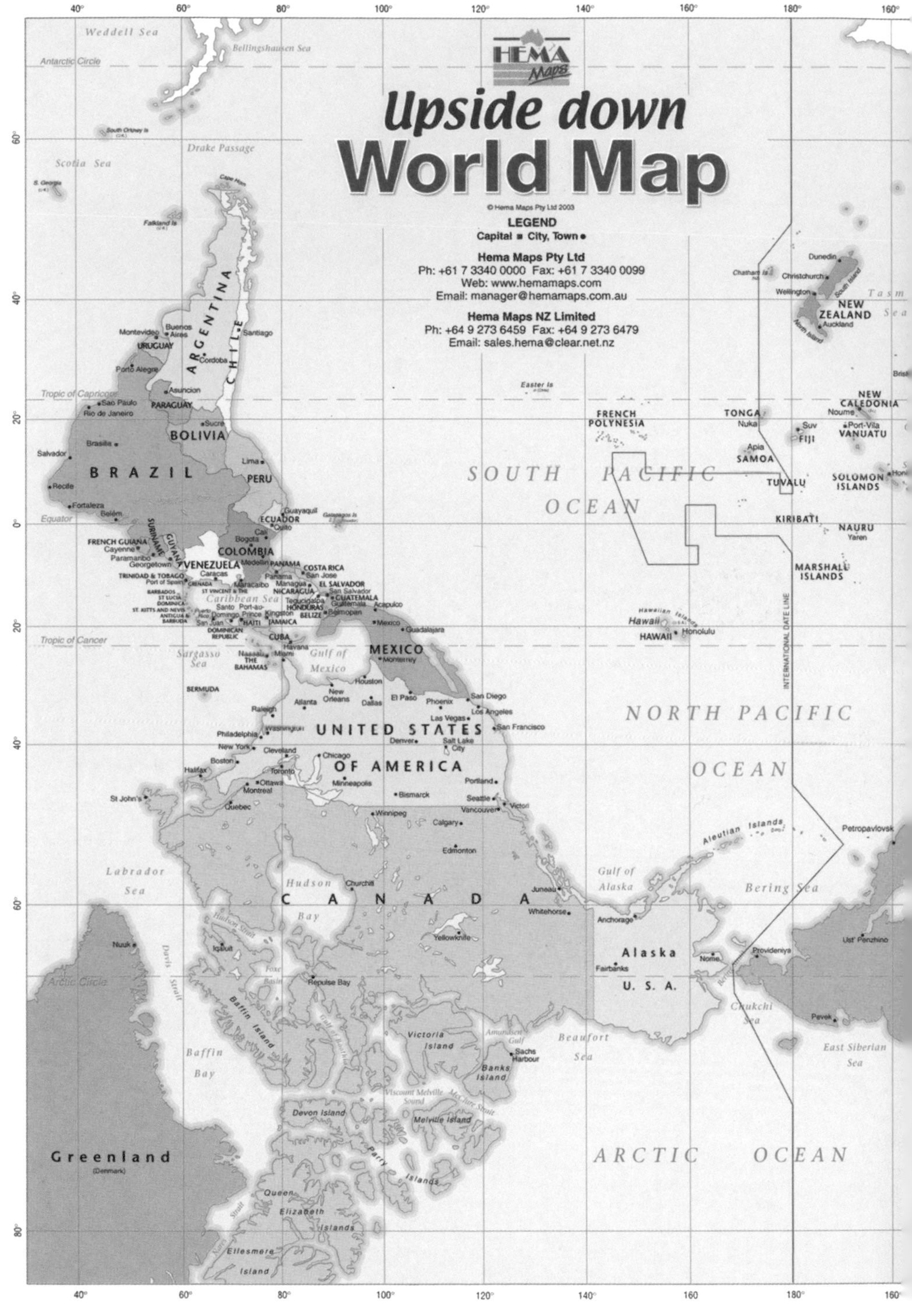

HEMA Maps
Upside down
World Map
© Hema Maps Pty Ltd 2003
LEGEND
Capital ■ City, Town ●
Hema Maps Pty Ltd
Ph: +61 7 3340 0000 Fax: +61 7 3340 0099
Web: www.hemamaps.com
Email: manager@hemamaps.com.au
Hema Maps NZ Limited
Ph: +64 9 273 6459 Fax: +64 9 273 6479
Email: sales.hema@clear.net.nz
Weddell Sea
Bellingshausen Sea
Antarctic Circle
Drake Passage
Scotia Sea
Falkland Is
ARGENTINA
CHILE
URUGUAY
PARAGUAY
BOLIVIA
BRAZIL
PERU
ECUADOR
COLOMBIA
VENEZUELA
FRENCH GUIANA
SURINAME
GUYANA
Tropic of Capricorn
Equator
Easter Is
FRENCH POLYNESIA
TONGA
SAMOA
FIJI
TUVALU
KIRIBATI
NAURU
MARSHALL ISLANDS
SOLOMON ISLANDS
VANUATU
NEW CALEDONIA
NEW ZEALAND
SOUTH PACIFIC OCEAN
PANAMA
COSTA RICA
NICARAGUA
EL SALVADOR
HONDURAS
GUATEMALA
BELIZE
JAMAICA
HAITI
DOMINICAN REPUBLIC
CUBA
THE BAHAMAS
BERMUDA
Caribbean Sea
Gulf of Mexico
Sargasso Sea
Tropic of Cancer
MEXICO
Hawaiian Islands
HAWAII
INTERNATIONAL DATE LINE
UNITED STATES OF AMERICA
NORTH PACIFIC OCEAN
Aleutian Islands
Gulf of Alaska
Bering Sea
Labrador Sea
Hudson Bay
CANADA
Alaska
U. S. A.
Arctic Circle
Baffin Island
Victoria Island
Banks Island
Beaufort Sea
Chukchi Sea
East Siberian Sea
Baffin Bay
Devon Island
Melville Island
Parry Islands
Queen Elizabeth Islands
Ellesmere Island
Greenland
(Denmark)
ARCTIC OCEAN

140°
120°
100°
80°
60°
40°
20°
0°
20°
ANTARCTICA
SOUTHERN
OCEAN
INDIAN
OCEAN
SOUTH
ATLANTIC
OCEAN
NORTH
ATLANTIC
OCEAN
AUSTRALIA
Adelaide
Perth
Alice Springs
Darwin
Timor Sea
EAST TIMOR
INDONESIA
Jakarta
Palembang
Borneo
Sumatra
SINGAPORE
MALAYSIA
Kuala Lumpur
Medan
BRUNEI
PHILIPPINES
Manil
VIETNAM
CAMBODIA
THAILAND
LAOS
MYANMAR
Yangon (Rangoon)
Hanoi
Hong Kong
TAIWAN
Taipei
Kaohsiung
Guangzhou
Fuzhou
Guiyang
Shanghai
Chengdu
CHINA
Lanzhou
Jinan
Beijing
SOUTH KOREA
Seoul
NORTH KOREA
P'yongyang
Shenyang
Tokyo
Osaka
Fukuoka
Sapporo
Vladivostok
Harbin
Khabarovsk
MONGOLIA
Ulan Bator
Ulan-Ude
Chita
Irkutsk
Urumqi
Novosibirsk
Omsk
KAZAKHSTAN
Astana
Almaty
KYRGYZSTAN
Bishkek
TAJIKISTAN
Dushanbe
Tashkent
UZBEKISTAN
TURKMENISTAN
Ashgabat
AFGHANISTAN
Kabul
PAKISTAN
Islamabad
Lahore
Karachi
INDIA
New Delhi
Kolkata
Mumbai
Hyderabad
Bangalore
Chennai
NEPAL
Kathmandu
BHUTAN
Thimphu
BANGLADESH
Dhaka
SRI LANKA
MALDIVES
Male
Bay of Bengal
Arabian Sea
IRAN
Tehran
IRAQ
Baghdad
SAUDI ARABIA
Riyadh
YEMEN
Sana
OMAN
Muscat
Salalah
SYRIA
Damascus
JORDAN
Amman
ISRAEL
Jerusalem
LEBANON
Beirut
CYPRUS
Nicosia
TURKEY
Ankara
Istanbul
ARMENIA
Yerevan
AZERBAIJAN
Baku
GEORGIA
Tbilisi
EGYPT
Cairo
LIBYA
Tripoli
TUNISIA
Tunis
ALGERIA
Algiers
MOROCCO
Casablanca
Rabat
Western Sahara
MAURITANIA
Nouakchott
MALI
NIGER
Niamey
CHAD
Ndjamena
SUDAN
Khartoum
ERITREA
Asmara
ETHIOPIA
Addis Ababa
DJIBOUTI
SOMALIA
Mogadishu
KENYA
Nairobi
UGANDA
Kampala
TANZANIA
Dodoma
Dar es Salaam
DEMOCRATIC REPUBLIC OF CONGO
Kinshasa
CONGO
Brazzaville
GABON
Libreville
CAMEROON
CENTRAL AFRICAN REPUBLIC
Bangui
NIGERIA
Abuja
Lagos
BURKINA FASO
Ouagadougou
COTE D'IVOIR
GHANA
Accra
GUINEA
Conakry
SIERRA LEONE
Freetown
LIBERIA
Monrovia
SENEGAL
Dakar
THE GAMBIA
Banjul
GUINEA-BISSAU
CAPE VERDE
Praia
ANGOLA
Luanda
ZAMBIA
Lusaka
ZIMBABWE
Harare
MALAWI
Lilongwe
MOZAMBIQUE
Maputo
MADAGASCAR
Antananarivo
COMOROS
Moroni
MAURITIUS
Port Louis
SEYCHELLE
Victoria
BOTSWANA
Gaborone
NAMIBIA
Windhoek
REPUBLIC OF SOUTH AFRICA
Pretoria
Cape Town
Durban
LESOTHO
Maseru
SWAZILAND
Mbabane
Cape of Good Hope
Gulf of Guinea
Mediterranean Sea
Black Sea
SPAIN
Madrid
PORTUGAL
Lisbon
ANDORRA
FRANCE
Paris
Monaco
ITALY
Rome
GREECE
Athens
BULGARIA
Sofia
ROMANIA
Bucharest
MOLDOVA
Chisinau
UKRAINE
Kiev
HUNGARY
Budapest
AUSTRIA
Vienna
SLOVAKIA
Bratislava
CZECH REPUBLIC
Prague
POLAND
Warsaw
GERMANY
Berlin
SWITZERLAND
Bern
LUXEMBOURG
BELGIUM
Brussels
NETHERLANDS
Amsterdam
UNITED KINGDOM
London
Edinburgh
Belfast
IRELAND
Dublin
DENMARK
Copenhagen
North Sea
BELARUS
Minsk
LITHUANIA
Vilnius
LATVIA
Riga
ESTONIA
Tallinn
RUS. FED.
Moscow
St Petersburg
Helsinki
Stockholm
Oslo
Bergen
FINLAND
SWEDEN
NORWAY
Norwegian Sea
ICELAND
Reykjavik
Denmark Strait
Greenland (Denmark)
Volgograd
Kazan'
Ufa
Perm'
Chelyabinsk
Yekaterinburg
Mezen'
Vorkuta
Murmansk
RUSSIAN FEDERATION
Okhotsk
Yakutsk
Olenek
Tiksi
Nordvik
Laptev Sea
Kara Sea
Barents Sea
Novaya Zemlya
Franz Josef Land
Svalbard (Norway)
Severnaya Zemlya
Ostrova
Sea of Japan (East Sea)
East China Sea
South China Sea
Bay of Biscay
Heard Is
Iles de Kerguelen
Iles Crozet
Prince Edward Is
Bouvetoya
South Sandwich Is
St Helena
Ascension Is
Chagos
Cocos (Keeling)
Christmas
60°
40°
20°
80°

These alternatives are not only dis-orienting to those of us who think of north as up, or ahead; they seem *wrong*. The modern convention is so strong—and as Americans we are so used to seeing the United States in the visually dominant position, as if this were the most obvious choice in the world—that we may find it difficult to make sense of a differently designed map. One Northern Hemispherean looked at my Australia-privileged map and asked, "Do they really *use* this?" The convention of orientation is not to be treated lightly; if we decide to orient our map to the west, or the south-southeast, we had better make that clear, and we must anticipate a good deal of misreading.

The "rules" put forth by well-intentioned teachers, and handbooks, and veteran writers indulging in Q&A after a reading, are of real use. While some are training wheels, designed to encourage competence by minimizing the risk of failure, others indicate proven ways of doing things effectively. Not all the rules come from others; individually, we discover techniques and strategies that seem to us effective. But simply discovering them isn't enough. We need to devote ourselves to the ongoing practice of questioning the rules we have found most useful (including those we hear ourselves offering as advice) and the fundamental assumptions of our work, constantly checking for empty routine, thoughtless employment. In *The Art of the Novel*, Milan Kundera writes:

> These days music can be composed by computer, but there was always a kind of computer present in composers' heads, in a pinch, they could compose a sonata without a single original idea . . . simply by following . . . the rules of composition. . . . Roughly the same idea applies to the novel: it too is weighed down by "technique," by the conventions that do the author's work for him: present a character, describe a milieu, bring the action into a historical situation, fill time in the characters' lives with superfluous episodes. . . . My own imperative is . . . to rid the novel of the automatism of novelistic technique.

Some maps are actually oriented in several different directions, yet are, nevertheless, quite easy to follow. In 1675 John Ogilby produced the first road atlas of Great Britain, and in doing so invented the route map (popularized in the twentieth century as the AAA trip-tik). Road maps date back at least as far as Roman times: in the name of conquest, that empire laid actual milestones. In medieval days pilgrims referred to prose "maps," used in conjunction with the other kind, that described shrines along the way, hostels, and the best places for changing horses and donkeys. In the thirteenth century, Matthew Paris drew strip maps of particular pilgrimage routes. But John Ogilby combined the road map, the strip map, and a scientific desire for comprehension into the first national road atlas.

Born in Scotland in 1600, Ogilby moved to London as a child and in his teens began a career as a dancer. Eventually he became a dance teacher and helped to build the New Theatre, in Dublin. After brief service in the military, and having won and lost a few small fortunes, he turned to translating and publishing Latin classics. In 1666, having lost virtually everything he owned in the Great fire of London, he began his last and most successful career: "shutting up the Fountain of the Muses," as he put it, to fall "into the beaten way, and more frequented paths of prose." He began by helping to create a plan of London, the purpose of which was to establish property boundaries as they existed before the fire. At the unlikely age of seventy-two he announced a boldly ambitious project: a six-volume atlas of Britain, including one that would contain "an Ichonographical and Historical Description of all the Principal Road-ways in England and Wales, in two Hundred Copper Sculptures, after a New and Exquisite method." The result was his *Britannia*, which was quickly reprinted, imitated, and pirated. The book's attention to detail was one reason for its success; its maps depict not only roads but hills and rivers, forests and bridges, towns and villages. Just as important, and most striking, was the maps' method of presentation. In a preface, Ogilby wrote:

OXFORD
By JOHN OGILBY
BUCKINGHAM SHIRE
Denham
To Denham
Uxbridge
To Colebrook
To Swackley
Hillingdon
Hillingdon heath
a Pond
Mayes
To Harrow
To Watford
To Northolt
MIDDLESEX
a Wooden bridge & Mill
Norcoat
To Greenford
Hanwell Church
To Harrow
To Drayton
LONDON
To Amersham
Pasture
Beconsfeild
To Amersham
To Burnam
To Fulmore
pond
Pas- ture

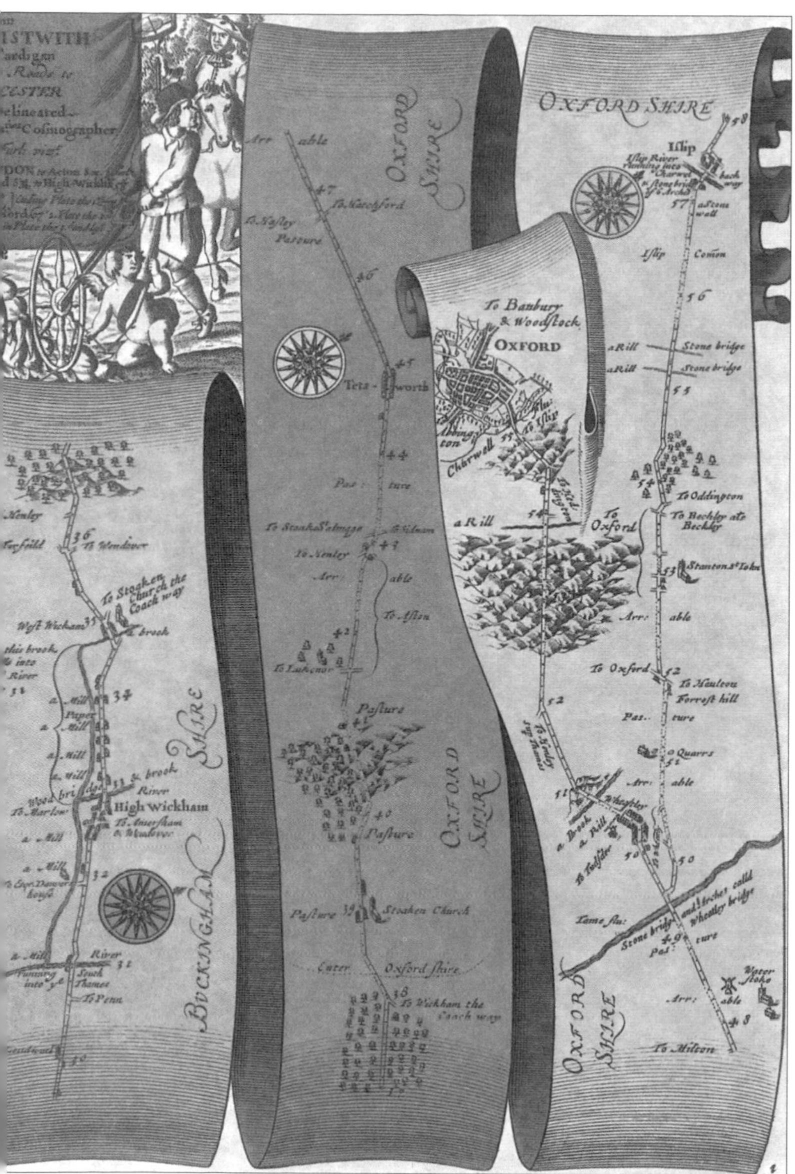

FIG. 27 **A COLORED REPRODUCTION OF THE ROAD MAP FROM LONDON (LOWER LEFT) TO OXFORD (UPPER RIGHT) IN OGILBY'S *BRITANNIA*. NOTE THE SHIFTING COMPASS ROSE**

"We have projected [the roads] upon imaginary scrolls, the initial city or town being always at the bottom of the outmost scroll on the left hand, whence your road ascends to the top of the said scroll; then from the bottom of the next scroll ascends again, thus constantly ascending till it terminates at the top of the outmost scroll on the right hand." As the strips follow the course of the roads, they change orientation; each segment of every "imaginary scroll" includes its own compass rose.

Ogilby explained his technique to his readers through a visual metaphor. Given the technical challenge of printing a series of maps several feet long, he tore the strips into even sections, in his mind, and presented them as if they were fragments of a scroll. Thus, *Britannia* hearkens back to those scraps of papyrus whereon Sappho is preserved, and it prefigures the use, over three hundred years later, of another imaginary scroll: the computer feature that asks us to perceive what we see on our screen as one section of a vertical image extending above and below, and invites us to tap a key in order to take an imaginary stroll.

As if writers didn't have enough competition from radio, television, and film, in the new millennium a disheartening portion of the American population—almost entirely male—is getting its fictive fix from video games.* A common premise of these games is that they show the player only a very limited portion of physical "space" at any one time. The key to success is to discover entrances and exits and avoid obstacles — to find your way through the game's landscape, which is revealed only in fragments, creating mystery and suspense.† This is a sort of disorientation we also find in writing, though the limitations of our "view" are, in prose, imposed by the fact that words are read one at a time, left to right in our language, and in sentences or grammatical units. Poets have the additional tool of the line and its companion, blank space. "In poems," Heather McHugh writes,

* While a few, like the now classic *Myst* (with its pitch line, "The Surrealistic Adventure That Will Become Your World"), offer something like story, the depressing majority (*Mortal Kombat*, *Halo*) are little more than justifications for shooting at someone.

† Which is to say that a significant percentage of the American population spends its leisure time playing virtual hide-and-go-seek.

> the convention of continuance is always being queried by poetic structure: a lineated poem is constantly ending. A sentence can have many line breaks in it, and each line break significantly reconceives not only the status of the sentence, but the status of the narrative the sentence stands for. Line breaks willfully remind us of the wordlessness that surrounds and shapes the verbal passage.

Like the strips in Ogilby's scroll, each line in a poem re-orients us.

In both poems and prose, the reader is guided by information delivered in a particular sequence. That sequence is determined by the work's purpose at any given moment. For the sake of clarity, exposition is often delivered straightforwardly. At other times, the purposeful withholding, suppression, or indirect revelation of information is key. We all know the satisfaction and delight afforded by those works that send us spinning back out into the world, dizzy and exhilarated. Alain Robbe-Grillet's "The Secret Room" doesn't offer plot, action, scene, or character in their most familiar forms; its primary mode of development is to disorient and orient us spatially—not just once, but again and again. "The first thing to be seen," the story tells us, "is a red stain, of a deep, dark, shiny red, with almost black shadows. It is in the form of an irregular rosette, sharply outlined, extending in several directions." In the rest of that paragraph, and the next, the claustrophobia and disorientation are relieved a bit as we're given context: we're told the room is "a dungeon, a sunken room, or a cathedral." Given the extraordinary range of dungeon to cathedral, and the wholly ambiguous "sunken room," it's a wonder we feel any relief, but we do. The *appearance* of information is comforting, even when it's as useless as an earlier map's hippogriffs and monoculi.

In the second paragraph we're allowed perspective—we see some columns "repeated with progressive vagueness." In the third we learn that the original image was a bloody wound on a white body; in the fourth, plot and story enter as we see "a black silhouette . . . a man wrapped in a long, floating cape . . . his deed

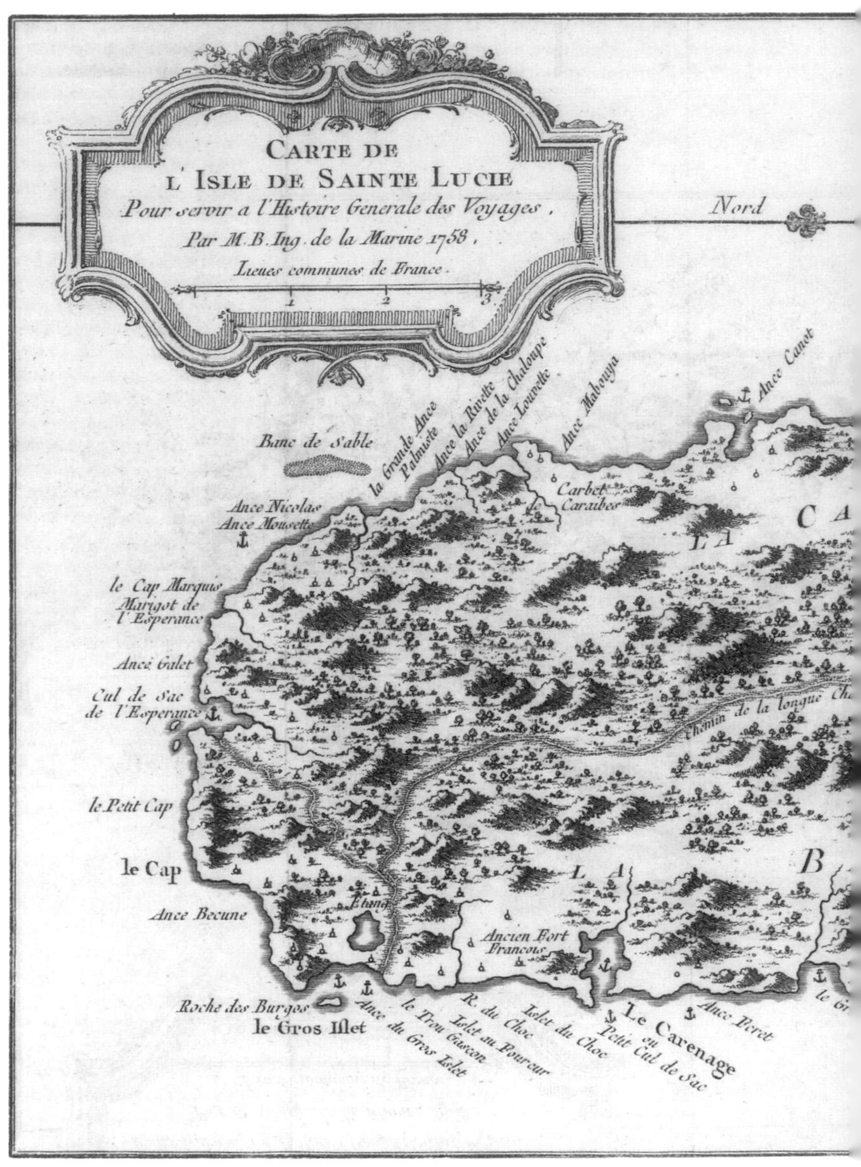
CARTE DE
L' ISLE DE SAINTE LUCIE
Pour servir a l'Histoire Generale des Voyages,
Par M.B. Ing. de la Marine 1758,
Lieues communes de France.
1 2 3
Nord
Banc de Sable
la Grande Ance
Palmiste
Ance la Rivette
Ance de la Chaloupe
Ance Louvette
Ance Mabouya
Ance Canot
Ance Nicolas
Ance Mousette
Carbet Caraibes
le Cap Marquis
Marigot de l' Esperance
Ance Galet
Cul de Sac de l' Esperance
Chemin de la longue
le Petit Cap
le Cap
Ance Becune
Etang
Ancien Fort Francois
Roche des Burgos
le Gros Islet
Ance du Gros Islet
le Trou Gascon
Islet au Fourour
R. du Choc
Islet du Choc
Le Carenage ou Petit Cul de Sac
Ance Peret

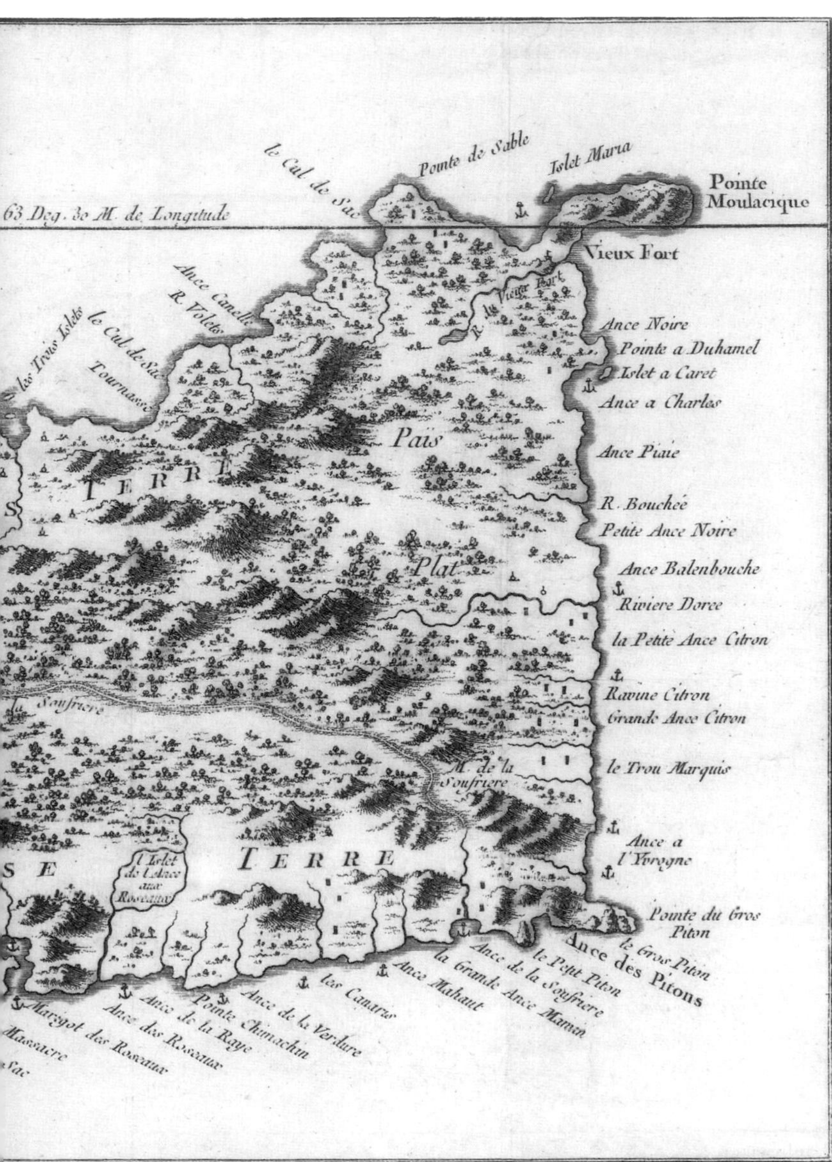

FIG. 28 **A MILDER CASE OF DISORIENTATION: THIS 1758 MAP OF ST. LUCIA, DRAWN TO TELL THE STORY OF THE TRAVELS OF A FRENCH NAVAL OFFICER, IS ORIENTED WITH NORTH TO THE LEFT**

accomplished." We return to what we are now told is "a fully rounded woman's body . . . lying on its back" on the floor. That cold, distant "its" seals off any hope of action.

One paragraph is devoted entirely to colors, another to the size of the room, yet another to light, as "no clue . . . suggests the directions of the rays." A paragraph describes the "vaguely outlined" stairs in the distance, another focuses on the escaping man's cloak. We keep returning to the body of what is now called "the young sacrificial victim," the implications more than enough to tempt us to imagine the morbid scenario. In the final paragraphs even the narrator seems compelled to speculate; just when we have surrendered any expectation of movement, the characters move, albeit in the past. The repetition of details— the staircase with no handrail, the man's cape—begins to provide rhythm, even structure.

The story's final sentence is also its last paragraph:

> Near the body, whose wound has stiffened, whose brilliance is already growing dim, the thin smoke from the incense burner traces complicated scrolls in the still air: first a coil turned horizontally to the left, which then straightens out and rises slightly, then returns to the axis of its point of origin, which it crosses as it moves to the right, then turns back in the first direction, only to wind back again, thus forming an irregular sinusoidal curve, more and more flattened out, and rising, vertically, toward the top of the canvas.

Ah-hah, we can hardly resist thinking. No wonder the narrator seemed so unconcerned about this poor naked woman chained to the floor with her legs spread, stabbed in the breast, and the man in black already escaping. But wait, the better reader in us says. Didn't we know from the beginning that this was "only" a short story? Why would we worry about a murdered woman in a story and not a murdered woman in a painting?

The second remove of art in the story's final sentence changes our perspective forever—just as it changes our reading forever to know all that is withheld in the beginning—but the word "canvas" is no answer. It is the electric shock that sends us running back through the story, reconsidering what we read, remembering our reactions. The corpse is mysterious at first, then made sense of, and finally familiar.

The movement of "The Secret Room" is movement through space and time. We are allowed so close a look at the wound in the first paragraph that it has no meaning—we don't know what we're seeing. As we back away, we (think we) begin to understand. We look back at the wound, understanding more. We look away, notice a new detail, look back. Understanding rises like a diver in murky water. We are reading a map—at least, this is about as close as prose fiction comes to recreating the experience of encountering a graphic image.* At the same time, this story stresses one of the significant differences between the linear unfolding of words on a page and a visual image. Sequence, or the controlled release of information, is one of the writer's most powerful tools.

The first American automobile road map, published in 1895 in the *Chicago Sun-Herald*, depicted the course of a road race—and was torn from the newspaper and put to use by the eventual winner. Nevertheless, for the next two decades drivers relied on prose maps, which offered directions the likes of, "At the fork at the foot of the hill, bear right," or "Turn left at the first red barn." Road maps as we know them appeared in the 1920s, as highways became more numerous. The "navigational systems" in cars today promise to show (and, in some cases, tell) the driver each turn on his journey from airport to hotel, from betting parlor to pawn shop.

Critics of realistic narratives might compare those of us who write them to the AAA employees who confidently move bold markers over narrow maps, clearly charting the route of the traveler's choice—shortest, fastest, most scenic. But unlike

* Through the words themselves, that is. Concrete poems "create a picture" in a different sense, and other typographical experiments, such as Mark Z. Danielewski's *House of Leaves*, create a variety of visual effects through the use of color, font, white space, etc.

auto club employees, even those of us who write realistic fiction are rarely interested simply in getting our clientele from one point to another. Rather, like another travel-oriented enterprise, we aim to provide an adventure in moving. We want our readers to find good (or bad) company at rest stops, overhear interesting conversation at roadside diners, have the occasional breakdown. We want them to be followed, like Humbert Humbert, by cars with drivers they only gradually identify. When we caution them about falling rocks, we fully intend to push a few into their path.

Even a self-proclaimed conventional realist and map-clutcher can appreciate a certain amount of disorientation. It is not for nothing that those of us who are passionate about reading can talk about being lost in a book. Two decades ago, I entered my studio apartment one afternoon with a stack of essays I was being paid to grade and a new novel by Italo Calvino, work I had paid to read. I opened the book to its disarming first sentence: "You are about to begin reading Italo Calvino's new novel, *If on a winter's night a traveler*." The first chapter is not the beginning of a story, at least not the sort of story we might expect; it offers instead a description of our own preparation for reading, a description both comically accurate and, the narrator acknowledges, mildly unsettling:

> Perhaps at first you feel a bit lost. . . . But then you go on and you realize that the book is readable nevertheless, independently of what you expected of the author, it's the book in itself that arouses your curiosity; in fact, on sober reflection, you prefer it this way, confronting something and not quite knowing yet what it is.

Hours later, I closed the covers. When I opened the book to reread a passage, I could not even find the words on the page; through my window, stars shone in a black sky. I had read the entire novel without once getting up, without even turning on a light. I had, gloriously, been lost in a book.

As readers, we are content, even delighted, to be lost, in the sense that we are both absorbed and uncertain of where we are or where we are going, as long as we feel confident we are following a guide who has not only the destination but our route to it clearly in mind. In *If on a winter's night a traveler*, Calvino appeals to our conflicting desires to know what we're reading and to be surprised. He draws us in at the start, with that direct address; then again in the second chapter and every "even" chapter, each of which purports to be the beginning of a different novel; in the ongoing story of the character called "The Reader"; and in what is, ultimately, an extended consideration of the relationships among readers and writers, translators and editors, publishers and books. While he appears to deny us progress through a narrative, he offers continuity. The novel makes both explicit and implicit use of the metaphor of seduction, or the cycle of arousal and denial.* The novel's story about a character called The Reader, combined with the clear structural pattern of alternating chapters and interwoven narratives, provide the necessary gratification of our desire for coherence. Logically, *If on a winter's night a traveler* is as methodical as a maze.

A prerequisite for finding our way through any story or novel is to be lost: the journey can't begin until we've been set down in a place somehow unfamiliar. And part of a reader's willingness to be led is a willingness to be betrayed, outwitted, jumped from behind. Like the main character in John Barth's "Lost in the Funhouse," a young fiction writer in the making, we envision "a truly astonishing funhouse, incredibly complex yet utterly controlled."

Utterly controlled? While we tolerate, even enjoy, some amount of dislocation, we also need to know where we stand in the world of a piece of fiction or a poem. With its opening line(s), the work asserts: You Are Here. Trust me in this and we may proceed. "You don't know about me without you have read a book by the name of *The Adventures of Tom Sawyer*," Huck explains, immediately

* Seduction is a metaphor Calvino employed on several occasions, including in a story that served as a precursor to the novel, titled "The Reader." There a man is increasingly distracted from the book he is reading by a beautiful young woman sunbathing nearby. Despite her advances, the man—a writer's fantasy—insists on finishing his book.

placing us, and himself, in both the real and fictional worlds—a dash of metafiction long before its time. "In my younger and more impressionable years," Nick Carraway begins, while Tolstoy insists, "Happy families are all alike." Shakespeare, who left no metaphor unturned, claims, "Thus is his cheek the map of days outworn, / When beauty lived and died as flowers do now," and we are firmly placed—in a figure of speech, a sentiment, a voice, and a poetic tradition. Every piece of writing establishes its basis for assertion, its orientation, and must immediately begin to persuade readers of its authority, its ability to guide.

> Perhaps, being lost, one should get lobster.
>
> — DEAN YOUNG

DEPARTURES FROM convention range in scale and import. "The Babysitter," "Lost in the Funhouse," "The Secret Room," and *If on a winter's night a traveler* are sufficiently unconventional that the reader is all but required to stop and take note. Kate Chopin's "The Storm" is surprising, but its defiance of conventions of technique is most noticeable to writers; its compression and quick shifts are not intended to jolt the reader out of "the story." In the middle ground, some stories appear to be conventional, only to stop the reader short at an unexpected turn, or depart from the norm in a way that seems—but only seems—minor.

Ernest Hemingway's "The Killers" opens like an old joke: two men walk into a diner. They order food, but only to pass the time. They are waiting for Ole Andreson, a regular customer, whom they mean to kill. This is alarming news to the man working the diner and to his young helper, Nick. To summarize: the killers wait, Nick Adams waits, we wait. Ole Andreson never shows. The men leave. The killers don't kill anyone, and neither do they decide not to kill the man they came for.

At this point, we do not have a story. We have an unresolved premise.

Nick's boss, George, decides that someone should warn Ole Andreson about the men who have come to town to kill him. Despite the cook's advice to "stay way out of it," Nick hurries to the boardinghouse where Andreson is staying, goes up to his room, and breaks the news. But again the potential for drama is undercut: the information is not news to the former boxer. He doesn't leap up and begin packing, and neither does he pull out a gun with which he means to counterpunch the hit men. Instead, unheroically, undramatically, Andreson says he will wait for the men, that he is resigned to his fate.

At this point, we have a story, one with a complete shape, even a surprising turn. But we don't have *the* story.

Nick returns to the diner. He isn't sure what to make of all this: the men are clearly dangerous, Ole Andreson is going to allow himself to be murdered, the Earth is wobbling off its axis. Nick tells George, "I can't stand to think about him. . . . It's too damned awful." George brings the story to a close with his response: "Well, you better not think about it."

In "The Killers," Hemingway leads us down a familiar trail, one we know from genre novels and from films. We know the trail so well that we know where it should end—or, more accurately, we know the several places it might end, and we might be content with any one of them. In frustrating our expectation, in stopping short of what we have anticipated, he risks leaving us behind. But of course, Hemingway is using our expectations, even our frustration, and depending on us to be good enough readers—looking around for ourselves, both eyes open for the unexpected—to ask, Why have we stopped here? The story stops where it does because it was never about whether the killers would kill Ole Andreson. The story is about Nick, and how he responds to the horror he is powerless to prevent. Hemingway forces us to consider the wisdom of the advice, "Well, you better not think about it"; he even comments on our reading in that line. In transforming the terms of the story, Hemingway provides a new perspective on a scenario we've seen countless times before.

The risk of defying readerly expectation is that the destination we offer in place of the one our readers thought they wanted to

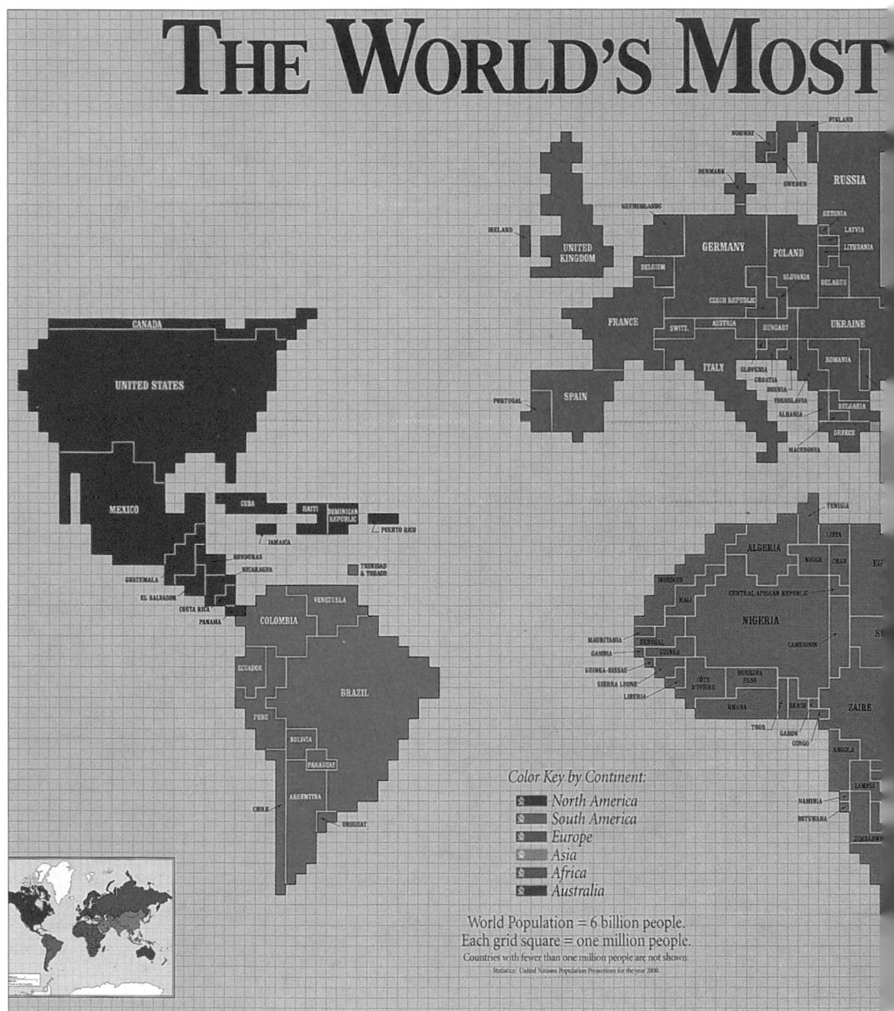

reach may be ignored, dismissed, or misunderstood. But we are not travel agents, nor mules carrying tourists down Bright Angel Trail. The film version of "The Killers" (starring Burt Lancaster as Ole Andreson) provides a lesson in the goals of art compared

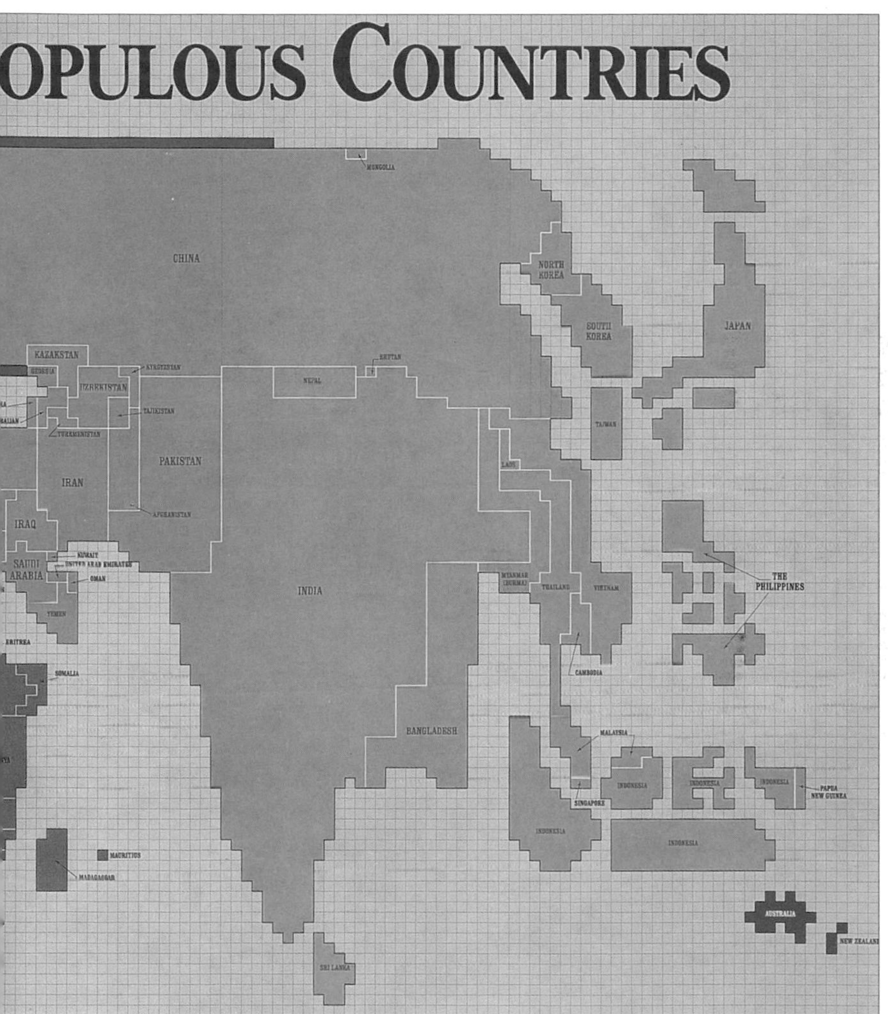

FIG. 29 **A CARTOGRAM**

to the goals of entertainment. The opening minutes of the film are surprisingly faithful to the story; but Hemingway's narrative doesn't take long to play out. The rest of the adaptation is devoted to a long explanation of Andreson's career as a boxer, his entanglement with organized crime, a fixed fight, betrayal. . . . But even if you haven't seen the movie, you know that story.

Some work, rather than defying our expectations for shape or content, reconsiders fundamental aspects of presentation. E. L. Doctorow's *Ragtime* discards technical conventions commonly accepted as necessary for clarity, as in this passage:

> He was a silhouette artist. With nothing but a small scissors and some glue he would make your image by cutting a piece of white paper and mounting it on a black background. The whole thing with the frame cost fifteen cents. Fifteen cents, lady, the old man said. Why do you have this child tied with a rope, Evelyn said. The old man gazed at her finery. He laughed and shook his head and talked to himself in Yiddish. He turned his back to her.

The "invisible" conventions are brought to mind by their absence. Doctorow shifts to dialogue without beginning a new paragraph or changing paragraphs with a change of speaker, and without using quotation marks. Nevertheless, the novel's scenes are easy enough to read and to understand, as he compensates for the omission of those markers with scrupulous attention to dialogue tags and sentence order. But this is not to say that the effects of the omissions, or deviations, are insignificant. The blending of dialogue into the narrative works to emphasize the novel's omniscient point of view, which never fully yields to mere depiction of scene, and it underscores our historical distance from the characters; we never "hear" them as intimately, as directly, as we hear characters in conventional novels. The de-emphasizing of dialogue reminds us of the narrator's constant

FIG. 30 (FOLLOWING SPREAD) **JOHNSON AND BROWNING'S MAP OF THE WORLD'S TALLEST MOUNTAINS AND LONGEST RIVERS, CIRCA 1864** presence, which in turn allows him to step back, away from the "action," without apology or transition.

> He began to create more and more intricate silhouettes, full-figured, with backgrounds, of Evelyn, of the little girl, of a drayman's horse plodding by, of five men in stiff collars sitting in an open car. With his scissors he suggested not merely outlines but textures, moods, character, despair. Most of these are today in private collections. Evelyn came nearly every afternoon and stayed for as long as she could.

It's as if the narrator walks a long hallway, peering in various rooms to see his characters at different moments of their lives, sometimes inviting us to lean through the doorways, but never fully entering. This freedom of movement allows him to take up scenes after they've "begun" and to leave them before they're "finished," showing us what he wants us to see, commenting as he likes, all for the purpose of de-emphasizing individual incidents, or threads, and so focusing on the larger weave.* As if in response to Kundera's call to "rid the novel of the automatism of novelistic technique," Doctorow goes to some lengths to prevent us from comfortably, thoughtlessly entering the world of the story, or what we might think of as the world of the story—a recreation of New York in a certain era. His choices regarding presentation define not only his novel's tone and texture but, ultimately, its subject.

Gerardus Mercator's projection dominated mapmaking for centuries for the excellent reason that it solved a critical problem of representation. It is still a useful projection—for certain applications. But its very familiarity ingrained its distortions so deeply that it literally affects how we see, or imagine, the world. The basic challenges facing mapmakers today are the same ones Mercator and Ortelius and Ptolemy faced, and our approaches to dealing with them are fundamentally unchanged. While new projections

* *Ragtime* was radically transformed when adapted to film, as film is absolutely dependent on visual presentation and scene; the novel is consistently, aggressively antiscene.

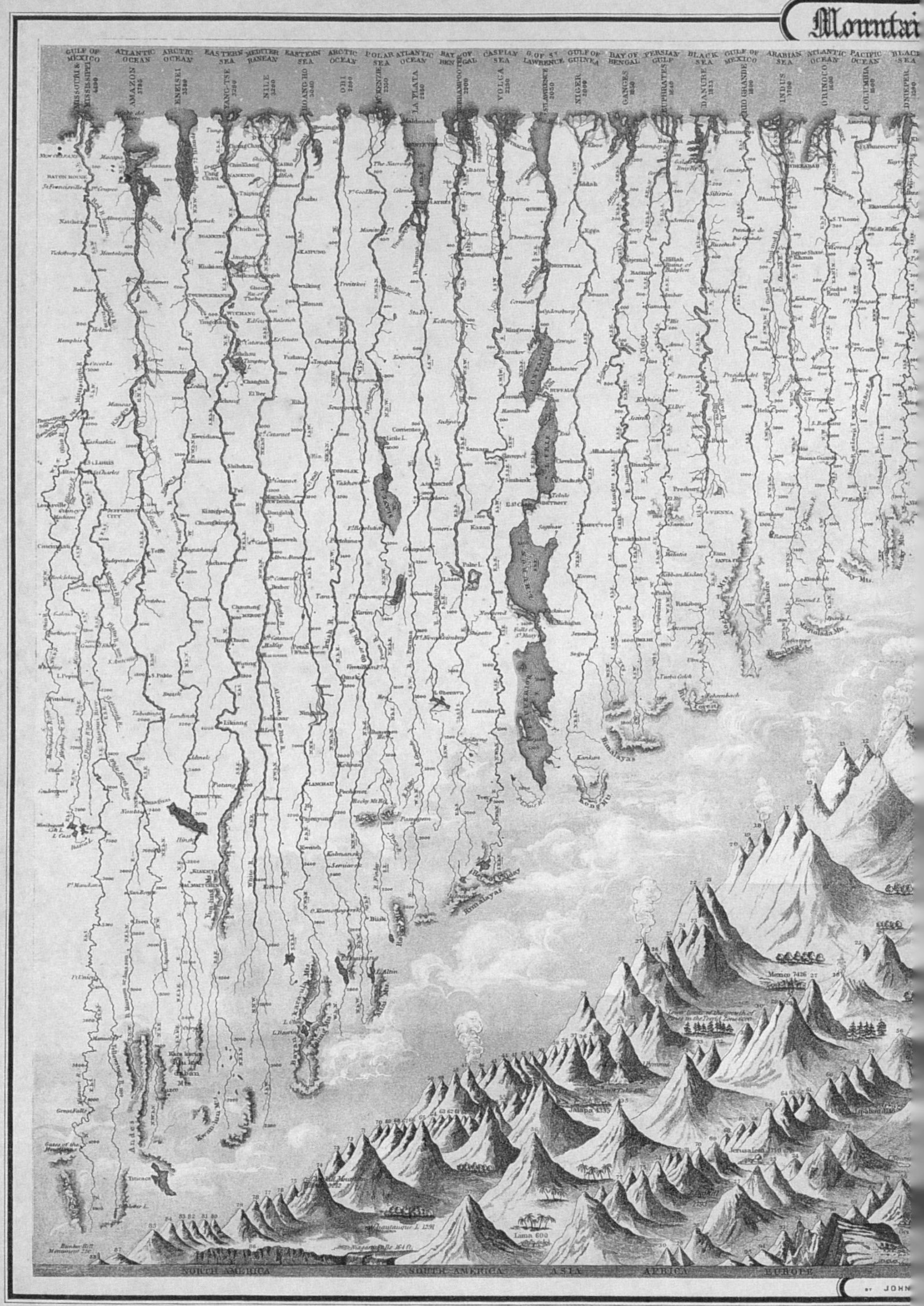

GULF OF MEXICO
MISSOURI & MISSISSIPPI
ATLANTIC OCEAN
AMAZON
ARCTIC OCEAN
ENESEI
EASTERN SEA
YANG-TSE
MEDITERRANEAN
NILE
EASTERN SEA
HOANG HO
ARCTIC OCEAN
OBI
POLAR SEA
ATLANTIC OCEAN
LA PLATA
BAY OF BENGAL
CASPIAN SEA
VOLGA
G. OF ST LAWRENCE
ST LAWRENCE
GULF OF GUINEA
NIGER
BAY OF BENGAL
GANGES
PERSIAN GULF
EUPHRATES
BLACK SEA
DANUBE
GULF OF MEXICO
RIO GRANDE
ARABIAN SEA
INDUS
ATLANTIC OCEAN
ORINOCO
PACIFIC OCEAN
COLUMBIA
Mexico 7426
Jerusalem 2750
NORTH AMERICA
SOUTH AMERICA
ASIA
AFRICA
EUROPE

Rivers
ATLANTIC OCEAN
CARIBBEAN SEA
NORTH SEA
NORTH SEA
ATLANTIC OCEAN
GULF OF MEXICO
BALTIC SEA
ATLANTIC OCEAN
GULF OF MEXICO
ATLANTIC OCEAN
MEDITERRANEAN
ADRIATIC SEA
ENGLISH CHANNEL
L. ISLAND SOUND
BAY OF BISCAY
BAY OF FUNDY
St GEORGES CHANNEL
ATLANTIC OCEAN
NORTH SEA
ATLANTIC OCEAN
SENEGAL
MAGDALENA
RHINE
ELBE
ALABAMA
ODER
TAGUS
RHONE
PO
SEINE
CONNECTICUT
GARONNE
ST JOHNS
SEVERN
HUDSON
THAMES
Andes
ASIA & OCEANICA
SOUTH AMERICA
AMERICA
AFRICA
EUROPE
Region of Lichens & Umbilicariæ
Potosi 13314
Quito 9638
La Paz 11983
Madrid 2220
Glacier of Haslingen
Splugen
Briançon 4285
Mont Louis
BRITISH ISLES
BRITISH ISLES

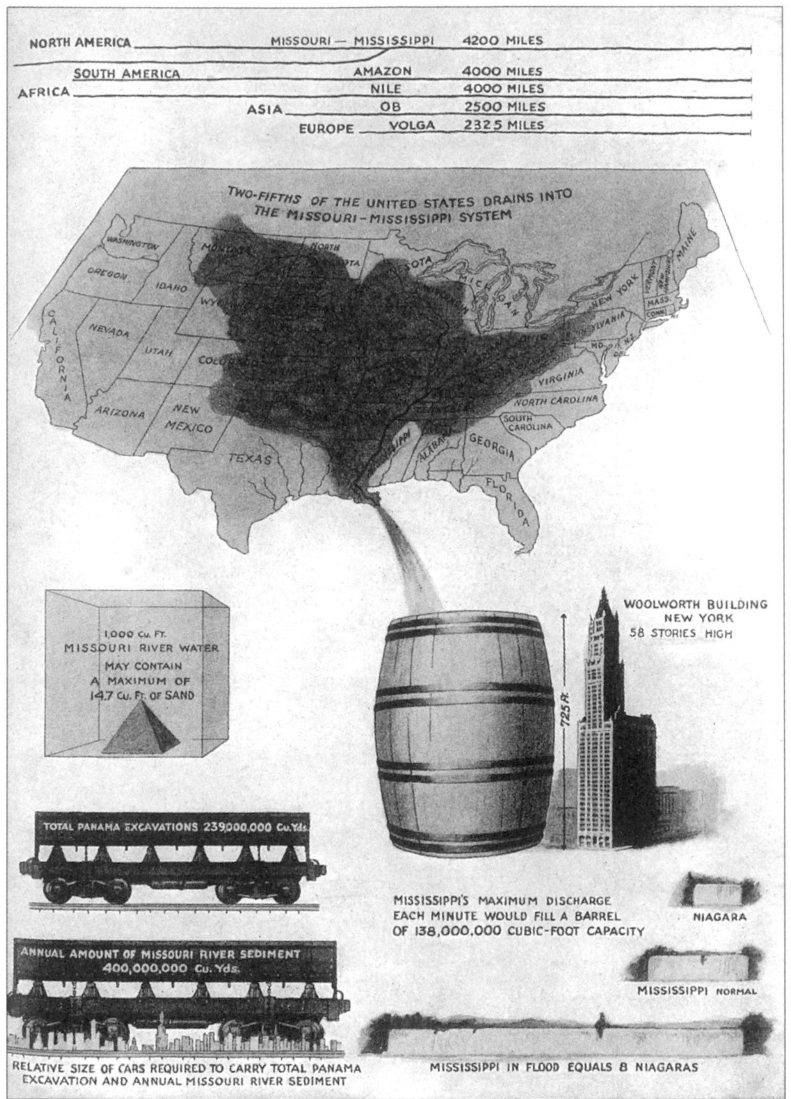

FIG. 31 **THIS DEPICTION OF THE WATER CHANNELED FROM THE LAND BETWEEN THE CONTINENTAL DIVIDES AND INTO THE MISSISSIPPI RIVER MAY GIVE THE VIEWER A NEW OUTLOOK ON NEW ORLEANS**

are being created, they build on the projections of the past, adjusting and adapting them to particular ends.

At the extreme of convention-defying were the dadaists, who aimed to frustrate the reader's ability to make sense. Among the sense-makers, but adamantly defiant of technical conventions, are such innovators as Samuel Beckett, James Joyce, and the notorious Austrian novelist and playwright Thomas Bernhard. In *The Loser*, Bernhard challenges the reader in several ways. The novel is written in just five paragraphs: in the University of Chicago Press edition, two are two lines long, one four, another (barely) five; the fifth paragraph goes on for just over 169 pages. As in *Ragtime*, there are no quotation marks; but there is very little dialogue. Over the course of the book the unnamed narrator arrives at an inn, goes to his room, speaks to the innkeeper, goes to the country home of his recently deceased friend, Wertheimer, speaks to a woodsman, and has a drink of water. But that summary overemphasizes the novel's events. Present "action" is deliberately minimal and, for most of the novel's duration, deep in the background; foregrounded are the narrator's thoughts as he contemplates his friend's suicide, their abandonment of their talent at piano playing, and their fellow student at Salzburg's Mozarteum, Glenn Gould.

Bernhard's stylistic tendencies are sufficiently unconventional that the English translator, Jack Dawson, felt compelled to add an introductory note:

> Bernhard's sentences are very long, even for a German reader accustomed to extended, complex sentence constructions. Further, the logical transitions between clauses ("but," "although," "whereas") are often missing or contradictory, and the verb tenses are rarely in agreement. Bernhard's frequent and unpredictable underlining also defies the conventional usage. Sometimes he italicizes the titles of Bach's compositions, sometimes he treats them like a common noun. . . . These and similar oddities have been rigorously maintained in the present translation.

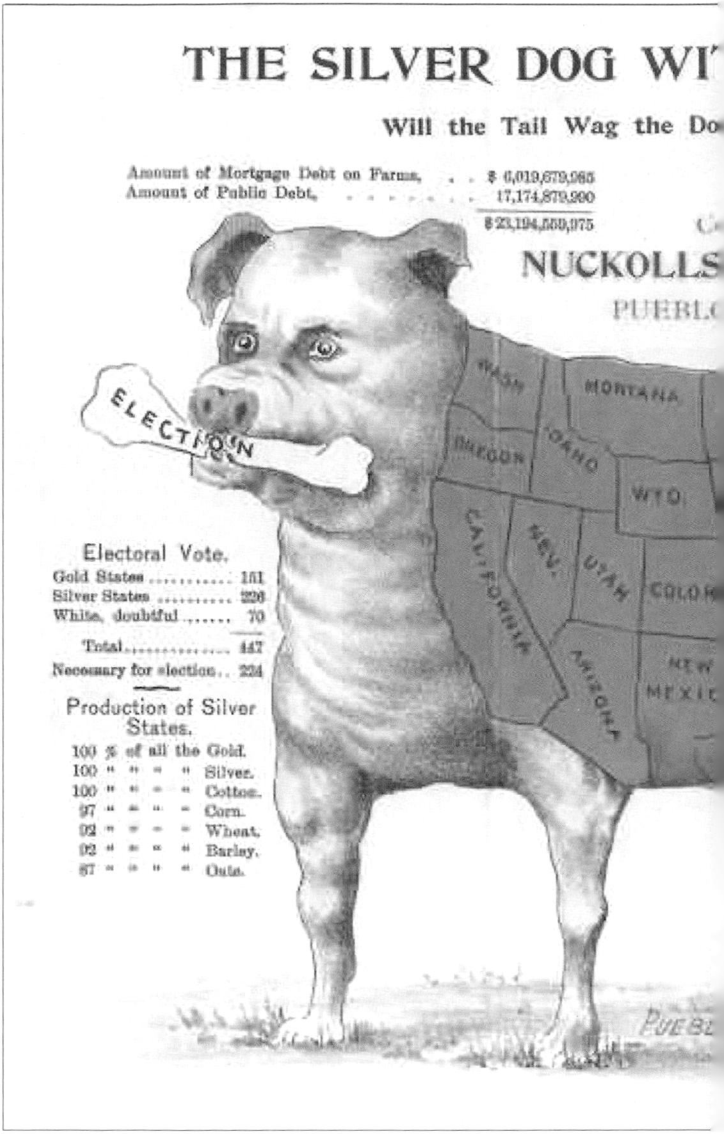

THE SILVER DOG
Will the Tail Wag the
Amount of Mortgage Debt on Farms, . . $ 6,019,679,985
Amount of Public Debt, ... 17,174,879,990
$ 23,194,559,975
NUCKOLLS
ELECTION
WASH
MONTANA
OREGON
IDAHO
WYO.
CALIFORNIA
NEV.
UTAH
ARIZONA
NEW MEXICO
Electoral Vote.
Gold States 151
Silver States 226
White, doubtful 70
Total 447
Necessary for election .. 224
Production of Silver States.
100 % of all the Gold.
100 " " " " Silver.
100 " " " " Cotton.
97 " " " " Corn.
92 " " " " Wheat.
92 " " " " Barley.
67 " " " " Oats.

FIG. 32 THIS 1896 LITHOGRAPH DID TRIPLE DUTY: AS A MAP, AS AN ADVERTISEMENT FOR THE NUCKOLLS PACKING COMPANY, AND AS A POLITICAL CARTOON ADVOCATING FOR FREE AND UNLIMITED SILVER COINAGE — A DEPARTURE FROM THE GOLD STANDARD — TO LIFT THE NATION OUT OF FINANCIAL DEPRESSION

So warned, some readers might choose a more compliant page-turner for company—while a more adventurous reader responds, On with the story. Prepared for a journey to new lands, we find that, as promised, some sentences are unusually long; as promised, the italicizing is unpredictable. In addition, there is a formidable amount of repetition, with variation (echoes of echoes of Gertrude echoes of Gertrude Stein), as well as an obsessive use of the most common attributives, or tags, as in this remembered conversation between the narrator and his deceased friend:

> But everything we say is nonsense, he said, I thought, no matter what we say it is nonsense and our entire life is a single piece of nonsense. I understood that early on, I'd barely started to think for myself and I already understood that, we speak only nonsense, everything we say is nonsense, but everything that is *said* to us is also nonsense, like everything that is said at all, in this world only nonsense has been said until now and, he said, only nonsense has actually and naturally been written, the writings we possess are only nonsense because they can only be nonsense, as history proves, he said, I thought. In the end *I fled into the notion of the aphorist*, he said, and when asked my profession I actually once responded, so Wertheimer said, that I was an *aphorist*. But people didn't understand what I meant, as usual, when I say something they don't understand it, for what I say doesn't mean that I said what I said, he said, I thought. I say something, he said, I thought, and I'm saying something completely different, thus I've spent my entire life in misunderstandings, in nothing but misunderstandings, he said, I thought. We are, to put it precisely, born into misunderstanding and never escape this condition of misunderstanding as long as we live, we can squirm and twist as much as we like, it doesn't help. But everyone can see this, he said, I thought, for everyone says something repeatedly and is misunderstood, this is the only point where everybody understands everybody else, he said, I thought.

That passage appears a little more than a third of a way through the novel. Part of Bernhard's genius is in teaching us to read, and understand, his style; by the time we reach those lines, they are not particularly difficult to comprehend, and the novel is anything but nonsense. Although we are denied some conventional handholds and guardrails, those barriers that allow us to sidle up to the rim of a canyon without plunging in, others are offered in such number and prominence that they serve an unconventional end, like an infinitely ascending Escher staircase. "He said" and "I thought" are used not as transparent clarifying devices but as intrusions and as crucial components of the rhythm of the prose. We are forced to read more slowly, more carefully; as a result we become attentive to other aspects of the prose, including its rhythm and its repetition of words, phrases, and meaning. Works of art do, after all, mean to lead us; only not to somewhere we've been before, or in the way we've gone there before. *The Loser* discusses, among other things, Glenn Gould's fascination with Bach's *Goldberg Variations*, and to some extent Bernhard's method mirrors his subject. But the novel is more than the execution of an imitative notion. To lead us into the world of its narrator, a world of obsession, bold assertion, and repressed self-doubt, Bernhard makes us read differently — so makes us listen — so makes us see the world anew.

THEATER OF THE WORLD

I believe that the earth is very large and that we who dwell between the Pillars of Hercules and the river Phasis live in a small part of it about the sea, like ants or frogs about a pond, and that many other people live in many other such regions.

ATTRIBUTED TO SOCRATES BY PLATO

PTOLEMY DEFINED GEOGRAPHY—a term he used as a synonym for cartography—as "a representation in pictures of the whole known world together with the phenomena which are contained within." Cartographic scholars focus on the word "known," as it indicates Ptolemy's appreciation of the need for exploration and discovery, as well as his scientific inclination—an inclination ignored by a millennium of medieval cartographers to follow, men who were more interested in mapping the spirit than the earth they stood on. But Ptolemy's definition was also precedent-setting in its use of "whole": he set geographers the goal of representing everything. In the time since, that goal has proven to be as compelling as it is elusive.

Our vision is limited, yet we want to see it all. Even in the Middle Ages, while *mappaemundi* weren't intended to map the physical world, their aim was, arguably, more ambitious: to diagram history and anthropology, myth and scripture. In 1570 Abraham Ortelius published what is now acknowledged as the first modern atlas: *Theatrum Orbis Terrarum*, or *Theater of the World*. The term "atlas" wasn't used, though, until 1585, when Ortelius's friend Mercator began to issue a three-volume collection of maps named after the mythical figure who both held and beheld the world.* Nearly three centuries later, soon after this country's Civil War, John Wesley Powell, best known for his explorations of the Colorado River, advocated a uniform set of topographical and geological maps of the entire United States (he estimated the job would take twenty-four years; it took closer to seventy, and revisions continue today). In a similar spirit, still in the nineteenth century, Albrecht Penck proposed an "International Map of the World," drawn with a common projection at a common scale. Over one hundred years later, that map remains unfinished.†

The challenge of mapping everything — even "everything" in a carefully circumscribed area—is made clear by such projects as the NYCMap (pronounced "Nice Map"), which has been described as "the first integrated, one-inch-to-a-hundred-feet, perfectly accurate map that has ever been made of the entire City of New York and everything in it." While that claim is exaggerated, it may be true that the map, or series of maps, is "the most nearly complete picture of a city that has ever been made." It set out to include "every building, street, tank, bridge, tower, antenna, courtyard, runway, curb line, railway fence, elevation, ventilation grate, cemetery boundary, river, lake, pond, stream, swamp, beach, shoreline, pier, pavement center line, alley . . . and ocean . . . every tax lot, sewer main, subway entrance, and power line . . . every parking meter, fire hydrant, manhole, and telephone booth."

* Other terms in the running to describe books of maps were *Mirror* and *Theater*. Shakespeare's playhouse was, in turn, called the Globe, as there the stage was all the world.

† The problems are geographical (some parts of the Earth remain tricky to get at), civil (some apparently accessible areas are not hospitable to visitors, scientific or otherwise), political, and financial.

Even so, the map doesn't include everything, and of course it can never be finished, as its very inclusiveness ensures that it goes out of date every time a power line is moved, or a pond is drained, or a building is extended or razed. As Adam Gopnik has written, such maps "look more like the time that made them than like the thing they were meant to show. We chart our cities, and we chart ourselves."

The desire to see it all, to contain it all, goes back as far as the Garden of Eden and Noah's ark. Eratosthenes, the first man to measure the Earth (circa 200 B.C.), wasn't an explorer or a cartographer but a librarian, at the Great Library of Alexandria—an institution created to gather, under one roof, a copy of every book (scroll) ever written. While no one of any imagination anticipates that even the finest education will result in knowing everything, a number of cultures have attempted, in one way or another, to recreate the Great Library. Thomas Jefferson, another arts and sciences type, supported and expanded the aims of the Library of Congress, which began as just that—a collection of books useful to the young nation's political leaders. After the collection was destroyed during the war of 1812, Jefferson sold his wide-ranging personal library to the government to "re-commence" the work of an institution whose mission became "to acquire, organize, preserve, secure and sustain for the present and future use of the Congress and the nation a comprehensive record of American history and creativity [and] the world's greatest treasury of recorded human knowledge." Even today the impulse continues, with such relatively old-fashioned publishing projects as the Library of America and such new-fashioned creations as the World Wide Web. The Web has resulted in the secular devotion to the belief that a glorious future is assured if only every child has access to a computer that is "wired." And yet, and yet—inevitably, these grand ambitions serve to make us newly aware of what is missing, what we can't contain.

For years television screens have gotten busier: not only in commercials and music videos (which have become virtually the same thing), but in shows themselves the jump cuts get jumpier, the images and text more crowded. Cable sports channels run scores and bulletins at the bottom of the screen, while CNN Headline News at its most florid presents the viewer, simultaneously, with (1) a primary clip, often the talking head dutifully reciting snippets of news, (2) a secondary, sometimes unrelated visual, (3) a bottom crawl of news conveyed in ten words or fewer, (4) a rectangular space devoted to the weather, (5) the time, and (6) a horizontal bar reporting, depending on the hour, stock prices or sports scores. At, say, 7:38 P.M., one might be confronted with the effects of a recent bombing in Israel, a nearly naked pop singer accepting a statuette, the prediction of a high of 86 and a low of 74 in Dallas, word that the president has arrived at a multinational conference in Europe, and the unsurprising fact that the Cubs dropped a game to the Mets in the fourteenth, 4–3. This audio and visual freneticism mirrors the barrage of information that greets us away from the television nearly every waking moment. This is most obviously the case in cities, where we have to ignore the majority of signs, store displays, billboards, and posters if we are to cross safely from one side of the street to the other — never mind the sounds of traffic, distant music, sirens, construction, voices, planes overhead, pigeons underfoot, and the smells of cinnamon buns, tar, steamed hot dogs, bus exhaust, french fries, and urine. It is too much to absorb; and yet we respond, almost unconsciously, blocking out the smells of food if we aren't hungry, blocking out the other smells if we are; attending to the crosswalk signal and traffic lights but not to the advertisements, or vice versa; concentrating through the din of the jackhammer to eavesdrop on the conversation taking place beside us, via cellphone, between the woman we see and someone distant — perhaps in the office building down the street — with whom she is vulgarly, spectacularly angry; while, above the din, the siren is growing closer.

Ah, we think, give us the country life. But even in the remote countryside our senses are constantly at work, our brain constantly sifting, attending to the evidence of a trail through the woods but not to the differences among plants; to the song of a bird but not to the rustling of the leaves and the murmuring of a stream; to the differences among plants but not to the clouds gathering above us or the blister on our toe; or, more likely, to all of it, to varying degrees. Faced with "everything," we filter—through our needs and desires and emotions, our knowledge and our curiosity.

The impulse toward comprehensive comprehension is most directly reflected in fiction and poetry in the epic—in works such as the *Thousand and One Nights* and *Beowulf*, *Moby-Dick* and *The Canterbury Tales*, *Bleak House* and *War and Peace* and the *Odyssey*. While not even those works claim to tell us everything, they take in the world with a wide embrace—even when, as in Proust's *Remembrance of Things Past* and Whitman's *Leaves of Grass*, the work is centered around an individual voice, an individual perspective. Ultimately, the route to the greatest knowledge of all that's around us combines an awareness of infinite possibility and the close examination of the individual.

Beginning writers are told to write what they know, and all too often they do, with wearisome results. Stories and novels and poems that never transcend the writer's self-interest might be beautifully executed, but they are executed nevertheless—not even well-built roads to nowhere but completely circular driveways. At its best, the emphasis on the individual leads to deeper understanding of others, an imaginative leap beyond the confines of the self—which we can never truly escape. "The most singular, most limited position," Ellen Bryant Voigt has said, "may be as close as we ever get to something we all share. There is a way, I think, in which the careful making of poems can distance or externalize the self—the gaze remains steadily outward, and the self becomes another small part of the world. The point is not to prohibit the personal, but to examine it with utter ruthlessness." Flannery O'Connor agreed: "The writer has to judge himself with a stranger's eye and a stranger's severity. . . . No art is sunk

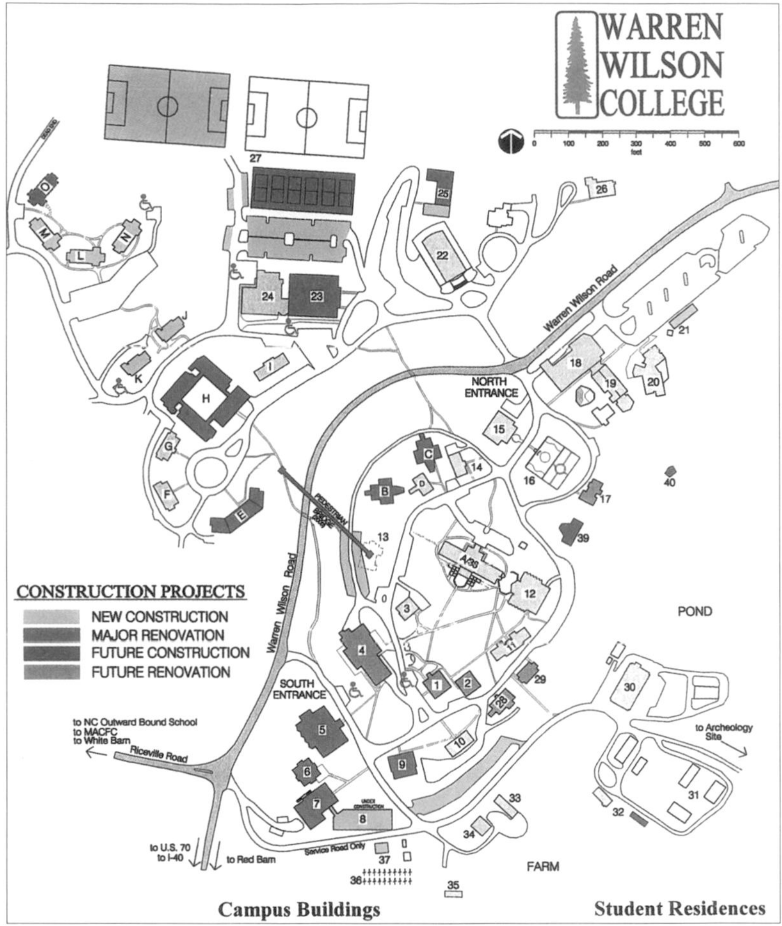

FIG. 33 AN "ACCURATE" CAMPUS MAP EMPHASIZING CONSTRUCTION PROJECTS

in the self, but rather, in art the self becomes self-forgetful in order to meet the demands of the thing being seen and the thing being made."* Whitman's most famous title only appears to be insufferably egotistical; "Song of Myself" is anything but self-obsessed. Emily Dickinson may not have gotten out much,

* Her identification of the writer as male underscores the point.

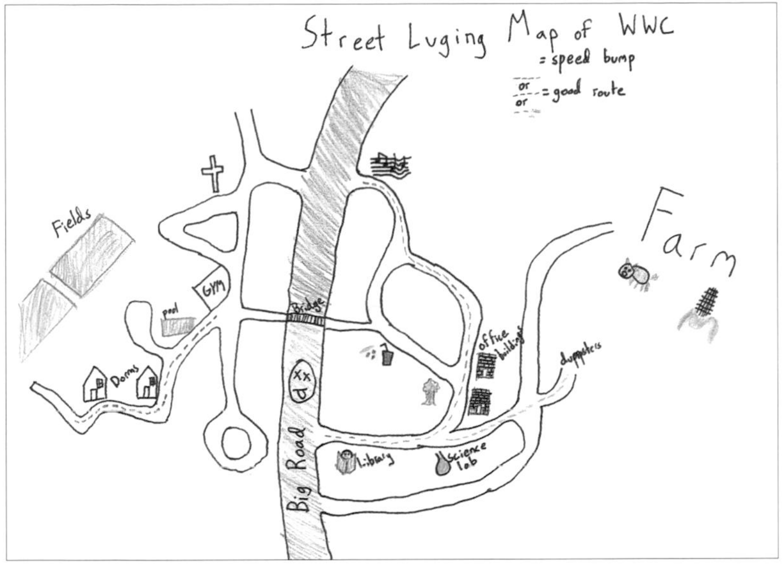

FIG. 34 A MENTAL MAP OF THE SAME SITE EMPHASIZING STREET LUGING RUNS, DRAWN FROM MEMORY BY THIRTEEN-YEAR-OLD REED TURCHI. NOTE THE DIFFERENCES IN DENSITY OF DETAIL, ORIENTATION, AND TONE (ONE MAP IS ABOUT WORK, THE OTHER ABOUT FUN), AND THE WARNING TO ANYONE FOOLISH ENOUGH TO LUGE THE STATE ROAD. EVERY MAP REFLECTS THE CARTOGRAPHER'S PERSPECTIVE AND CONCERNS

but her poems create a universe. The challenge is not only what to select for telling and how to present it, but how to evoke, simultaneously, the Theater of the World—how to make the leap from ego-vision to omnivision.

We want our writing to reflect the world in which we live, and of which we must constantly make sense. We impose order on chaos, which keeps resisting, so we keep trying to include more of the chaos, without yielding to it. One result of this striving is the testing of traditional forms. Today we see novels that combine fictional narrative with memoir and other nonfiction or presumed nonfiction (recipes, newspaper clippings, e-mail messages reproduced in all their crude typographical urgency). David Foster Wallace attaches to his narratives countless footnotes and asides, in the tradition of Borges and Nabokov, but more conversationally, as if to say, "If only we could head off in every direction at once."* Nicholson Baker's hypersensitivity to the moment in books such as *The Mezzanine* attempts to capture the richness we sense around us, ours to contemplate if only we could stop, or slow, time. Anne Carson consistently questions forms, calling *The Autobiography of Red* a novel, referring to what most readers think of as her poems "essays," and subtitling one book *A Fictional Essay in 29 Tangos*. The naming alone is inconsequential — a writer might refer to his latest collection of stories as a soufflé for violin and banana—but Carson's productions don't look, or read, exactly like much else. "I think the forms are in chaos," she has said. "I seize upon these generic names like *essay* or *opera* in despair as I'm sinking under the waves of possible naming for any event that I come up with. I really don't know what to call anything. . . . It's like closing the windows on a rainy night. It just feels a little safer to have a genre to be in, but I don't think most of them work." Forms, by definition, have boundaries; when they won't allow us to play the games we want to play, we search for new ways to reflect our communication with the world.

Much of this searching goes on within the friendly confines of realism, the dominant mode of our day, due in large part to one of the great gifts of literary modernism: the representation of the complexity of characters' minds. Attempts to reflect the effects of the disorder of the world on the individual in James Joyce, William Faulkner, Katherine Anne Porter, T.S. Eliot, Ezra Pound, and e. e. cummings continue to influence what we call conventional realism — or, more usefully, since realism has taken many forms over the past 150 years, contemporary psychological realism.

Mental mapping is a field of interest not only to cartographers but to psychiatrists, psychologists, sociologists, and many others, including urban planners and architects. It includes the paths or routes we store in our heads but also our more general impres-

* Far from a by-product of technological cacophony, genre-combining goes back at least as far as Xenophon's *Anabasis*, an amalgamation of history, biography, and memoir.

sions of places. In their book *Mental Maps*, Peter Gould and Rodney White include drawings of the Mission Hill area of Boston made by three African American boys who lived there. The drawings depict the same streets, but are entirely different in proportion and in detail. In one, the white residential area is an enormous blank, terra incognita; in another, the street between the boy's home and the white residential area is dominant, illustrating the substance of the barrier; the third, drawn by a boy attending Boston Latin, puts the white neighborhood in proportion, and includes among its primary landmarks five carefully identified educational institutions. Similar experiments led to similar results, confirming that a neighborhood, like a home, is a state of mind. Perhaps the most famous depiction of a mental map is Saul Steinberg's Manhattanite's view of the world, which appeared on the cover of the *New Yorker*. Intended as a comment on New York provincialism, it was quickly copied and imitated, indicating that the joke hits home, wherever our home might be. (In the 1400s a Venetian senator confronted with Fra Mauro's world map saw his home city represented as a tiny dot and said, "Why so small? Venice should be bigger and the rest of the world should be smaller.") Just as mapmakers have traditionally put their homeland at the center, the part of the world we know best, the place or places we live, loom largest.

WHEN I WAS very young—four, five—I would go with my mother to the place she called the beauty shop and, while a woman named Beulah washed her hair, I would crawl behind the chairs, under the counters, and collect stray bobby pins and curlers. A small thing, but memorable enough that after I had started school, whenever I would see any of the women who worked in the beauty shop, they would ask when I was coming back, since now, they claimed, there was no one to pick up after them.

Skip ahead nearly twenty years. My family has long since

moved, and I have gone off to college. I have occasion to return to our old house—and there, standing on the sidewalk, waiting for the bus home, is Beulah. I introduce myself. Beulah exclaims, "You've changed your hair!" Never mind that I had

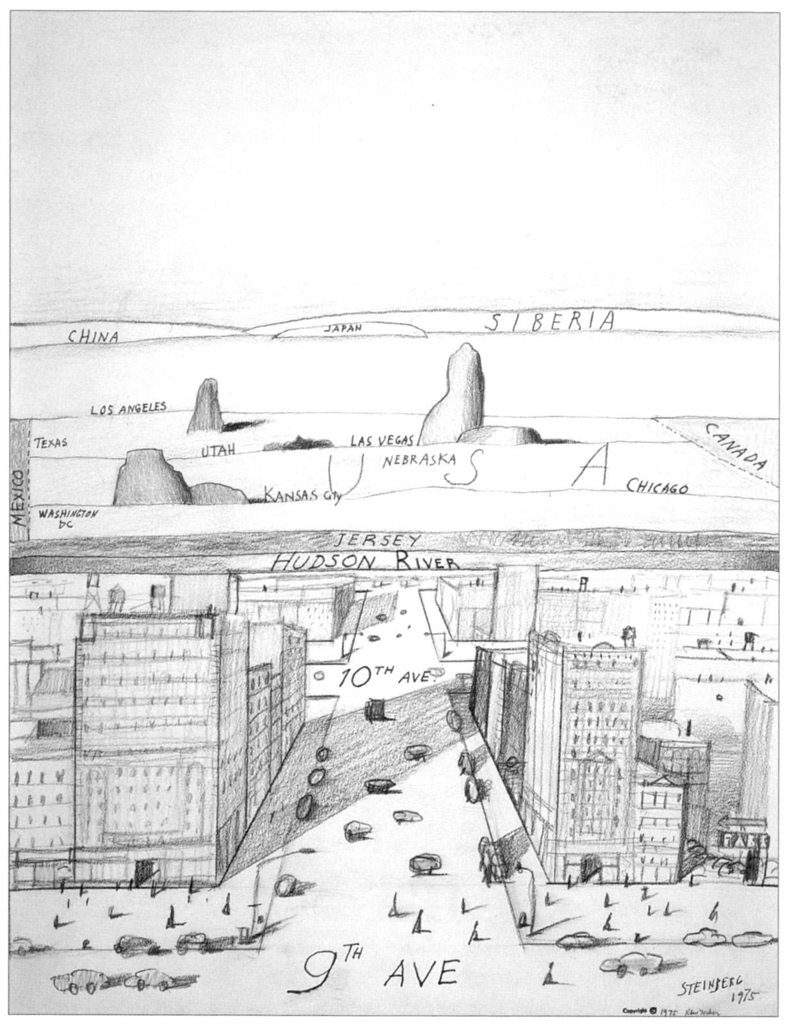

FIG. 35 **SAUL STEINBERG'S *VIEW OF THE WORLD FROM 9TH AVENUE*, 1975; WAX CRAYON AND GRAPHITE ON PAPER; 20 X 15 INCHES**

grown three feet taller and added a hundred pounds, a beard, and glasses.

In his stories and novels, John Updike is particularly alert to details related to occupation, details that lend authority to characterization and immediately convey a defining aspect of the character's view. In "A&P," Sammy refers to the keys of the cash register in shorthand (4, 9, GROC, TOT); in *Rabbit is Rich*, Toyota salesman Harry Angstrom spends his days staring out through the showroom window, reading the huge paper banner spanning the glass wall: .TI TOG EW ,TI ROF DEKSA UOY Like it or not, the work that occupies most of our time also occupies our minds, and as a result we see the people around us as an assortment of hairstyles, car owners, or various states of health. (Once, on a plane, I struck up a conversation with my seatmate, who happened to be a doctor. After the initial give-and-take, he asked, "What did you do to your thumb?" — having noticed a three-year-old scar the size of a kernel of corn.)

While our perspective and understanding are undeniably limited, in some sense we each have the world — or we each have *a* world, one that includes not only our hometown and our favorite vacation spot but Victorian England, volcanoes we have only read about, and Vietnam, which has a place in our mind even if we can't find it on a globe. We compile mental maps that are wildly skewed, a mental atlas so large and complex that we can never fully convey it to anyone else. Then we live in the world those maps create.

> In *Ulysses* I have recorded, simultaneously, what a man says, sees, thinks, and what such seeing, thinking, saying does, to what you Freudians call the subconscious.
>
> — JAMES JOYCE, IN A LETTER TO EZRA POUND

IN ALLOWING US an intimate view of another individual's perspective, psychological realism moves from the nineteenth century's Theater of the World toward a Theater of the Mind. In *Ulysses*, Joyce conveys disorder by attending with greater care than ever before to the "stream of consciousness" — a term that is misleading, since no matter its width and speed, a stream flows in one direction, within its banks. Our thoughts are rarely linear and logical; rather, they tend to spin out in all directions, responding to all of those aforementioned intellectual, emotional, and sensory impulses. What we call our Train of Thought is more like a Tornado of Thought—a huge, swirling mass capable of picking up cows, fenceposts, salsa, and talcum powder with no single purpose, yet moving in one general direction at any given moment. *Ulysses*, like *Absalom, Absalom!* and "The Love Song of J. Alfred Prufrock," Katherine Anne Porter's "Pale Horse, Pale Rider," and much of the best modernist work, presents us with a simulated storm of information and experience.

"A state of mind," Rita Carter writes in *Mapping the Mind*, "is an all-encompassing perception of the world that binds sensory perception, thoughts, feelings and memories into a seamless whole. To produce it millions of neural brain patterns fire in concert, creating a stream of 'mega-patterns' — one for every conscious moment. This constellation of neural activity shimmers with constant change as one thought dies away and another comes forward. But so long as your attention is held by the basic theme, the overall pattern, a sort of mega-mega-pattern, will remain recognizable."

Virginia Woolf re-creates this "neural shimmer" in *Mrs. Dalloway:*

> "I love walking in London," said Mrs. Dalloway. "Really it's better than walking in the country."
>
> They had just come up—unfortunately—to see doctors. Other people came to see pictures; go to the opera; take their daughters out; the Whitbreads came "to see doctors." Times without number Clarissa had visited Evelyn Whitbread in a nursing home. Was Evelyn ill again? Evelyn was a good deal out of sorts, said Hugh, intimating by a kind of pout or swell of his very well-covered, manly, extremely handsome, perfectly upholstered body (he was almost too well dressed always, but presumably had to be, with his little job at Court) that his wife had some internal ailment, nothing serious, which, as an old friend, Clarissa Dalloway would quite understand without requiring him to specify. Ah yes, she did of course; what a nuisance; and felt very sisterly and oddly conscious at the same time of her hat. Not the right hat for the early morning, was it? For Hugh always made her feel, as he bustled on, raising his hat rather extravagantly and reassuring her that she might be a girl of eighteen, and of course he was coming to her party to-night, Evelyn absolutely insisted, only a little late he might be after the party at the Palace to which he had to take one of Jim's boys,—she always felt a little skimpy beside Hugh; schoolgirlish; but attached to him, partly from having known him always, but she did think him a good sort in his own way, though Richard was nearly driven mad by him, and as for Peter Walsh, he had never to this day forgiven her for liking him.

Essentially simultaneously, Mrs. Dalloway walks through the city, engages in conversation, considers her history with the Whitbreads, and worries over how she's presenting herself. In the opening pages of Woolf's novel, we are being introduced to Clarissa's mental map. Like every other mental map, hers might seem arbitrary at times and unreliable, but we don't always want objective information—we *want* to understand how others see the world, and so grow beyond the confines of our own perspective.

Even in more conventional psychological realism, we mean to evoke a large and complicated world, one with potentially overwhelming detail and sensation—within the confines of a thoroughly considered, many-times-revised piece of writing. Michael Ryan reminds us that an original function of language

> was to exclude from attention what was unimportant to the task at hand, thereby providing an ordering of the experience of the world. That exclusion, which characterizes rationality and discursiveness, is also useful to poetry, because it is in the balance between order and inclusion that poems are made. As Stevens said, "The poem must resist the intelligence *almost* successfully." The "blessed rage for order" must win in the end because it is that which allows us to survive. However, if the battle against it . . . is not a raging battle, the poem will seem to have excluded too much.

All writing imposes order, eventually, in the same way that we impose order on our thoughts every day so as to get things done and to hold conversations. To truly speak our mind — to give voice to all our thoughts—would be to risk sounding out of our mind. In the course of daily interactions we constantly edit, revise, and suppress. We make sense.

In this regard, the differences among, say, Joyce's portrayal of the working of a mind, and Faulkner's, and Nicholson Baker's, is a matter of degree. We simplify or clarify a speaker's or character's thoughts, reducing or confining them in the name of "clarity" or "purpose," even as we attempt to acknowledge the cacophony of emotions, sensations, questions, and understandings that propel her or paralyze her. The challenge in any given work is to find the most appropriate and effective ways to evoke complexity-bordering-on-chaos.

FIG. 36 TERRA CARTA™

Don DeLillo's *White Noise* is a study of contemporary American culture, of contemporary American academic culture (still ringing true almost twenty years later), and of the timeless challenge of living in the face of death. The novel begins with two techniques of inclusion. The first paragraph includes a long list of items the narrator, Jack Gladney, observes or imagines being carried to campus, from blankets and books to soccer balls and popcorn, by students and their parents. Gladney, who teaches at the College-on-the-Hill, is watching what he calls "the day of the station wagons": the day just before the start of the fall semester when students arrive and lug their belongings into the dorms. The scene is representative of ritual and tradition, a spectacle Gladney says he's witnessed "every September for twenty-one years."

In the book, DeLillo's characters find themselves trying to make sense—and to make a life—of a perplexing combination of information, misinformation, first-hand observations, gossip, fear, rumors, and hope. Typical is a scene in the family car, which begins as Denise asks her mother about medication she suspects her mother is taking:

> "What do you know about Dylar?"
>
> "Is that the black girl who's staying with the Stovers?"
>
> "That's Dakar," Steffie said.
>
> "Dakar isn't her name, it's where she's from," Denise said. "It's a country on the ivory coast of Africa."
>
> "The capital is Lagos," Babette said. "I know that because of a surfer movie I saw once where they travel all over the world."
>
> "*The Perfect Wave*," Heinrich said. "I saw it on TV."
>
> "But what's the girl's name?" Steffie said.
>
> "I don't know," Babette said, "but the movie wasn't called *The Perfect Wave*. The perfect wave is what they were looking for."
>
> "They go to Hawaii," Denise told Steffie, "and wait for these tidal waves to come from Japan. They're called origamis."
>
> "And the movie was called *The Long Hot Summer*," her mother said.
>
> "*The Long Hot Summer*," Heinrich said, "happens to be a play by Tennessee Ernie Williams."
>
> "It doesn't matter," Babette said, "because you can't copyright titles anyway."

Jack goes on to tell us,

> The family is the cradle of the world's misinformation. There must be something in family life that generates factual error. Overcloseness, the noise and heat of being. Perhaps something even deeper, like the need to survive. Murray says we are fragile creatures surrounded by a world of hostile facts. Facts threaten our happiness and security. The deeper we delve into the nature of things, the looser our structure may seem to become. The family process works toward sealing off the world. Small errors grow heads, fictions proliferate.

Murray is right, and Murray is wrong. The family is the world in microcosm. DeLillo portrays the "world of hostile facts" not by imitating the swirling consciousness of Stephen Dedalus or Mrs. Dalloway but by including, in the midst of the narrative, snippets of dialogue from the television and observations of objects and events, without comment. These juxtapositions can almost always be read as absurd humor, but they come to define Jack Gladney's, and to some extent his family's, view of the world.

The disorder of the world is a constant presence. But that isn't to say there isn't order; in fact, the opening of the novel is a recognition of some of the order in Jack's world. He believes the day of the station wagons "tells the parents that they are a collection of the like-minded and the spiritually akin, a people, a nation." While he stands apart, observing, he is also fully involved in the life of the college and its students. He has started a program, an organization. As chairman of the world's first department of Hitler Studies, he has both subscribed to the life of the institution and refused to be part of what his friend Murray calls "a collective perception." "Collective perception" is the focus of Murray's department, American Environments, which he says aims "to decipher the language of our culture" as it's expressed through television, film, comic books, cereal boxes, and Elvis. But in the novel it is Jack who deciphers our culture, from the vantage point of an active participant in the struggle between order and chaos, between sense and absurdity.

> When I came to measure the mark with my own foot, I found my foot not so large by a great deal. . . . These things filled my head with new imaginations.
>
> — DANIEL DEFOE, *ROBINSON CRUSOE*

WE CHART OUR CITIES, so we chart ourselves. To chart the external world is to reveal ourselves — our priorities, our interests, our desires, our fears, our biases. We believe we're mapping our knowledge, but in fact we're mapping what we want — and what we want others — to believe. In this way, every map is a reflection of the individual or group that creates it. By "reading" a map, by studying it, we share, however temporarily, those beliefs. This explains why we can enjoy, collect, and hang on our walls maps of places we've never been and never expect to go to — even places that don't exist. Because the map takes us there.

Recently I found a treasure map, one that had been the subject

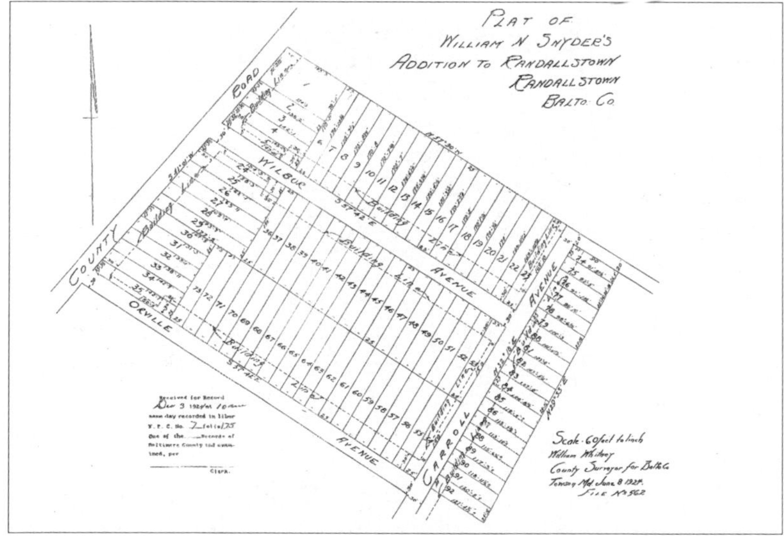

FIG. 37 **ONE MAN'S DREAM MAP, COMMITTED TO PAPER JUNE 8, 1924**

of family lore for most of a century. The map, a plat, shows the intended division of some farmland owned by my great-grandfather in the 1920s, outside of Baltimore. My great-grandfather was, apparently, a beloved local figure. He hosted community dances and parties, and when he returned each week from Lexington Market he was generous with his leftovers, to the extent that for years elderly strangers would tell me about summer afternoons eating William Snyder's homemade ice cream. But farming is farming, and with four children there were plenty of bills, so he agreed to borrow against his land so a local builder could construct a house on speculation, with the aim of developing a modest neighborhood. The house was constructed on the eve of the Great Depression, and in its wake the bank repossessed the farm, evicted the family, and auctioned the farmhouse. Before the auction my great-grandfather died, some said of heartbreak, and his wife fell into a depression that lasted the rest of her life.

The neighborhood came into being years later. The only remnants of William Snyder's original plan are the old farmhouse, now hidden by suburban homes; two street signs, which bear the names of two of his children; and the map: a piece of paper that brings me as close to him as I'll ever get.

Every brain constructs the world in a slightly different way from any other because every brain is different. The sight of an external object will vary from person to person because no two people have precisely the same number of motion cells, magenta-sensitive cells, or straight-line cells. For example, one person — someone with a particularly well-developed colour area, say — may look at a bowl of fruit and be struck by the gleaming colours and the way they relate to each other. Another — with a more active depth discriminatory area — may be caught instead by the three-dimensional form of the display. A third may notice the outline. A fourth may home in on some detail. In each case the raw data would be identical but the image brought to consciousness would be different.

— RITA CARTER

THE FILM *Memento* uses a variety of narrative and technical strategies to give the viewer two perspectives on the unusual situation of its main character. Leonard Shelby has suffered a severe blow to the head, damaging the hippocampus, with the result that he can form no new memories. This makes his hold on order particularly tenuous. Leonard's memory of events before his injury is normal, and he is able to function reasonably well. And yet, day after day, he fails to recognize the clerk of the hotel he's staying in, and he wouldn't be able to return to the hotel, or recognize other people, or remember their significance, without his Polaroid photographs and the notes he has written on them, as well as crucial "facts" he has tattooed on his body. Leonard suffers from the inability to make new mental maps. Largely through unconventional narrative sequence, the film simulates his disorientation for the viewer; at the same time, the film provides a second view, from a greater distance, to allow us to understand Leonard's story in a way he cannot.

The urgency of dramatic necessity is supplied by the fact that Leonard's wife was raped and (we are told) murdered, and he is intent on revenge. When we meet Leonard, he is standing over a bloody corpse. The drama of the scene is immediately undercut, though, as we see a Polaroid photograph undevelop and slide back into the camera Leonard is holding. A moment later, a gun leaps into his hand, a bullet rolls around on the floor, jumps, and reinserts itself into the barrel, the dead man's glasses return to his face, the man rises to his knees, and screams. While we don't know it yet, this backward movement through time reflects Leonard's confusion. In that Leonard can't remember what he did a few days, or hours, or even minutes ago, we don't *know* what he did; like him, we are constantly trying to figure things out. But this strategy presents a challenge to the filmmakers, as putting the scenes in reverse order would eventually lead to a kind of predictability—albeit an uncommon one—and because the film needs to release explanatory information. And so while part of the story is told backward, beginning with the murder of John Gammell (who Leonard believes killed his wife) and ending with Leonard murdering a young drug dealer named Jimmy Grantz (who Leonard believes killed his wife), another series of scenes runs forward in time, beginning with Leonard waking up in a hotel room (the film's second scene) and ending when he murders Jimmy Grantz. To add to the narrative braid, a number of flashbacks are inserted along the way, scenes from Leonard's past—at least some of which, we come to understand, are not reliable.

Writer-director Christopher Nolan and editor Dody Dorn are careful to provide just enough clues, in a variety of ways, so that we can make sense of what we see and hear. In addition to the backward action in the first scene, the film offers assistance via a visual device: the reverse-chronological scenes are in color, while the forward-moving scenes are in black and white. (The two meet near the end of the film, when Leonard dresses in Jimmy Grantz's suit.) Just as video games teach their players how to negotiate the landscape and avoid or overcome various obstacles by carefully introducing both the obstacles and their solutions, the makers of *Memento* teach us how to "read" the film. The first scene is the only one actually played in reverse, with the developed Polaroid undeveloping and sliding back into the front of the camera, the gun leaping back into Leonard's hand, and so on. The scene is a purposeful exaggeration, designed to call our attention to the film's strategy. Slightly less explicit indications of the film's ordering are offered in the next brief scene, when Leonard doesn't know where he is except that it's a hotel room, and in the next, when the dead man appears, perfectly healthy, in the building where we just saw Leonard murder him. Leonard takes a Polaroid from his pocket to identify the man—Teddy, a close acquaintance—and the film's narrative methods are in place.

Leonard Shelby's mind is, to the viewer, terra incognita. (While there are people who suffer similar afflictions, the very nature of their disability makes it impossible for them to comprehend a feature-length film.) By drawing us in, the filmmakers not only make his strange land familiar but provide us a new perspective from which to view our own world. *Memento* is entertaining because it's clever. It is also amusing, perhaps frightening, and, ultimately, compelling in its depiction of a willfully simplified life, a life impoverished by its being reduced to a single idea, the quest for revenge. It draws us into a consideration of our dependence on memory; on people who claim to act as our friends and who confirm or correct our memories; and on our very sense of reality. In the final scene, after we've learned the extent of Leonard's self-deception, he thinks: "I have to believe in a world outside of my own mind. . . . We all need mirrors to remind ourselves who we are."

Dody Dorn has said the film "puts the viewer in Leonard's head. . . . The only difference between the viewer and Leonard is that the viewer at least has a cumulative recollection of what will happen." That "recollection of what will happen" is crucial—it is the distance that allows us to step back from Leonard's nightmarish life, to make sense of it, to imagine it.

In one of the film's quieter moments, a flashback, Leonard and his wife are in their bedroom; she is reading an already well-worn paperback.

> "How can you read that again?" Leonard asks.
>
> "It's good," she says.
>
> "You've read it a hundred times."
>
> "I enjoy it," she says.
>
> "Yeah," he allows, "but the pleasure of a book is in wanting to know what happens next — "
>
> "I'm not reading it to annoy you," she tells him. "I enjoy it."

Leonard's wife knows the pleasures of repetition, of anticipation, and of expectation fulfilled. The reader of a book, like the viewer of a film, is a kind of traveler; the book, story, poem, or film "seizes moments out of time." Leonard and his wife are both right: there is the pleasure of not knowing what comes next, and there is the pleasure of knowing. The pleasure of knowing what comes next requires a drastic reduction of the world, a reduction most of us would not place on our lives even if we could. In writing, however, reduction, selection, and order are key. "Mapping," according to G. Malcolm Lewis, "may . . . have served to achieve what in modern behavioral therapy is known as desensitization: lessening fear by the repeated representation of what is feared." Like maps, fiction and poetry enable us to "see" what is literally too large for our vision.

> What we remember is continually being changed by new learning, when the connections between nerve cells are being modified. . . . Meaning is different for every person, because it depends on their past experience. Since the sensory activity is washed away and only the construction is saved, the only knowledge that each of us has is what we construct within our own brains. . . . The world is infinitely complex, and any brain can only know the little that it can create within itself.
>
> — WALTER J. FREEMAN

WRITING ADDS TO "the little the brain can create within itself" by presenting vicarious experience: alternate lives in alternate worlds. This needn't necessarily entail entering a world as unusual as Leonard Shelby's, or exaggerated for comic effect, like Jack Gladney's. There is plenty to discover much closer to home.

Heather McHugh's "Not a Prayer" recounts and considers the death of a close friend of the speaker, an elderly woman who spends "the livelong time that's left" at home with her "half-deaf" socialist and cardiologist husband, her son, the speaker, and various relatives and attendants. The poem is told in thirty sections, and while several are quite short (one is a single line), the majority have internal stanza divisions or space breaks—which is to say, the structural components are marked but irregular. The poem's narrative is concerned primarily with the last three days of the dying woman's life, but the sections describing those days are not in chronological order and are interspersed with memory and reflection. The opening scene of *Mrs. Dalloway* introduces us to the workings of Clarissa's mind; the opening scene of *White Noise* has Jack observing the flotsam and jetsam of college life; the opening scene of *Memento* exaggerates technique to instruct the viewer and to explain the narrative logic. In an early section of McHugh's poem, the speaker acknowledges the absence of such a logical strategy, a surrendering to "time's unrecoverable flow."

> Who tells the time?
>   . . . Two days from today
> (is it today?) I took the red-eye. One
> AM: is anyone awake? Arrived
> a life ago. But time is going
> to be unkept. It has
> to tell itself.

The speaker is unable to "keep" time, in the sense that time continues to move (toward death) and will not be stilled, and in the sense that the speaker's attention to her friend, coupled with exhaustion and emotional distraction, make it impossible, and unimportant, to note the hours or to maintain a normal schedule—she will stay awake with her friend through the night. But while the speaker is unable to keep time, stop time, or move back in time (except through memory and imagination), her dying friend exerts a measure of control:

> To put some sense together, she takes
> time: ten minutes, twenty, half an hour.
> The others come and go.

Each thinks her thinking
incoherent. But if anybody
listens long enough he hears
(among the many dozings)
something terribly intelligible.

We are invited to listen long enough, carefully enough, to make sense of the apparently senseless, and so to share the speaker's grief, fascination, and admittedly limited understanding. The poem's movement through time and space reflects both the fading consciousness of the dying woman and the competing claims of the speaker's intellect and emotion; it moves along a circuitous, but ultimately clear, path. In the next stanzas, the speaker charts for us the woman's attempt to utter a sentence:

"Yesterday yesterday I was [and here she falls asleep for seven minutes]
yesterday I was full of new [she falls asleep for three] new life new life
but today but today new life but today [she falls asleep eleven minutes]
I am full of full of yesterday I was [she falls asleep] was full of new life
but today I am full of [come back, come back, I tell one of her sons,
the sentence has a structure, when she falls asleep she's not forgetting]
but today [she falls asleep, he can't believe me] I am full of but today
I'm full of [somebody is calling him from somewhere else and then
he's gone] but today I am full of . . . [now she'll tell me, now I'll know]
. . . I'm full of finished . . ."

[Full of finished? is that last word AFTER the ellipsis? should it be
attached to how, instead of what, she meant? which parts were talking
about talking, should I put some
quotes in quotes? some kind
of mind inside the mind, some
time inside, or out? This bracket

is the writer's. Who
are you? are you? are you?]

The passage offers the reader a number of overlapping but distinct trails as it works to make sense of an incomplete utterance. First there is the dying woman's speech, with all of its repetition and restarting, its gradual syntactical progression. If the speaker merely wanted us to understand what the woman said, she could assemble the pieces for us, edit the unfinished sentence to its most complete form. But while she helps us to see that version—by collapsing time, by bracketing the material that isn't the woman's speech—she leaves in the diversions, as the passage is as much about the effort to speak, to communicate, as it is about what's being said. The second trail we're given through the material is provided inside the brackets, where the speaker explains the lapses, offers some of her own thoughts at the time, and provides narrative context, including the response of the woman's son. These bracketed sections also employ repetition and variation, making them a musical counterpoint to the dying woman's speech. Finally, McHugh has created a third trail, one that moves not in sentences but through lines and stanzas. The first of the three stanzas above is unlineated—the poet has relaxed her control over the line, and so emphasizes the dying woman's stuttering syntax — but with "I'm full of finished . . ." she reasserts her poetic presence, combining longer and shorter lines, using uppercase for emphasis and neglecting to use uppercase to begin new sentences.

"A lineated lyric," McHugh says, "draws a reader's attention, by design, more to immediate spatial and structural relations — to the course the reader travels from departure to arrival point, the pattern of curves en route." The effect of the above passage from "Not a Prayer" is the equivalent of a reverse zoom, as the stanza with fewer overt poetic devices encourages our intimacy with the woman, while the following stanzas, with increasingly explicit devices, draw us away from the woman's words, first to the speaker's frustration, and her own attempt to make sense, and then, through particularly aggressive enjambment, to ours:

This bracket

is the writer's. Who
are you?

The poem takes us deep into the terror of death and loss and voicelessness. And yet, reading it, we experience the satisfaction afforded by art that recognizes and re-creates the complexity of our thoughts and feelings and simultaneously imposes order, shaping experience, so transforming it. Such work maps meaningfully the way we think, the way we live.

How can we imagine what our lives should be without the illumination of the lives of others?

— JAMES SALTER

THAT PLAT I have from 1924 is a cold document. It shows only how William Snyder, or more likely someone he hired, subdivided a portion of farmland. It doesn't mention that roads were laid out, utilities were installed, a house was built on speculation. The map offers no indication that the Depression hit or that, in 1931, William Snyder died from a combination of heartbreak and exhaustion, his family was evicted from the farmhouse, and the house and land were auctioned off by the bank. My only evidence of those things is family gospel, as it was told and retold for over sixty years. And that tale, it turns out, isn't quite true.

In fact, my great-grandfather died of epilepsy, which his family considered shameful; and the pain of his death, combined with the shame of the poverty that followed, led his four children to romanticize those early years on the farm through their adulthood and well into old age. To recognize that is not to blame them. "The various dwelling-places in our lives," Gaston Bachelard writes in *The Poetics of Space*, "retain the treasures of former days. . . .

We comfort ourselves by reliving memories of protection . . . by recalling these memories, we add to our store of dreams; we are never real historians, but always near poets, and our emotion is perhaps nothing but an expression of a poetry that was lost." Over the years, my aunt and uncles each bought a small piece of the old farm from strangers; but now even that land belongs to other strangers, people who have no way to know or reason to care that the streets they drive on each day are named for my grandfather and one of his brothers. My mother grew up in a house on the street named for her father; and in a house around the corner I saw, the only time I remember, my great-grandmother. My copy of that plat is important to me less because it was a kind of treasure map, in its promise of wealth, for a man I never met, than because it serves as a reminder of the distance between past and present, between what is and what might have been, between the lives we live and the lives we imagine. And of course, that map isn't what brings me closest to my great-grandfather. What truly summons a man who died long before I was born are the stories his children have told me. No one of their stories captures him; rather, he exists, for me, in vivid fragments, a collection of shards I've assembled into the shape of a pot, with more gaping holes than clay.

One of the impulses behind nineteenth-century realism was to tell the stories of people whose lives had not, previously, been deemed story-worthy. Another was to describe the world as it is. While we might fault Dickens for sentimentality and melodrama, in his large-canvassed novels he sought to represent a world in which many stories are happening at once, stories that intersect directly and indirectly, in ways no one participant can see. Melville quickly grew dissatisfied with simply describing places and events, no matter how multilayered or exotic, and so integrated philosophy and meditation. The modernists brought us more fully inside the mind, at the same time experimenting with the arrangement of information, requiring the reader to join in the process of composition.

When we grow frustrated with received literary forms, it is because we feel the forms are reductive, placing artificial constraints on what can be represented on the page. But no matter whether we work within those forms or try to make them more elastic, the challenge is to find ways to express, not everything in the world, but some part of the world in its complexity. The tension between our vision for the work and the form we choose mirrors the tension between the world in its incomprehensible vastness and our attempts to make sense of it.

As writers, we refuse simply to share and thereby reinforce the collective perception; we want to get at something else, something that hasn't been perceived or hasn't been presented the way we see it. By asserting our vision, we strive not to impose our view on others, as an act of aggression, but to share it, as an act of generosity. Eudora Welty said that her goal in writing fiction was "not to point the finger in judgement, but to part a curtain, that invisible shadow that falls between people, the veil of indifference to each other's presence, each other's human plight." Our interest in maps of places we've never been, and may never go, is evidence of our curiosity not only about where others live but about how they live, and how we would live if we were among them. We can never move entirely beyond the limits of our physical confines, or even beyond our perceptions and understanding; but fiction and poetry, in expanding the world of our imagination beyond the world of our experience, allow us a more intimate—and so more thorough, and perhaps more compassionate—imaginative knowledge of our fellow beings than we are likely ever to have in the course of our daily lives.

A RIGOROUS GEOMETRY

Philosophy is written in this grand book (I mean the universe) which stands continuously open to our gaze, but it cannot be understood unless one first understands the language and recognizes the characters in which it is written. It is written in the language of mathematics, and its characters are triangles, circles and other geometric figures. Without knowledge of this medium it is impossible to understand a single word of it; without this knowledge, one is wandering about in a dark labyrinth.

GALILEO GALILEI

I. THE LINE (OF ARGUMENT) FORMS HERE

WHILE MATHEMATICS may or may not be the language of the universe, it is one of the man-made tools that have long helped us to understand our world. From the very start, people wanted to know more about the Earth: how much of it there was, what shape it was, if and where there were other people on it. By paying attention to the sun and the stars, the moon and the sea, even the ancients understood the Earth was more or less a ball. And they knew it was a big ball.

How big?

Too big to measure by foot.

Eratosthenes, credited as the first man to measure the girth of the Earth with any kind of accuracy, acted on one crucial assumption (that the Earth is a sphere), a few observations (that the sun appears to move across the sky and, as it does so, shadows change length; also, that over the course of the year, the sun appears to be higher or lower in the sky), and a knowledge of geometry. He knew that if the sun's rays are essentially parallel when they reach the Earth, then by measuring the angle of a shadow in Alexandria and the height of the object casting it at the time the sun shone straight down onto shadowless Syene, in the tropics, he could learn what fraction of the Earth's circumference was represented by the distance between the two cities. By his calculations, the answer was nearly one-fiftieth. Multiplying that figure by the distance between Syene and Alexandria produced the circumference of the Earth.

Early man had taken note of the movement of the sun, and the change of seasons, and recognized that in spring and fall the sun changed direction; its northernmost and southernmost paths are the imaginary lines we call tropics (after *tropos*, Greek for "turn," for the apparent turning of the sun across the sky). The tropics are named after the constellations Cancer and Capricorn—imaginary figures in the sky, remnants of an ancient

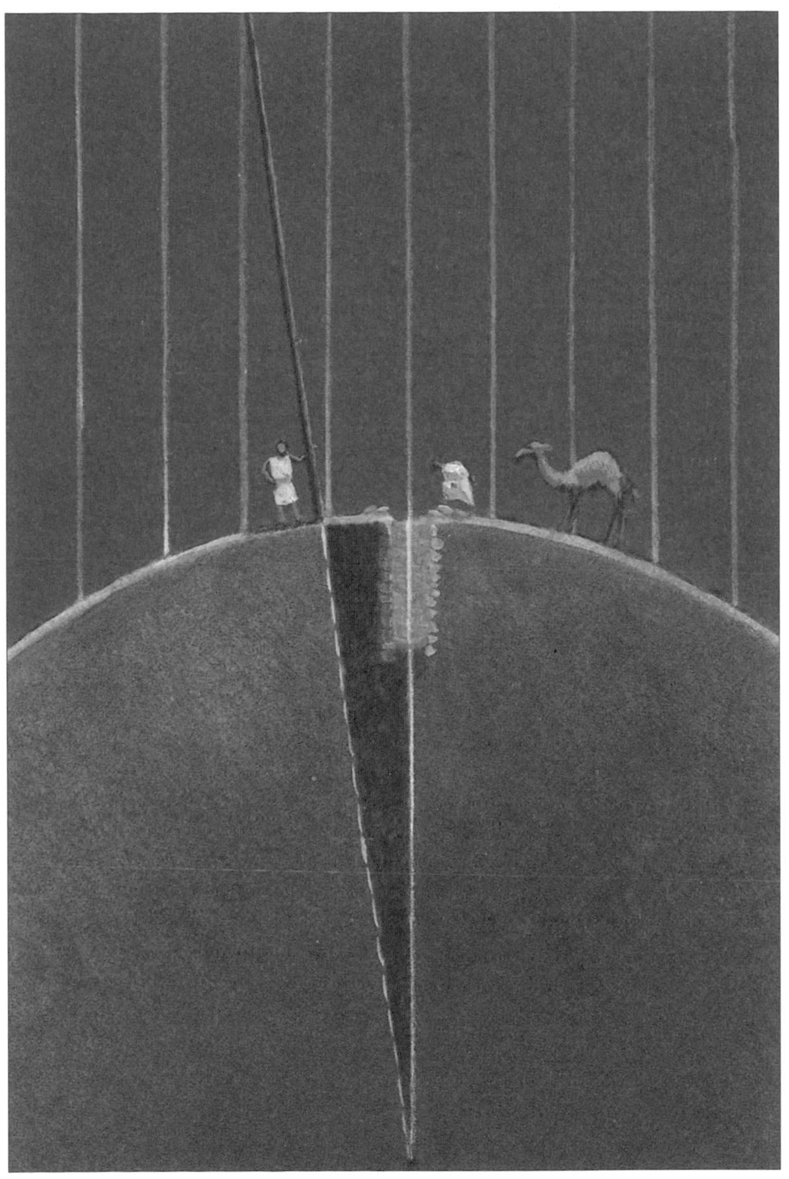

FIG. 38 **ERATOSTHENES AND FRIENDS**

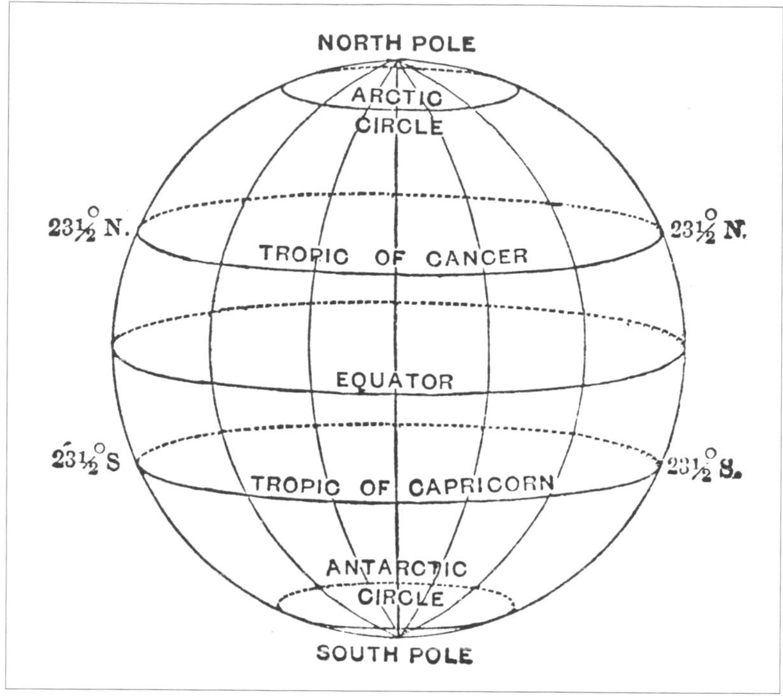

FIG. 39

game of connect-the-dots. The equator is another imaginary line, this one on the Earth itself. Long before any man was able to stand (or sit) far enough away to see the entire planet, people conceived of the Earth as a ball with imaginary lines of latitude parallel to the equator and imaginary lines of longitude running perpendicular to it, connecting the poles (points determined not by any natural feature of the land but by mathematicians).

For much of our existence, then, mankind has used the invented system of geometry to gain a better understanding of the Earth. We have literally imposed geometry on the planet, flattening the ground and building cities on grids of roads laid parallel and at precise right angles or, as in Washington, D.C., like spokes extending from a wheel.* As our buildings, streets, and cities are mathematical constructs, it comes as no surprise that our maps of them are. The road map tells us that our destination lies at G8 and we read across, then down, identify the appropriate rectangle, and spot it. If we give the activity a moment's thought, we're simply grateful someone has taken the trouble to divide the world up so neatly.

II. A STORY IS A KIND OF MAP

> Nothing can remain immense if it can be measured. Prior to the shrinkage of space and the abolition of distance through railroads, steamships, and airplanes, there is the infinitely greater and more effective shrinkage which comes about through the surveying capacity of the human mind, whose use of numbers, symbols, and models can condense and scale earthly physical distance down to the size of the human body's natural sense and understanding. Before we knew how to circumscribe the sphere of human habitation in days and hours, we had brought the globe into our living rooms to be touched by our hands and swirled before our eyes.
>
> — HANNAH ARENDT, *THE HUMAN CONDITION*

The oldest extant terrestrial globe, dating to 1492, was made by Martin Behaim. Behaim, who lived in Nuremberg, called his globe *erdapfel*, or "earth apple." (An "earth apple" is no kind of apple but a potato, a small brown planet imbedded in the earth.) Even in its roundness, a terrestrial globe is not so much a model of Earth as a metaphor for the earth. A map is at yet another remove.

The world of a story is not merely the sum of all the words we put on a page, or on many pages. When we talk about entering

* Early roads evolved from footpaths, many of which followed the twisting courses of streams, creeks, and rivers. As our speed increased—by horse, iron horse, then Ford Mustang—the turns of those roads grew hazardous. Unnatural speed led to unnatural, and carefully calculated, routes.

HALLE DES BOUCHERIES
HOTEL DE VILLE
(F) THEATRE D'ORLEANS
DOUANE
(M) GOUVERNEMENT année 1761
PLAN
of the City and Suburbs of
NEW ORLEANS
City Surveyor.
FAUBOURG
PLACE
BATTURE
MISSISSIPI

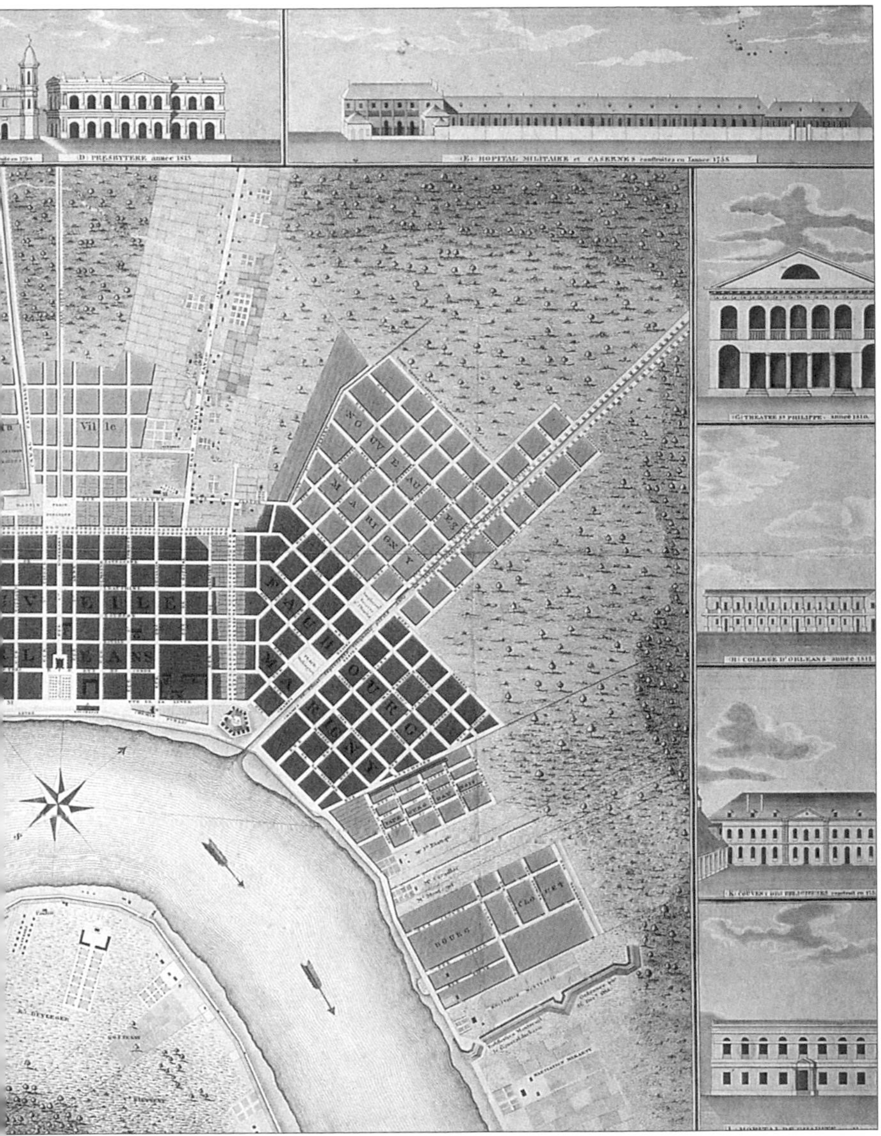

FIG. 40 **CHARLES DEL VECCHIO'S *PLAN OF THE CITY AND SUBURBS OF NEW ORLEANS*, FROM 1817, ILLUSTRATES THE JUXTAPOSITION OF MAN'S GEOMETRY WITH NATURE'S COURSE**

the world of a story as a reader we refer to things we picture, or imagine, and responses we form—to characters, events—all of which are prompted by, but not entirely encompassed by, the words on the page. As writers we know that to be true, because we don't write everything out; we trust the reader to understand why a young American man might be apprehensive to learn that his fiancée's work will take her to Libya, or what is implied when a narrator says his family's ideal vacation is a weekend at Dollywood. When we send a character to a suburban subdivision, we might rely on our reader to conjure a picture of the place. When a character is making a joke or when a line is intended to be sarcastic or ironic, we want our tone to be clear, but we resist explaining our intention in so many words, since to do so would be to defeat that intention. We expect, we require, the reader to understand more than we spell out.

So the world of a story is a thing we create or summon into being, but which the reader participates in creating and understanding. A story or novel is a kind of map because, like a map, it is not a world, but it evokes one (or at least one, for each reader).

III. MAPS ARE BASED ON GEOMETRY

Modern maps that mean to be scientifically accurate are the product of a complex geometry. The Earth is not perfectly round; we can refer to it as an oblate spheroid, but as anyone who has ever walked up a mountain or fallen off one can attest, it's an irregular oblate spheroid. As we have noted earlier, there is no way to plot points from the lumpy ball we call Earth on a sheet of flat paper with a uniform degree of accuracy; there is, unavoidably, some degree of distortion. The maps in our glove compartment, the ones we bought for their accuracy and usefulness, their clarity and simplicity, lie on an invisible but essential bed of mathematics.

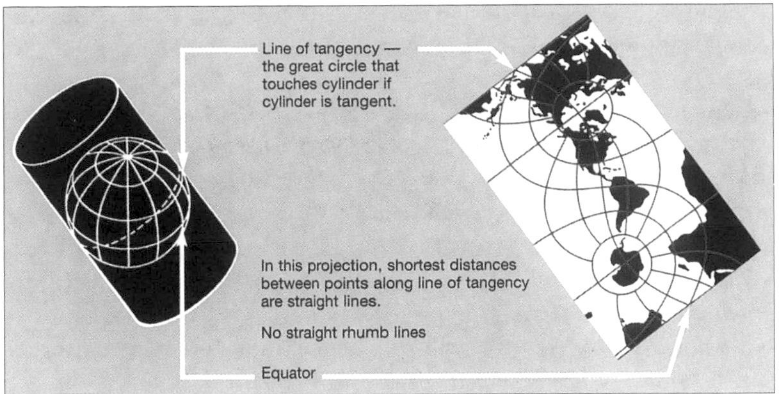

FIG. 41 THE SPACE OBLIQUE MERCATOR IS A CONFORMAL PROJECTION DEVELOPED FOR THE CONTINUOUS MAPPING OF SATELLITE IMAGES

IV. FORM IN FICTION

> The work proceeded, step by step, to its completion with the precision and rigid consequence of a mathematical problem.
>
> — EDGAR ALLAN POE

Form in Fiction: Part 1

IF A STORY IS a kind of map, and maps are created through the use of projections, or distortion formulas, (1) What are the analogous projections, or distortion formulas, for fiction?, and (2) On what sort of geometry are they based?

Contemporary fiction is essentially without defined forms. We have the story, the novella, and the novel. The short short, the long story, the novelette, and the novelleeny. But those terms describe only length. While the novella may once have been more fully defined, today it is a piece of fiction all but impossible to publish. Essentially, the forms of fiction are small, medium, and large.

A story can imitate other kinds of writing and so can take the "form" of a letter, a myth, a condemned man's journal, a scrapbook, an instruction manual for a photocopier, or a clothing retailer's fall catalog. But such imitative forms are very loosely defined. We don't talk about formal fiction versus "free" fiction. We may talk about the episodic novel, the bildungsroman, the picaresque, and so forth, but those terms don't describe the shape or size of a narrative in any detail. To call a story a dramatic monologue tells us only that it is written in one character's voice within a dramatic context.

Writers from Aristotle to Flaubert to Flannery O'Connor have argued that form is essential; yet fiction writers have no defined forms to choose from.

Woe is us.

Tie Me Up, Tie Me Down (Constraints)

SOME FICTION WRITERS invent forms. One example is the Oulipo, or the Workshop of Potential Literature (Ouvroir de Littérature Potentielle), begun in Europe in 1960. Members of the Oulipo are interested in investigating "scientific" ways of generating poems, stories, and novels, or "the systematic application of text-generating methods." In his "Second Manifesto," François Le Lionnais writes:

> The activity of the Oulipo and the mission it has entrusted to itself raise the problem of the efficacy and the viability of artificial (and, more generally, artistic) literary structures. The efficacy of a structure—that is, the extent to which it helps a writer—depends primarily on the degree of difficulty imposed by rules that are more or less constraining. Most writers and readers feel (or pretend to feel) that extremely constraining structures . . . are mere examples of acrobatics and deserve nothing more than a wry grin, since they could never help to engender truly valid works of art. . . . At the other extreme

> there's the refusal of all constraint, shriek-literature or eructative literature. . . . Between these two poles exists a whole range of more or less constraining structures which have been the object of numerous experiments since the invention of language. The Oulipo holds very strongly to the conviction that one might envision many, many more of these.

A few of the constraints the Oulipo has yielded include the Belle Absente, a form of acrostic encoding in which the letters of a given name are the only letters not used in the text; the

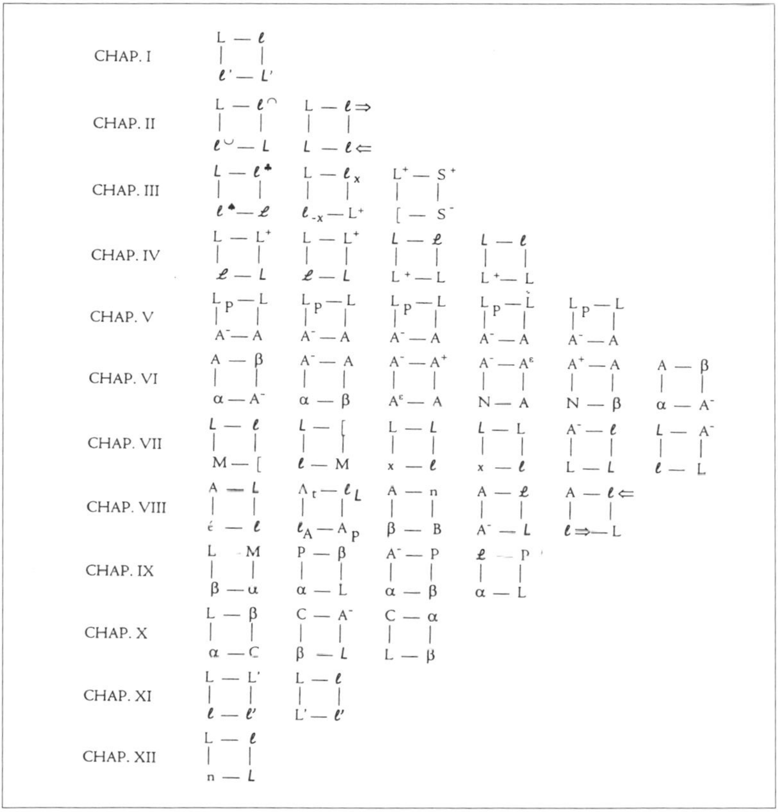

CHAP. I	L — ℓ / ℓ' — L'					
CHAP. II	L — ℓ⌒ / ℓ⌣ — L	L — ℓ⇒ / L — ℓ⇐				
CHAP. III	L — ℓ♣ / ℓ♣ — ℓ	L — ℓ_x / ℓ_{-x} — L^+	L^+ — S^+ / [— S^-			
CHAP. IV	L — L^+ / ℓ — L	L — L^+ / ℓ — L	L — ℓ / L^+ — L	L — ℓ / L^+ — L		
CHAP. V	L_P — L / A^- — A	L_P — L / A^- — A	L_P — L / A^- — A	L_P — L / A^- — A	L_P — L / A^- — A	
CHAP. VI	A — β / α — A^-	A^- — A / α — β	A^- — A^+ / A^ε — A	A^- — A^ε / N — A	A^+ — A / N — β	A — β / α — A^-
CHAP. VII	L — ℓ / M — [	L — [/ ℓ — M	L — L / x — ℓ	L — L / x — ℓ	A^- — ℓ / L — L	L — A^- / ℓ — L
CHAP. VIII	A — L / ε — ℓ	A_t — ℓ_L / ℓ_A — A_P	A — n / β — B	A — ℓ / A^- — L	A — ℓ⇐ / ℓ⇒ — L	
CHAP. IX	L — M / β — α	P — β / α — L	A^- — P / α — β	ℓ — P / α — L		
CHAP. X	L — β / α — C	C — A^- / β — L	C — α / L — β			
CHAP. XI	L — L' / ℓ — ℓ'	L — ℓ / L' — ℓ'				
CHAP. XII	L — ℓ / n — L					

FIG. 42 **ITALO CALVINO'S DIAGRAM OF THE STRUCTURE OF PART OF *IF ON A WINTER'S NIGHT A TRAVELER***

Cento, a text composed entirely of passages from other texts; Eye Rhymes, a poetic form in which the end rhymes are visual, not sonic (e.g., know, cow); the Heterogram, a text in which no letter is repeated; the Lipogram, a text in which a given letter(s) does not appear; and various replacement formulae. A poem might by created by taking a currently existing poem and replacing each word with, say, the eleventh word following the given word in a particular dictionary (cookbook, auto repair manual, etc.).

The most famous Lipogram is George Perec's novel *A Void*, which avoids the letter *e*. Another product of the workshop is Italo Calvino's *If on a winter's night a traveler*. Calvino's essay about composing that book includes a diagram of part of its structure.

The writers in the Oulipo believe constraints can inspire writers to be creative in new ways; they believe constraints can lead to a kind of freedom. They're joined by artists as diverse as Igor Stravinsky ("The more constraints one imposes, the more one frees oneself of the chains that shackle the spirit. . . . The arbitrariness of the constraint only serves to obtain precision of execution") and Paul Valéry ("My delight is in precision — I feel myself putting on chains to free myself — taking my own form"). Poets continue to use forms hundreds, even thousands of years old. In a discussion of Elizabeth Bishop's revisions of "One Art," Ellen Bryant Voigt suggests how they provide artistic opportunity:

> Neither Wordsworth nor Heaney nor Bishop's biographers can quite translate for the general reader the extent to which the working poet sees, in initial drafts, a formal challenge. The essential problems presented by this draft center on tone . . . and the high degree of repetition. . . . Bishop's response: the discipline of an existing traditional form that converts reiteration into refrain. . . . By the next draft Bishop is committed to the villanelle with a secure opening (and recurrent) line. . . . Now the work will have purpose and focus.

All of this may sound foreign to those who believe in the essential role of impulse, intuition, good fortune, "the muse," the subconscious, or whatever we call the source that we call on but cannot control. Embracing form requires an appreciation of the pure products of the mind—an eye for the beauty of, say, a mathematical proof.

V. ANYMORE, WE'RE NOT IN KANSAS—OR ARKANSAS

One of the tensions of our day—and of much of the last century—is that between realists, who see all the material they'll ever need in simulations and considerations of people's lives, and others — modernists, magical realists, metafictionists, hypertextualists—who feel realism has done what it can do. They feel realists are writing, and rewriting, nineteenth-century fiction. The realists counter that postrealistic* work is cold, overdetermined, lifeless. Art, they argue, is reduced to idea. Design is everything. This debate is useful to the extent that it helps us to recognize like-minded fellow artists and, just as important, to understand and consider what others are doing, so that we might further define and develop our own practice.

According to Milan Kundera,

> Two centuries of psychological realism have created some nearly inviolable standards: (1) A writer must give the maximum amount of information about a character: about his physical appearance, his way of speaking and behaving; (2) he must let the reader know a character's past, because that is where all the motives for his present behavior are located; and (3) the character must have complete independence; that is to say, the author with his own considerations must disappear so as not to disturb the reader, who wants to give himself over to

* A graceless but useful label. "Postmodern" has been defined too many ways, by too many people, to be simply adopted. "Postrealist" is both more inclusive and more direct: having discovered and explored realism, artists have gone on to try any number of other methods, no one of which has clearly replaced realism—which trundles on like the crocodile, unaware that dinosaurs are extinct.

> illusion and take fiction for reality. . . . [But] a character is not a simulation of a living being. It is an imaginary being. An experimental self. Understand me, I don't mean to scorn the reader and his desire, as naïve as it is legitimate, to be carried away by the novel's imaginary world and to confuse it occasionally with reality. But I don't see that the technique of psychological realism is indispensable for that.

When we read a realistic novel, we "make believe" the characters and places described exist. (It isn't just that we *can* imagine a world created through words; the power of tales, tall and short, is that we *want* to enter their world.) We are engaging in an act similar to the one that allows us to look at, say, a Monet, and talk about a water lily when in fact we are looking at an oil-stained canvas. While Kundera sees this as naïve, and others may call it a romantic act of denial or self-deception, this ability and inclination is essential to imaginative understanding. We imagine ourselves in Kundera's fiction, albeit in a different way. We don't "merely" read the work; we enter into dialogue with it. To the extent that we engage in discussion with black marks on pieces of paper, we allow ourselves to confuse those pages with something like reality.

Postrealistic work simply asks us to imagine other ways of imagining. Some of it draws the reader's attention to the artificial nature of its construction. Jorge Luis Borges's stories, like Nabokov's and Calvino's novels, are intricately mapped, as carefully explored, played, and designed as their metaphoric labyrinths, chess games, and invisible cities. At the same time, explicitly or implicitly, postrealism takes as its subject our ability to imagine ourselves in a world created entirely by the placement of ink on a page. John Barth's "Lost in the Funhouse" provides a simple, metaphorically potent narrative—a boy's trip to a boardwalk amusement park—as the spine to which are attached countless asides discussing the techniques and conventions of fiction, and so engages us in both the world of "the story" and that of a playful essay—or, even better, in some new world, one that includes them both as well as the space in between. "Let's pretend to believe in *that*," the work says to us, "but let's remember we're pretending." Kundera puts it this way:

> A novel examines not reality but existence. And existence is not what has occurred, existence is the realm of human possibilities, everything that man can become, everything he's capable of. Novelists draw up *the map of existence* by discovering this or that human possibility. . . . The Kafkan world does not resemble any known reality, it is an *extreme and unrealized possibility* of the human world.

In *Arctic Dreams*, Barry Lopez reprints a map of the Alaskan coastline drawn by a Native American fisherman. The product of years of mental mapmaking, the map shows the coast as seen from above—that is, it offers a view the fisherman had never seen—yet the map is extraordinarily accurate. The fisherman's knowledge came from walking the shoreline. "The map presents us with the reality we know," Denis Wood explains, "as differentiated from the reality we see and hear and feel." Similarly, as writers, we are able to—we need to—project ourselves, so we can recreate what we may have never actually seen, or experienced, but can imagine. Kafka presents readers with a reality he knew, and readers recognize it. Something similar happened when Calvino read Borges:

> The major reason for my affinity with him . . . is . . . my recognizing in Borges of an *idea of literature as a world constructed and governed by the intellect*. This is an idea that goes against the grain of the main run of world literature in this century, which leans instead in the opposite direction, aiming in other words to provide us with the equivalent of the chaotic flow of existence, in language, in the texture of the events narrated, in the exploration of the subconscious. But there is also a tendency in twentieth-century literature, a minority

> tendency admittedly . . . which champions *the victory of mental order over the chaos of the world*. . . . The discovery of Borges was for me like seeing a potentiality that had always been toyed with now being realized: seeing *a world being formed in the image and shape of the spaces of the intellect, and inhabited by a constellation of signs that obey a rigorous geometry*.

Calvino also read Galileo and wrote about the astronomer's notion of a mathematical alphabet, the Renaissance key to unlocking the universe.* The goal of postrealistic work is not to reduce the universe, any more than Galileo wanted to reduce it; rather, like that astronomer, it aims to find a way to understand it.

Nabokov's *Pale Fire* is in the form of a madman's annotation of another man's unfinished thousand-line poem. Kundera writes his novels in seven sections. Robert Coover's "The Babysitter" asks us to consider several contradictory versions of one theoretical night's events, just as some hypertexts allow us to "choose" what happens, like certain children's books, in a sort of binary progression: if the girl says no, click here; if she says yes, click there. Such work reminds us that any story is a single option among a realm of possibilities. The presentation of that notion within a narrative is at least as old as the *Thousand and One Nights*, in which Scheherazade is said to know everything—even more stories than she tells. (Some scholars interpret the "1,001" of the title as "forever and a day.") Where realism confronts us with an equivalent of what Calvino calls "the chaotic flow of existence," postrealists remind us of the infinite universe of narrative and potential narrative and question the choices we, as writers, make from it. If nineteenth-century realism—say, *Great Expectations*—represents the Theater of the World, and twentieth-century psychological realism shifts toward the Theater of the

* Galileo himself was surprisingly unsympathetic to certain experimentation in the arts. "Those who impart such strict laws on themselves," he wrote, "remind me of those whimsical painters who as a game set themselves constraints such as that of trying to depict a human face or some other figure by simply juxtaposing agricultural implements or fruits or flowers of different seasons. All of this bizarre art is fine and gives pleasure as long as it is done for amusement."

Mind, postrealistic work moves still further in that direction, emphasizing the exploration of the mind's constructs.

Borges invented elaborate games for his stories, sometimes writing them as if they were scholarly articles about old or lost books. This is "potential literature." Borges had no interest in creating those texts—that is, in creating books that would serve as mere illustrations of ideas. Instead he wrote stories that referred to those texts as if they already existed, thus avoiding tedium and still allowing himself to play with the ideas they suggested. In "The Library of Babel," Borges takes the library at Alexandria and the Library of Congress a step further. He tells a tale of a repository containing not only every known book, or every written book, but every conceivable book (and so every conceivable imitation, variation, facsimile, misprinting, etc.). At the end he notes that "Strictly speaking, *one single volume* should suffice: a single volume . . . of infinitely thin pages." He returns to that notion in "The Garden of Forking Paths." The title refers not only to the story, and to a garden labyrinth, but to a metaphorical labyrinth, an infinite novel. A character explains:

> In all fiction, when a man is faced with alternatives he chooses one at the expense of others. In the almost unfathomable [book by] Ts'ui Pên, he chooses—simultaneously—all of them. He thus *creates* various futures, various times which start others that will in their turn branch out and bifurcate in other times.

While "the web of time . . . embraces *every* possibility," the Library of Babel is "useless" and drives men to madness; the novel called *The Garden of Forking Paths* is "tortuous . . . interminable." Not only can we not have every book or one book of infinite possibilities, but, Borges says, we don't want it. Simply to imagine such a volume is quite enough. Postrealism often focuses on our unquenchable desire to enter the worlds we can imagine.

In the board game Risk, players are challenged to conquer the world, region by region, continent by continent. But the game's

FIG. 43 A MAP OF THE PLANET DISTORTED IN THE INTEREST OF GOOD-NATURED WORLD DOMINATION

world is curious: the United States is divided in two, East and West, while France, Spain, and Portugal are replaced by "Western Europe." Thanks to Risk, countless Americans who can't locate Kentucky know where Irkutsk is. (Or was; despite real-world changes, only recently has the Risk game board been updated. One new version is played on a map of the world as it might be, in the future.) Even larger numbers of people play Monopoly, on its highly stylized depiction of Atlantic City, with an immediate understanding that they are buying and selling real estate by entire streets and avenues, "improving" the properties by building houses and hotels, moving around the board and so through high- and low-rent districts. The streets of the real Atlantic City have been organized into color-coded rectangles, increasing in value, interrupted by train lines and public services. That map, or graphic presentation, has proven to be remarkably accurate and useful — not for someone planning a vacation, but for the purposes of the game.

FIG. 44 A MAP OF ATLANTIC CITY DISTORTED IN THE INTEREST OF HIGH ROLLERS

Chess presents its players with a greater level of abstraction: the battle between two kingdoms staged on a square board, with restrictions set on each piece meant to reflect the relative worth of castles and knights, bishops and foot soldiers. The chessboard map does away with names and other distinguishing features of place, emphasizing relative location. Only the most fundamental narrative context remains: two equal kingdoms are at war, and they will fight by rigid rules until one prevails. At a still higher level of abstraction we have checkers, another game of two competing sides, but with identical pieces of equal value and very few rules. Only the ascension to kingship reminds players of the conquest being reenacted by round tokens moved diagonally over a geometrically uniform surface.

Some people feel fiction based on constraints, fiction that doesn't pretend to be "real," seems false, lifeless. And some of it does. (Far from celebrating the results of every experiment, members of the Oulipo themselves are quick to acknowledge that many of the poems created by replacement strategies are tedious.) But

FIG. 45 A MAP OF TERRITORY TO BE CONTESTED BY TWO KINGDOMS

we all use constraints, and we all not only tolerate but work at a very high level of abstraction. We even play at a high level of abstraction. If we've abandoned board games for television, the evidence is just as strong: the constraints on the script of a network situation comedy are as knotty as a sestina's. The most popular fiction of our day, on screens large and small and in genre novels, is by far the most rigid.

"You don't lose when you restrict, no, you gain. That's true of all Art. . . . (What had killed off a theater the glory of which was Shakespeare, had been, Eliot postulated, its limitless appetite for Realism.)" So says Hugh Kenner in his contribution to the Portraits of American Genius series, *A Flurry of Drawings*, which takes as its subject animator extraordinaire Chuck Jones. Fiction writers with no taste or inclination for the formal constraints of Oulipo could do worse than spend an afternoon watching Chuck Jones's work. It isn't enough to watch one Road Runner cartoon

FIG. 46 **CHUCK JONES'S ARCHETYPAL CHARACTERS, IN CONFLICT EVEN AT REST**

or three; you need to immerse yourself in them (there are over forty) to see all the conventions, all the restrictions, to understand the few options of the Road Runner world—and then to see how, again and again, the cartoons surprise.

"The Road Runner saga," writes Kenner, "all four-plus hours of it, relies on just one theme, seemingly inexhaustible. That is Wile E. Coyote's persistence in pursuit of what was once a potential snack and has long since mutated into an ideal conquest. The viewer of a new installment has seen it all before and yet seen none of it before." This is both meaningfully and literally true: Jones made it a point of pride never to reuse footage, even footage of virtually identical chases or the coyote's fall. The point, he said, was to allow the animator to have some fun in making each one a little bit different. But his use of "fun" is misleading; those differences are serious work put to deliberate effect. Jones points out that a character runs differently when he's being chased than he does when he's chasing. Animation needs to be able to express character without words, and since animation is movement, character is expressed through the way a character moves. Jones's notebooks contain countless sketches of hips and leg bones, feet and shoulders, comparisons of how, say, real coyotes lope, heads hung down, with the way Wile E. Coyote slouches. All mammals share similarities of construction, so the keys to distinctive movement are the subtle differences. (If an animator of cartoons pays this much attention to physiology, it stands to reason that writers of realistic fiction should be students of syntax and, for instance, the many different ways in which a populated room can be silent.)

In the days when cartoons were a standard part of the package film studios sent to theaters, each was required to be six minutes long. That works out to 540 feet of film or, at 12 drawings per second (each used twice) for 360 seconds, 4,320 frames. Movement, pacing, and rhythm are discussed in terms of frames. Wile E. Coyote's inevitable fall off a cliff requires eighteen frames for him to fall into the distance and disappear, then fourteen frames later to hit. "It seemed to me that thirteen frames didn't work in terms of humor," Jones said, "and neither did fifteen frames. Fourteen frames got a laugh." The punch line, or tonal effect, is calculated to within one-twelfth of a second.

In his biography, Jones identifies some of the constraints he gave himself for that one series (he made many others):

Rule 1. The road runner cannot harm the coyote except by going "beep-beep!"
Rule 2. No outside force can harm the coyote—only his own ineptitude or the failure of the Acme products.
Rule 3. The coyote could stop anytime—if he were not a fanatic. (Repeat: "A fanatic is one who redoubles his effort when he has forgotten his aim."—George Santayana)
Rule 4. No dialogue ever, except "beep-beep!"
Rule 5. The road runner must stay on the road—otherwise, logically, he would not be called road runner.
Rule 6. All action must be confined to the natural environment of the two characters—the Southwest American desert.
Rule 7. All materials, tools, weapons, or mechanical conveniences must be obtained from the Acme Corporation.
Rule 8. Whenever possible, make gravity the coyote's greatest enemy.
Rule 9. The coyote is always more humiliated than harmed by his failures.

Some viewers might be tempted to think of the results as a visual equivalent of pulp romance novels, working the same material in essentially the same ways, with barely discernible and inconsequential variation. But those cartoons' constraints were dictated not by sales departments, marketing surveys, or audience polls; they were self-imposed by the artist. For all their looniness, Road Runner cartoons are not so far removed from the experimental formalism of the Oulipo. Chuck Jones, however, was still telling stories. Some postrealistic fiction abandons both character and narrative, concentrating instead on ideas, form, or language alone. Writers of such work might be more geometers than mapmakers, interested primarily in calculating new projections.

VI. THE DISTORTION FORMULA WE CALL "REALISM"

Some writers (and readers) delight in stories and novels that bring formal properties to the foreground, while others—perhaps the sort of people who go blank at the thought of congruent triangles and the challenge of transcribing spheres onto cylinders—prefer something more "natural," something less "intellectual": the mode we call realism. But realism is perfectly unnatural, and as writers we need to understand how it is created. We may want the world of our stories to be rich and complex, even (apparently) unpredictable, filled with surprise. But surprise depends on expectation. If

FIG. 47 ALBRECHT DÜRER'S *MAN DRAWING A LUTE.* "AT LENGTH THERE HAS BEEN DISCOVERED A METHOD OF GETTING IT PERFECTLY TRUE" (LEON BAPTISTA ALBERTI, *ON PICTURE MAKING*)

we have no expectations, there are no surprises; that's why it's hard to tell jokes to dogs. While we may want to evoke unpredictability and complexity, we ultimately want our work to be shapely. And the study of shapes is the study of geometry.

Given that our capacity for abstraction is great, greater than we may realize, it isn't necessary for a map user to know the first thing about projection formulas. A map *maker*, however, is obliged to understand exactly what he is doing.

In *The Art of the Novel*, Kundera decries the historical movement toward verisimilitude, away from astonishment and enchantment. Mark Twain's call for accuracy in detail and in observation of the natural world can lead to submission to the oppression of actuality, a limited subset of the realm of human possibility. But that doesn't mean we should reject realism; only that, if we are to practice it, we need to keep in mind the distinction between realism and reality. To confuse the two is to lose sight of the difference between art and life.

Perspective Is a Distortion Formula

THE GEOMETRY OF realism dates back roughly six hundred years, to the discovery of perspective—a distortion formula designed to fool the eye. Until that time, figures were painted against flat or solid backgrounds, and larger scenes were depicted without attempt to convey a viewer's perspective of three dimensions. The desire to replicate the—or a—viewer's view is realism's reason for being.

But we do not see things the way they are. The simplest demonstration is the now-elementary art-class exercise of representing a road receding into the distance. The "correct" drawing will show two lines converging toward a vanishing point. Everything in the picture is drawn with angled lines, so that the "back" of the building is actually shorter than the "front," and the two sides of the road meet at a point in the "distance." But there isn't any distance, or back or front; everything in the picture is on the same thin plane, a piece of canvas or paper. It's the Orange Peel problem all over again. The two sides of a street don't actually touch or vanish, and both sides of a building are the same height. An "accurate" realistic drawing requires distortion.

Thanks to the artists of the Italian Renaissance, especially Filippo Brunelleschi, Leon Baptista Alberti, and Leonardo da Vinci, perspective was developed as a tool and a method. To understand the goal was not enough; artists had to train themselves in this new way of seeing so they could portray on canvas not what they knew to be true, but what they perceived. Brunelleschi, a goldsmith turned architect, is credited with being the first to portray three-dimensional objects (the buildings of Florence) on two-dimensional surfaces through the use of mathematical calculations. In 1472 Piero della Francesca wrote, "First is sight, that is to say the eye; second is the form of the thing seen; third is the distance from the eye to the thing seen; fourth are the lines which leave the boundaries of the object and come to the eye; fifth is the intersection, which comes between the eye and the thing seen, and on which it is intended to record the object." Mathematical perspective — a calculated illusion — grew to dominate the visual arts, to the point that other methods of representation seemed, and still seem, "unnatural."

Alberti's Veil, which he compared to a mullioned window, aids an artist in transferring three dimensions to two. By lightly drawing a grid on his paper or canvas, the artist could transfer what he saw through the veil, square by square, preserving the relationship of the lines of the subject ("the thing seen") to the horizontal and vertical lines of the grid. Alberti's veil served—and continues to serve—as a training device.

A realistic painting is a kind of map drawn on an imaginary window. It is based on a geometric projection that fools one of our senses and so helps us to enter the world of the painting.

Is There "Perspective" in Fiction? If So, What Are Its Rules?

WHAT IS THE equivalent of perspective in writing? What are the tools by which we create realistic fiction, as opposed to some

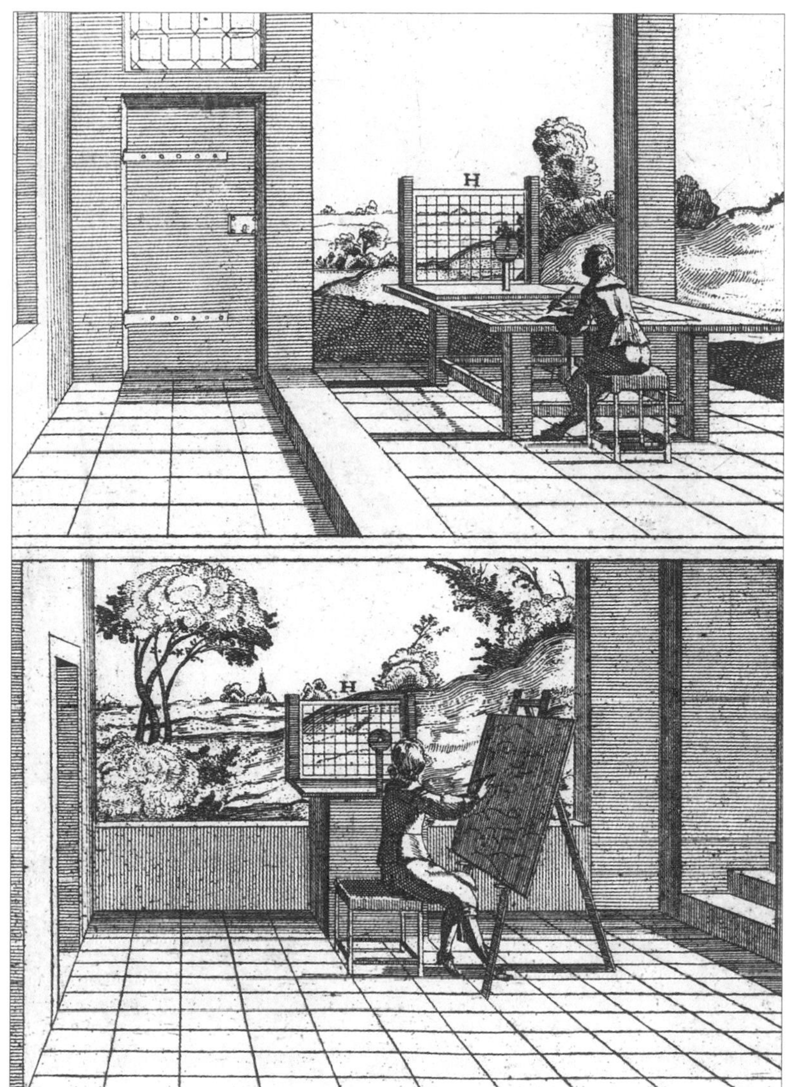

FIG. 48 **ALBERTI'S VEIL EMPLOYED**

other kind of fiction? If we hold up Alberti's Veil and, instead of drawing, write sentences, how do we transcribe what we see—and hear, touch, smell, and think—to the page? Clearly, this is far more complicated than wrapping a sheet of paper around a globe, or recreating the illusion of our vision alone.

In "The Decay of Lying," Oscar Wilde writes: "What art really reveals to us is nature's lack of design, her curious crudities, her extraordinary monotony, her absolutely unfinished condition. . . . If nature had been comfortable, man never would have invented architecture, and I prefer houses to the open air. In a house we feel all the proper proportions."

Just as the construction of a house requires relatively regular lines and curves, realistic writing relies on a kind of geometrical neatening. Whereas a realistic painting creates an illusion for one of our senses, realistic writing evokes the world in all its dimensions—physical space, time, sound, smell, et cetera—through the abstract code of those inky squiggles. Far from being "natural" or "straightforward," realistic works may be among the most deceptive, as they go to great lengths, heights, and widths to conceal their geometric underpinning.

One example: dialogue in fiction is not true to life. While our presentation of speech may not be as mathematically determined as the figures in da Vinci's *The Last Supper* (in which the vanishing point is the head of Christ), it is, nevertheless, rule-bound. We strive to represent the voice, vocabulary, sentence structure, and speech rhythms of our characters and thus be "accurate" in our depiction, even as we edit out verbal static— those *um*s and *er*s, as well as mispronunciations and false starts—that, in life, as listeners, we edit out in order to focus on meaning. We also attend to matters of presentation that have no direct relationship to real-life conversation: beginning a new paragraph for each speaker, using quotation marks, and identifying speakers either through sentences describing them or their actions or through dialogue tags. Those tags (he said, she asked, he exclaimed) are meant to guide the reader without being obtrusive (*not* he exhorted, she maintained, he amplified). Of course, we are free to depart from these conventions, but to do so is to draw the reader's attention to our "unnatural" presentation.

Beyond that, dialogue in fiction is purposeful in a way actual speech most often is not. Among other things, it reveals character, it expresses conflict, and it conveys necessary information. Even work that depends on "conversation" to the extreme, such as *Waiting for Godot* or Nicholson Baker's *Vox*, presents dialogue that is unusually intriguing, and encapsulates, in one way or another, dramatic structure. In writing dialogue, we create an equivalent of the Way Finder.

We are obliged to describe the physical appearance of our characters, even though physical appearance often plays a minor role in narratives. In such cases, our descriptions are an acknowledgment of our unspoken agreement with the reader that we are not simply telling a tale but evoking an imaginary world. (In the seventeenth and eighteenth centuries, mapmakers were sometimes called "world describers." In geometry, to *describe* a shape is to draw or trace its outline.) When the description of a character is important, we return to it from time to time, to keep the image in our reader's mind. There is no simple formula for the frequency of mentions of, for instance, an otherwise beautiful woman's lazy eye; but as we write we experiment with frequency and placement until the effect is satisfyingly clear without being distractingly "artificial."

Much of what we learn as fundamental to "good" fiction writing — from descriptions of character, avoiding stereotype, conveying mood through detail in setting, and not calling attention to attributives — is fundamental to the distortion formula of realism. Can we write that formula out, in so many words? People do it all the time. Every writing handbook — no matter whether it addresses fiction, poetry, screenwriting, essays, or job application cover letters — sets out to explain the "rules" of a distortion formula. Mark Twain's essay on Fenimore Cooper's literary offences is, ultimately, less about Cooper or even about romanticism than it is the assertion of a new aesthetic. Twain was, in his own slant way, defining the rules for his own work, and encouraging others to join him.

Freytag's . . . What's That Shape Again?

FOR "INSTANCES WHERE evidence makes a difference," says Edward Tufte, "the design logic of the display must reflect the intellectual logic of the analysis. . . . Clear and precise seeing becomes as one with clear and precise thinking." In a piece of writing, the "evidence" is all we have. While fiction writers may not talk about the "design logic of the display," we do engage in discussions of "narrative arc," "narrative distance," and "shape": the "design reasoning" of a story or novel.

Perhaps the most common invocations of geometry in discussions of narrative concern plot. A *plot* is a piece of ground, a plan (as in the plan of a building), or a scheme; *to plot* is to make a plan or, in geometry, to graph points on a grid. When we create a story, even a character- rather than event-based story, we make a plot or map out the narrative's essential moments. Gustav Freytag depicted Aristotle's description of plot as an isosceles triangle, with "rising" action on the inclining left, "falling" action on the declining right.

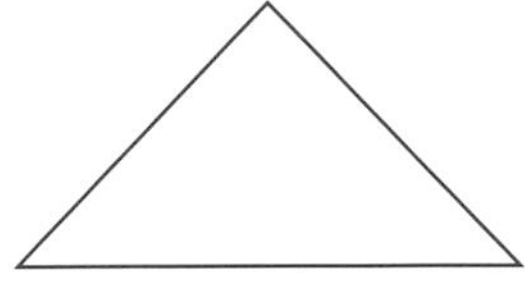

FIG. 49 **FREYTAG'S TRIANGLE**

One useful way to think about geometry in fiction is to build on that simple triangle. Freytag's figure is commonly revised to indicate that there is often some change of direction within the rising action, and that the portion of a narrative from dramatic climax to conclusion is, typically, much shorter than what precedes it. The result is no longer a simple triangle, but an irregular quadrilateral.

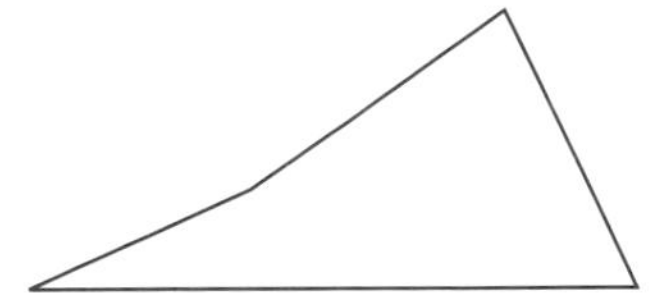

FIG. 50 "FREYTAG'S" QUADRILATERAL

While some narratives might involve a single rising action, most employ a series of dramatic movements. A graph of the rising and falling of dramatic tension, or plot complication, in any but the very simplest story would result in an even more irregular figure — it would approximate a drawing of peaks in a mountain range.

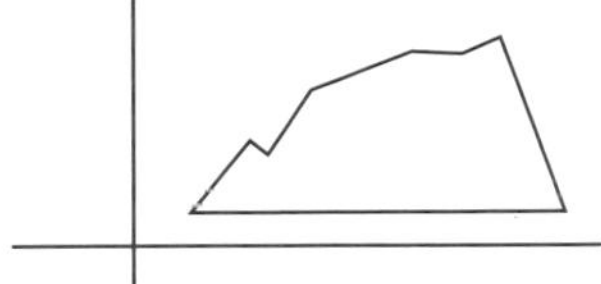

FIG. 51 FREYTAG'S TRIANGLE APPLIED, HYPOTHETICALLY

Even that more irregular figure falls far short of accurately depicting the movement of plot in a story, and a moment's consideration reveals why. The axes on which the figure is graphed are unspecified. The horizontal (X) axis might be time, or the story's progression from first word to last, or the infinite plane from which all narratives arise. The vertical (Y) axis indicates something even more vague: "action," "conflict," or "tension." If what we want to chart is the "rising action" for each of a story's main characters, we might use action as our Y-axis (we'll ignore, here, the question of how one measures that quality) and the pages of the story as our X-axis to plot a series of overlapping lines, each representing the increasing and decreasing dramatic tension for one character. Since these are not likely to rise and fall at the same moments, to chart the story more accurately, we need either overlapping figures or a three-dimensional field.

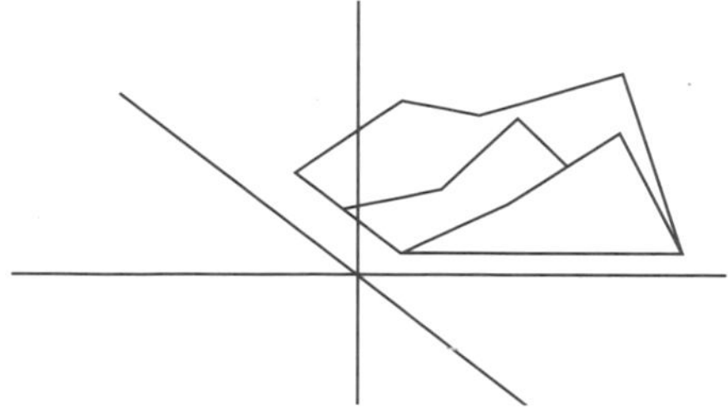

FIG. 52 FREYTAG'S TRIANGLE APPLIED, HYPOTHETICALLY, IN THREE DIMENSIONS

We might imagine a graph in which the X-axis again represents the duration of the story but the Y-axis represents levels of explicitness. Above the X-axis we could chart what the reader "sees" or is told and, below it, what is implied. In other words, above the X-axis, we could plot the story's statements and events, while below we could chart the development of subtext. For other purposes, we could use the horizontal axis to represent a story's "present" and chart current action above, past events and memories below.

Freytag's triangle suggests countless useful ways of mapping. Beneath the surface appearance of "reality" in a story are carefully considered patterns and rhythms of significant details, metaphors, motifs, and even themes. A chart of Alain Robbe-Grillet's "The Secret Room" might indicate when and how often he mentions and returns to key images, such as the corpse, the columns, and the man in the cape; a bar graph of Kate Chopin's "The Storm" might depict the lengths of the sections, to illustrate the story's proportions and tempo. Whereas most of us would resist providing our readers anything resembling a map's fortuitously named legend, we do, deliberately, lead our readers toward something as bold as Meaning or as modest as a momentary glimmer of sympathetic understanding, something that burns as brightly or beckons as elusively — our choice — as the green light at the end of Daisy Buchanan's dock.

Few if any of us are likely to begin composing fiction by creating a series of elaborate charts and graphs. But many writers rely on something very much like charts and graphs as part of their process of composition, and others do a sort of prose mapping.

This is easiest to observe in cases where form is predefined. A traditional sonneteer may not carry in her head a visualization of the Shakespearean sonnet, but she must necessarily have an ear toward the rhyme scheme and meter of the form, line length and the number of lines, and, superimposed above them, the poem's argument. The poet has chosen the sonnet as her projection. For the *Divine Comedy*, Dante chose to project the world of the poem via a form of his own design: three sections of thirty-three cantos each, plus one introductory canto to make an even hundred. He wrote the poem in tercets (three-line stanzas), in terza rima *(aba / bcb / cdc)*, using a hendecasyllabic line (eleven syllables, with the accent on the tenth).

Novelists may find themselves forced to come up with some sort of chart or map sooner than short story writers, if only because it is harder to riffle through the entire manuscript of a novel, to keep track of a long narrative's movements through time and place. Of course, when a novelist says she stopped to "map out" her narrative, she usually means she wrote a summary version or an outline. We might, at least occasionally, find it useful to be more analytical than that. Since those of us writing "free narrative" are likely to resist what we feel are arbitrary constraints (every chapter must begin with a surprise, every chapter must consist of thirty-five paragraphs, no character can be seen outdoors), we could do our mapping after the fact, looking at one of our drafts, and charting, oh, the duration of our scenes. What does it tell us if they are invariably two pages long? What does it tell us if our first-person narrator has less dialogue than any other character? What does it tell us if no more than ten pages elapse without narrative intervention, flashback, or passages of introspection? What does it tell us if all our sentences are perfectly balanced, or if all our lists contain three items? Among other things, it might tell us that we were writing under constraints we didn't recognize. Maybe we have failed to fully explore a scene; maybe our first-person narrator is observing rather than acting; maybe we've fallen into an unconscious rhythmic pattern. The purpose of such mapping isn't necessarily to recognize and then sustain those patterns or to recognize and then depart from them. Rather, the goal is to recognize unconscious constraints so that we can make conscious choices.

In Poe's famous discussion of the composition of "The Raven," he asserts:

> Nothing is more clear than that every plot, worth the name, must be elaborated to its dénouement before anything be attempted with the pen.* It is only with the dénouement constantly in view that we can give a plot its indispensable air of consequence, or causation, by making the incidents, and especially the tone at all points, tend to the development of the intention. . . . I prefer commencing with the consideration of an effect. . . . I say to myself . . . "Of the innumerable effects, or impressions, of which the heart, the intellect, or (more generally) the soul is susceptible, what one shall I, on the present occasion, select?"

After having settled on the matter of length, he tells us that for "The Raven" he aimed for beauty ("the sole legitimate province of the poem") and sadness ("Melancholy is . . . the most legitimate of all the poetical tones"). Searching for "some pivot upon which the whole structure might turn," he chose a single word refrain,

* John Irving echoed the sentiment when he said writing a story without knowing the ending is like telling a joke without knowing the punch line. It isn't necessary to know the end before we put pen to paper, but it is necessary before we pen the final draft. Writing a story is more like writing a joke than telling one: once we know the punch line, we can fashion the telling for greatest effect.

one "sonorous and susceptible of protracted emphasis. . . . These considerations led me to the long *o* as the most sonorous vowel, in connection with *r* as the most producible consonant." Coupling those sounds with the tone of melancholy made it "absolutely impossible to overlook the word 'Nevermore.'" Poe continues in that fashion, explaining his choice of a talking bird (or "*non*-reasoning creature capable of speech") and so the raven, the death of a beautiful woman, and even his choice of rhythm and meter. The icing on the cake of analytical construction came, he claims, at the end of the poem, because "there is always a hardness or nakedness, which repels the artistic eye. Two things are invariably required — first, some amount of complexity, or more properly, adaptation; and, secondly, some amount of suggestiveness — some under current, however indefinite of meaning."

More than one reader has proposed that Poe's explanation of the creation of his most famous poem is suspiciously neat, a better example of creative logic after the fact than a true report of his process. Yet even if the explanation overstates the role of the analytical in invention, the discussion of meter and rhythm, tone and proportion, offers insight both into how one particular poem works and how others might work. The "Philosophy of Composition" is one example of a writer's prose map of his creation. Here's another:

> For my nymphet I needed a diminutive with a lyrical lilt to it. One of the most limpid and luminous letters is "l." The suffix "ita" has a lot of Latin tenderness, and this I required too. Hence: Lolita. However, it should not be pronounced as most Americans pronounce it: Low-lee-ta, with a heavy, clammy "L" and a long "o." No, the first syllable should be as in lollipop, the "L" liquid and delicate, the "lee" not too sharp. Spaniards and Italians pronounce it, of course, with exactly the necessary note of archness and caress. Another consideration was the welcome murmur of its source name, the fountain name:

> those roses and tears in "Dolores." My little girl's heartrending fate had to be taken into account together with the cuteness and limpidity. Dolores also provided her with another, plainer, more familiar and infantile diminutive: Dolly, which went nicely with the surname "Haze," where Irish mists blend with a German bunny—I mean, a small German hare.

This self-annotation, or mapping of a single word, reveals the possible effects of the sound and sense of something as fundamental as a character's name. Nabokov composed chess problems, and he composed his novels on index cards, a sentence at a time. The level of intention and analysis in his process was extraordinarily high. Some would say that explains the density, or the ornateness, of his prose; some would say that accounts for its beauty.

> In each of the narrative lines [of *The Possessed*], theme is considered from a different angle, like a thing reflected in three mirrors.

IN HIS "DIALOGUE on the Art of Composition," Milan Kundera talks at length about the proportions of his novels, compares them to musical forms, and repeats with interest the discoveries made by a Czech literary critic in an essay titled "The Geometry of *The Joke*." He calls it "a revelation," and adds that "that 'mathematical system' emerges completely naturally as a formal necessity, with no need for calculation. . . . The seven-part structure doesn't represent some superstitious flirtation with magical numbers, or any rational calculation, but a deep, unconscious, incomprehensible drive, an archetype of form I cannot escape. My novels are variants of an architecture based on the number seven."

No matter whether they came to an understanding of the relationship between presentation and intention at the outset (as Poe claims to have done), after the fact (as Kundera says he did), or, as we might presume happens most often, at some point(s) during the creation of the story, novel, or poem (as Voigt concludes Bishop must have, by studying the drafts of "One Art"), the relationship exists. Fitzgerald labored to make Gatsby the focal figure of his novel and yet elusive; in *Catch-22*, Joseph Heller offers the reader fragments of the scene leading to "Snowden's secret" at carefully determined intervals, waiting for the moment of greatest dramatic effect to show the reader what Yossarian saw. While the process of exploring, taking notes, and drafting may make us feel we're searching for a route through a labyrinth, in the final version of what we write we are creating the labyrinth: moving walls, creating dead ends and profitable turns. The act of drafting and revising is essentially an act of gaining authority over the work — and our understanding of the work is an important element of its authority.

Form in Fiction: Part 2

IF A SINGLE particular sonnet is a map, a map that evokes a world, the sonnet *form* is the geometric projection for that sonnet. It's the mesh screen to which the plaster of paris is applied. It's the checkerboard on which the game is played.

What, then, is happening in other poems poets call sonnets? In Gerald Stern's *American Sonnets*, the poems are in free verse. If the sonnet is defined by its meter, its length, its rhyme, and its argument, and a poet does away with meter, length, rhyme, and argument, what's left? In what, if any, meaningful way does the projection still apply?

A single point on the page does little to provoke the imagination:

•

FIG. 53

While the introduction of a companion and the tension of white space are not insignificant, two points are hardly more intriguing:

FIG. 54

With three points, however, the imagination gets to work:

FIG. 55

Most people looking at those three dots will "see" a triangle, even though no triangle is drawn. Our imagination, combined with our desire to make sense of what is put before us, creates the lines:

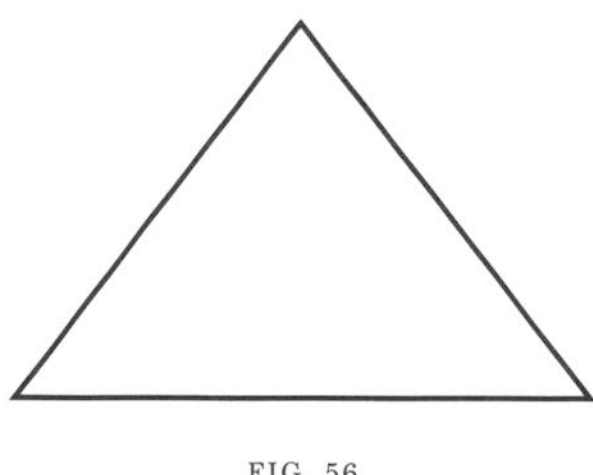

FIG. 56

Curiously, the figure itself, once drawn, becomes nearly as static, or unprovocative, as a single point. There is nothing for the imagination to do. By removing bits of the figure, we reintroduce tension:

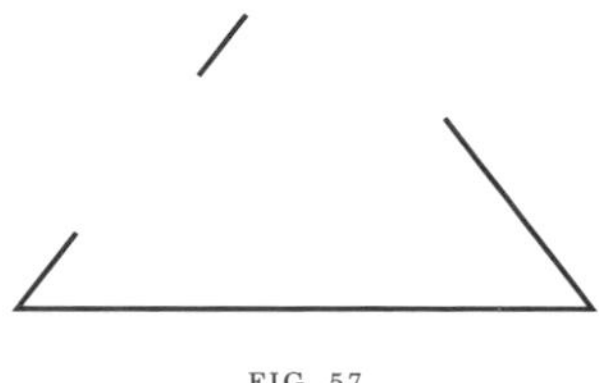

FIG. 57

In the figure above, most people will see a triangle partially erased. As we continue to erase, though, the geometrical shape will eventually become a vague assortment of points and line segments:

FIG. 58

In any particular instance, we might ask:

> What does it take to suggest the shape?
> When is the shape vague, or undetermined?
> When is it usefully ambiguous?
> When does it become explicit, or essentially explicit?

The first word of a short story, even the first sentence, doesn't usually imply a complete shape; but as the story goes on, no matter how "linear," fragmented, or collagelike it may be, the reader will work to find the story's shape or possible shape. This is how we make sense of what we read: we work to put the parts together. We expect to discover an intended whole.

As writers, we have many options. We can, if we're writing stories for young children or fill-in-the-blank genre fiction like those old Hardy Boys books, simply provide the reader with the expected shape. Alternately, we can remove certain transitions and information and allow the reader to participate more actively in discovering the shape of the narrative.

Take, for instance, that brief Kate Chopin story. In its first two sections, "The Storm" introduces an age-old scenario: her husband (and son) away, a woman has extramarital sex. In the familiar figure of the romantic, or sexual, triangle below, A = Alcée, B = Bobinôt, and C = Calixta.

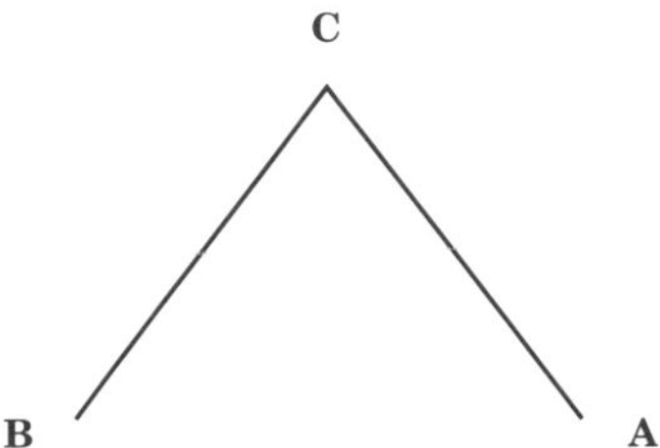

FIG. 59 **THE APPARENT "STORM" TRIANGLE**

Based on our experience with the scenario, we might anticipate tension along one or more of the three lines: between Bobinôt and Calixta (either because he learns of his wife's infidelity or because she resents the repression he represents); between Alcée and Calixta (as they continue their illicit relationship, or don't); or between Bobinôt and Alcée, rivals for Calixta's attention.

But the triangle is only implied; and instead of drawing the third line connecting the two men, Chopin takes the story in another direction. A descriptive figure of it might look like this:

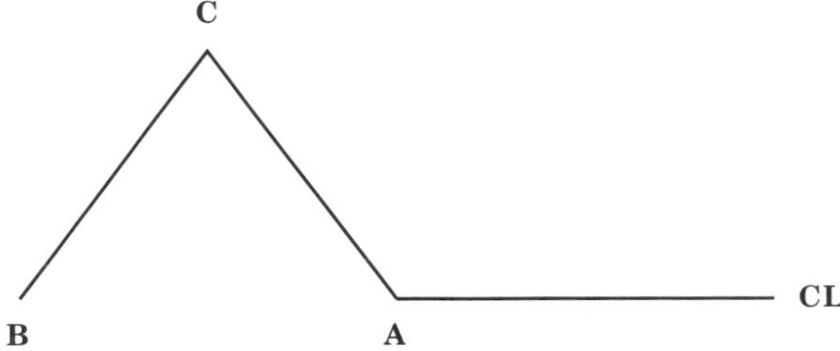

FIG. 60 **THE STORM TURNS**

Here, CL = Clarisse. What led us to see the triangle was our anticipation of a familiar shape; in this case, while the shape may be familiar from life, it is even more boldly and repetitively drawn in popular entertainment, from Hollywood films to soap operas to country and western songs. If we give greater attention to our life experience, we recognize that marriages, romantic relationships, and sexual affairs are complex and wildly varied (the odds are good that we know of some circumstance at least as uncommon as the one Chopin describes). Chopin's story doesn't rely on a trick or gimmick; it simply defies our expectation. In her short tale she goes to great lengths to prepare us for the story's turns: by employing an agile omniscient narrator, one who demonstrates at the outset the ability to move through space and among characters; by making, in each section, an assertion of peace ("Bibi . . . was not afraid," "[Calixta and Alcée] seemed to swoon together," "[Calixta, Bobinôt, and Bibi] laughed much and . . . loud," "[Alcée] was getting on nicely," and "[Clarisse] and the babies were doing well") leading to the concluding assertion ("every one was happy"); and by choosing a central metaphor that supports the closing statement (storms do, after all, blow over). If we miss all those signs the first time through, it's because we have been prepared, by our previous reading, to see something else.

An even more arresting departure from expected shape is demonstrated by Hemingway's "The Killers." When the two strangers enter the diner and say they're waiting to kill Ole Andreson, we anticipate Andreson's arrival. We know what this story looks like. It, too, can be drawn as a triangle, one with the killers (K) at the apex. They threaten George, Nick, and Sam the cook (GNS), and they pose a threat to Andreson (A). Whereas in the love triangle we have implicit tension between a woman's two lovers, here we have a protective bond between the men in the diner and Ole Andreson.

Based on versions of this scenario we've seen before, we might reasonably anticipate the killers to kill Andreson; the killers to

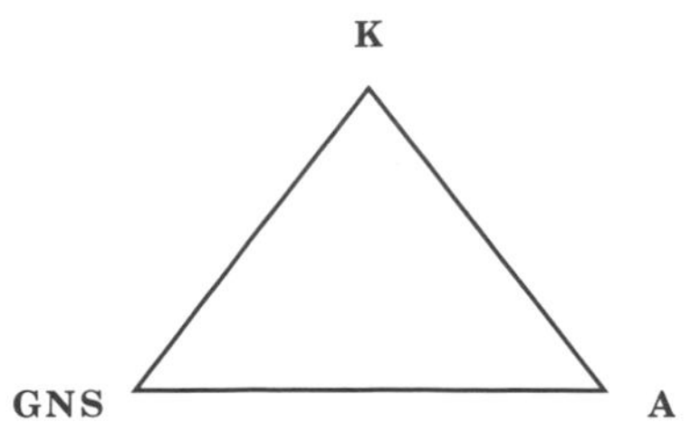

FIG. 61 THE APPARENT "KILLERS" TRIANGLE

fail to kill, or be persuaded not to kill, Andreson; the killers to be killed; or the killers to kill one or more of the men in the diner.

When Ole Andreson doesn't show up, the killers leave, and Nick Adams runs off to the boardinghouse where Ole Andreson is staying. We may adjust our expectations (to include, in addition to all of the above, Ole Andreson defending himself or getting out of town), but this, too, is a story we recognize.

Ole Andreson tells Nick he already knows about the men, and makes clear that he's going to wait for them and not fight them. He literally rolls over. If the story ended here it would be surprising, but neither complete nor satisfying.

Nick goes back to the diner and says the situation is "too damned awful" to think about. George tells him, "You better not think about it," and while that may, at first, seem to leave us with nothing but loose ends, on closer examination it is both satisfying and, like Chopin's story, provocative—which is to say, unsettling. "The Killers" asks us to put aside the scenario's more familiar options of flee or fight (options familiar thanks to films, television, etc.) and instead confront the dilemma faced when a character is aware of a great wrong about to be done but is, or believes himself to be, incapable of affecting the course of events.

But our concern is the story's shape. It's as if we were riding a bus, waiting to get off, but the bus kept passing what looked like stops, only to park in the center lane of a highway. We could see what we thought was going to be the story's shape so clearly, we're acutely aware of what the story has failed to do, what it

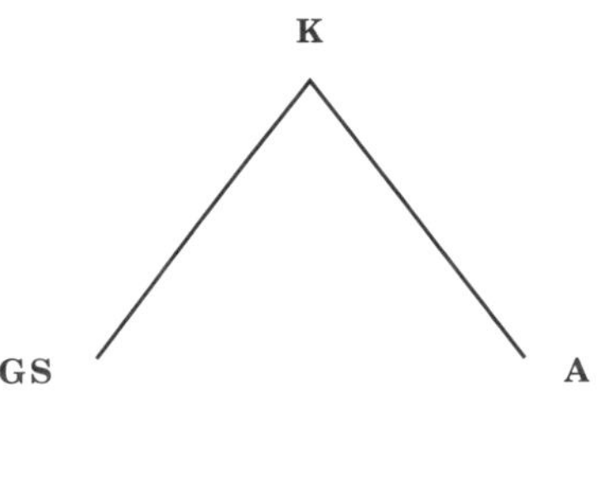

FIG. 62 NICK FINDS HIMSELF ALONE — NO LONGER A SMALL PART OF A FAMILIAR TRIANGLE, BUT AN ISOLATED OBSERVER BEARING UNSEEN PRESSURE

has failed to be. That sense of absence might lead to frustration, but it forces a better reader to ask, What's wrong here? Eventually we realize that the story has been trying to get us to ask that question all along. The diner clock is always wrong (for no disclosed reason, it's twenty minutes fast); the killers look and sound "like a vaudeville team"; Henry's lunch room, which was once a saloon, is run by a man named George; Mrs. Hirsch's boardinghouse is run by a woman named Mrs. Bell; Ole Andreson, the former boxer, is "a gentle man." And the story isn't the triangle we thought it was; yet we're pleased to be invited to recognize a new shape. Surprise jolts us into a state of heightened perception, and so opens us to the possibility of new understanding.*

* The combination of expectation and surprise is the essence of comedy; it can also be found in a poem's enjambments, and in the blues: "Bop doo wop / Baby I'd chop / off my right arm / for your love"; "I ain't never loved / but three women in my life. / My mother, my sister / and the woman who wrecked my life."

CALVINO'S SLENDER volume *Cosmicomics*, a model of potential literature, suggests the infinite universe of all stories. The title promises a sort of playful science fiction, and indeed the stories stretch the boundaries of place, time, and character. The unpronounceably named narrator, Qfwfq, tells us he was young back in the days of a soundless, timeless void when the only things in the universe were hydrogen atoms. "The Distance of the Moon" begins with an epigraph from the nineteenth-century English astronomer Sir George H. Darwin. On the basis of a mathematical theory of solar tides, Darwin suggested the Moon originally had been part of the Earth but was broken away by tidal action and receded from the planet. In the first lines of Calvino's story, "Old Qfwfq" promises his audience a yarn about the old days, when the moon was "on top of us all the time," each month drawing to within a few yards of the Earth's surface. He explains how he and others would journey out in a cork rowboat, hold up a ladder, and scramble onto the Moon.

Before long, a triangle is revealed: Qfwfq admits he was in love with the sea captain's wife, while she had eyes only for his cousin. Or is it a rectangle? Qfwfq's cousin, The Deaf One, is enamored of the Moon. But can we draw the triangle, or rectangle, when all the relationships are pointed in one direction? There are no interpersonal conflicts; this is only a string of unfulfilled desires. The story has more sides than three, and many more angles. It is a tale of unrequited loves; of a love triangle, or rectangle, or love shape = x; of ritual and tradition; of the end of an era, so a coming of age, or loss of innocence; and of a myth (the Moon's relationship to Earth, and the power the Moon has over lovers). In telling all these stories and drawing on science, the oral tradition, and folktales, Calvino's story is a hybrid, as if he had rooted around in the scrapyard of fiction, emerged with a wheelbarrow full of appealing parts, and welded them into something strangely wonderful, something that manages to satisfy our expectations and transcend them with its rumination on love and attraction. If we were forced to draw it, the story might look something like this:

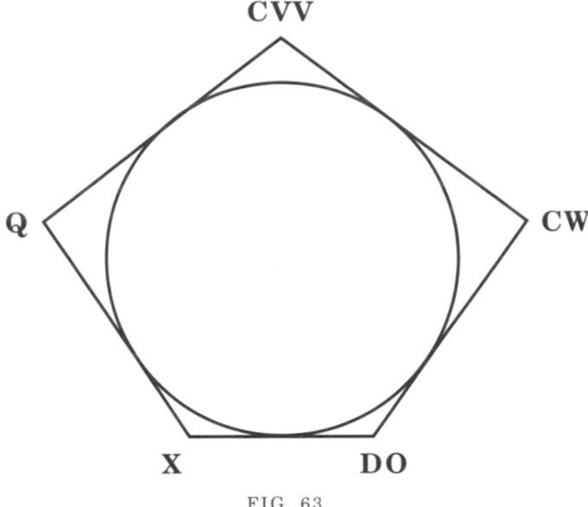

FIG. 63

Here, the central characters (Qfwfq, Captain Vhd Vhd, the Captain's wife, the Deaf One, and little Xlthlx) act out their human dramas against and around the Moon.

Most fiction offers us a shape that is, to some degree, familiar. Sometimes the familiarity is in the basic outline of the plot; in other cases the familiarity is in a character's movement toward insight. We read a story, we recognize its template, and we regard it as an effective or ineffective variation. If we are confronted with isolated points and line segments, if we can't find pattern, order, or coherence, we're frustrated. Perhaps, if just one or two of those line segments were extended, or if two arcs were added, we might, like a child connecting the dots, suddenly see a figure emerging. "How delightful!" we would say. "How wonderful!" We would, for a moment, be looking up into the sky, seeing Orion's belt for the first time.

When we enjoy a novel or story, we sometimes say we wish it hadn't ended. What we mean is we enjoyed being in the world of the story, "under its spell." We're sorry to leave. And that sorrow — that bittersweet ending — is itself part of what we cherish. The wholeness, the shapeliness, that forces the work to come to an end is a crucial element of our pleasure.

> Everybody knows what a house does, how it encloses space and makes connections between one enclosed space and another and presents what is outside in a new way. This is the nearest I can come to explaining what a story does for me, and what I want my stories to do for other people.
>
> — ALICE MUNRO

OUR DESIRE FOR shape, combined with our desire for surprise, explains not only the importance of careful selection but also the power of fragments. The general outline of a biography provides context for the brief passages of Michael Ondaatje's *The Collected Works of Billy the Kid;* our desire to have the promise of biography satisfied leads us to meet the challenge issued by the first (blank) photograph of its subject. We've been handed pieces of a puzzle. Fragments create tension because of our expectation that there will be, or is, a shape. Alice Munro writes conventional psychological realism yet challenges the shapes we know and expect. Munro not only leaves things out of her stories but arranges the parts so that a story's ultimate shape is often unpredictable. It's as if she's taken a narrative line and applied the Munro Projection.

Readers get one kind of pleasure from a complete shape and another kind of pleasure from perceiving a shape only partially represented—from playing a role in bringing the work to completion. As writers we need to determine how much of the shape to supply, how clear to make it—and to understand how much work we're asking the reader to do. If we provide too little, we fail to communicate. If we provide too much, there is no room for the imagination. But when we get it right, we're the best of guides, leading the way to a place that allows for the reader's discovery.

None of this is meant to imply that we should start stories or novels with a predetermined shape in mind or that we should both start with and adhere to any particular constraints. We *might* start with a shape in mind, or with a constraint, but we must be prepared to change or adapt that initial notion to suit the thing we create; and we might start without a sense of the whole, but our drafts will lead to the discovery of shape and to the recognition of the distortion formula that will allow us to create the most appropriate vision of the world for the particular purpose of that story or novel.

In 1921, when he was thirty-seven, Hermann Rorschach published a monograph he had originally subtitled "Methods and Results of a Perceptual-Diagnostic Experiment: Interpretation of Arbitrary Forms." An amateur artist who made detailed ink drawings on a small scale, Rorschach had been especially intrigued by Klecksographie, or Blotto, a popular late-nineteenth-century game. Players would buy or make inkblots, then either create poemlike associations or play a form of charades. In school, children would compete by creating elaborate descriptions of what they saw in the blots. But when preparing his famous experiment, Rorschach opted not to rely on the arbitrary; instead, he carefully chose blots, or what he came to call "figures," that fulfilled "certain requirements of composition," as otherwise "they [would] not be suggestive, with the result that many subjects [would] reject them as 'simply an inkblot.'" Some scholars believe he went so far as to embellish the puddles of ink by hand.

Rorschach died a year later, without claiming to have created any sort of definitive "test"; his monograph reported results of a preliminary investigation. The man whose name is forever linked to ink blots was just beginning to see something. . . .

VII. NEW GEOMETRY, NEW (?) SHAPES

Fractal geometry, still relatively new, has been applied in ways that offer intriguing possibilities for the geometry of fiction. Like some of the experiments of the Oulipo, fractals create shapes through replacement formulas. A very simple one would replace every line segment

FIG. 64

with

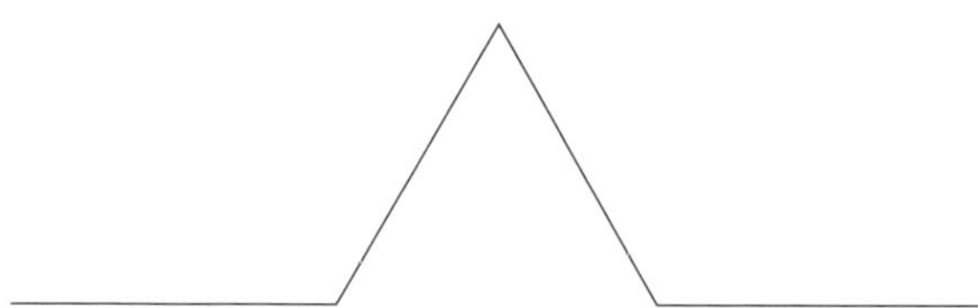

FIG. 65 **FIRST ITERATION**

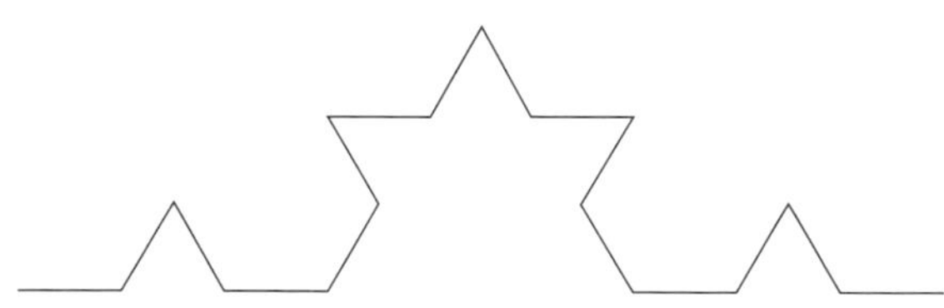

FIG. 66 **SECOND ITERATION**

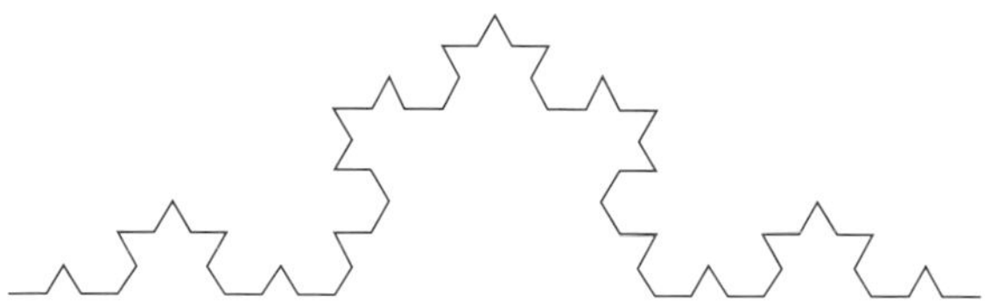

FIG. 67 **THIRD ITERATION**

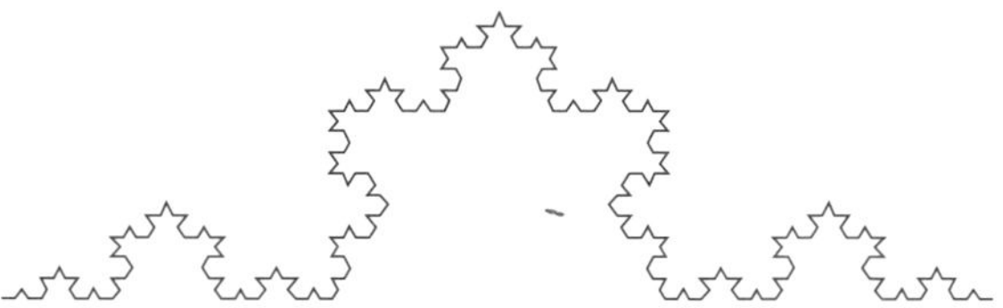

FIG. 68 **FOURTH ITERATION**

In each successive iteration the figure becomes increasingly elaborate. The replacement can continue infinitely—with the result that the distance between the beginning and the end of the figure is, theoretically, infinite. By extension, a shape in nature, such as a shoreline—even the perimeter of a garden pond—is infinite. The closer we look, the more detail we find. The only limitation to our view is the limitation of our ability to see. In order to find something new, we simply have to be willing to look more closely, more carefully. And so, realism is inexhaustible.

A fractal landscape, a kind of fictional map, is made by similar replacements. A rectangle, say, will be replaced by that same shape divided in quarters, the smaller rectangles sloping toward the center.

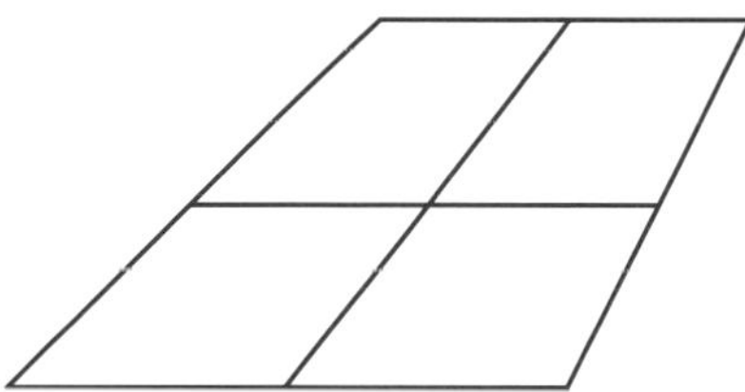

FIG. 69 **A DIVIDED PLANE**

An artfully placed random generator makes the landscape seem irregular, so "realistic."

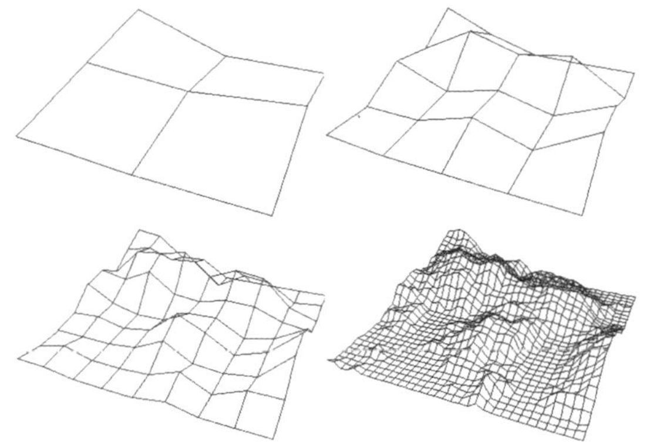

FIG. 70 **FOUR STAGES IN THE EVOLUTION OF A FRACTAL LANDSCAPE**

Fractals can also be used to imitate—some would say duplicate—shapes found in nature.

FIG. 71

The fractal above is not identical to a fern, but to make it more nearly so is simply a matter of being patient with the math and of deciding whether the goal is to recreate one particular fern or to create an "ideal" image of a type of fern. While Euclidean geometry describes man-made objects, fractals are more useful for describing shapes found in nature.

The lesson for writers of realism is that the representation of natural shapes is achieved not by abandoning geometry but by embracing a more rigorous geometry.

VIII. IS THIS ARGUMENT CIRCULAR? POINTED? THE END OF THE LINE

As a young artist, Chuck Jones was a fan of the work done by the Disney studio, but he grew to believe that believability was more important than realism. Inspired by the exotic landscape of Arches National Monument, he pushed further and further into a stylized American Southwest, until it became otherworldly. His trains and trucks had no human drivers, his coyote looked like a hobo, and his Road Runner was impossibly clever. Yet Wile E. Coyote retains some of the physical characteristics and apparent forlorn desperation of actual coyotes, and Road Runner is based on an actual running bird. The challenge in the cartoons was to strike a balance between two worlds. Kenner writes about a Jones-directed Bugs Bunny classic called "Bully for Bugs," in which the hero takes on the role of a matador:

> If we don't think of a bull the cartoon gets trivial, whereas thinking of a beast in pain expels us from the cartoon world. But that is not a beast, therefore not in pain; it's a wondrous arrangement of lines and color and movement. . . . Jones . . . [works] close to the mysterious zone where we viewers connect pen-and-ink artifice with the world we inhabit.

In some way or another, all writing connects "ink artifice" with the world we inhabit. When we read "Lost in the Fun-

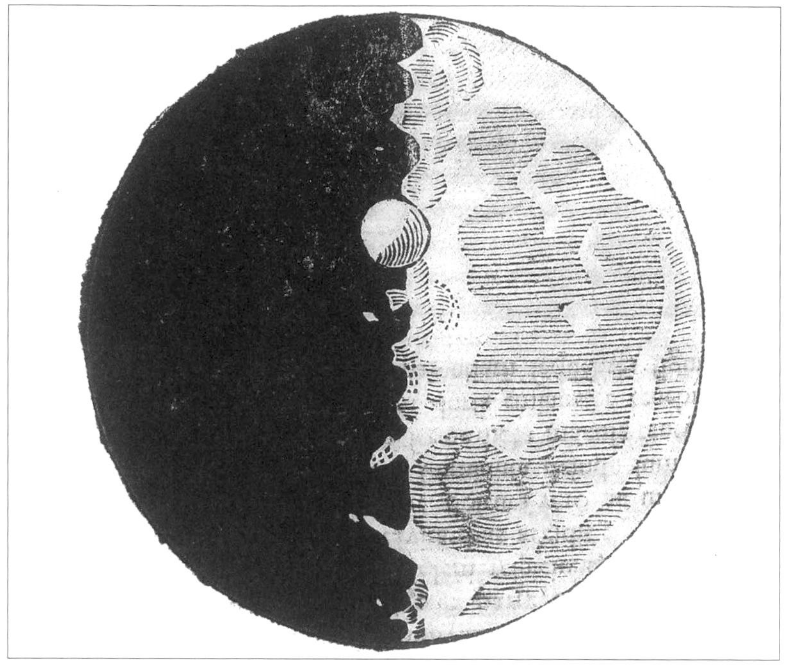

FIG. 72 ONE OF A SERIES OF COPPER ENGRAVINGS OF THE MOON BY GALILEO, ILLUSTRATING LUNAR SHADOWS

house," *The Unbearable Lightness of Being*, and *Lolita*, if we aren't persuaded to think of the characters in those narratives as people — if we aren't repulsed by Humbert Humbert, and occasionally amused—the fiction fails. But if we only feel impatient, in Barth's story, because it seems we'll never get to the beach, or feel exasperated, in Kundera's novel, because the narrator keeps "interrupting," if we only *feel*, we're missing the opportunity provided by fiction that means to engage our mind in other ways as well. Some of the work referred to as "postmodern" that is most difficult to access, even for dedicated readers, reads like integral calculus. Such work is more likely to be a tangent, in its extremity, than the next prevailing tradition. Nevertheless, a visit with the Oulipo-ets and other postrealists, via their work, is likely to be provocative and inspiring even to writers who have no intention of creating new methods of text generation.

John Barth used a phrase of Borges's to describe the blind librarian's stories; he said they combine "the algebra and the fire." Borges himself said, "I think that cleverness is a hindrance. I don't think a writer should be clever, or clever in a mechanical way." And while Nabokov called his characters galley slaves, the locations for scenes "sets" he "constructed," and his narrative structures "mechanisms," he also wrote:

> For me a work of fiction exists only insofar as it affords me what I shall bluntly call aesthetic bliss, that is a sense of being somehow, somewhere, connected with other states of being where art (curiosity, tenderness, kindness, ecstasy) is the norm. There are not many such books.

Tenderness. Kindness. Ecstasy. Nabokov's definition of art would surprise those who find him overly "intellectual." Elsewhere, he added, "you read an artist's book not with your heart (the heart is a remarkably stupid reader), and not with your brain alone, but with your brain and your spine. 'Ladies and gentleman, the tingle in your spine tells you what the author felt and wished you to feel.'"

Again and again, the best of the postrealists strike this note. Kundera writes that Cervantes and other early novelists "were not looking to simulate reality; they were looking to amaze, astonish, enchant. They were *playful*, and therein lay their virtuosity. . . . The great European novel started out as entertainment, and all real novelists are nostalgic for it!" This is a call for freedom, for play—but for serious play. "If I believed my writing were no more than . . . formal fun-and-games," Barth has told us, "I'd take up some other line of work. The subject of literature, says Aristotle, is 'human life, its happiness and its misery.' I agree with Aristotle. . . . What we want is passionate virtuosity. If these pieces aren't also *moving*, then the experiment is unsuccessful."

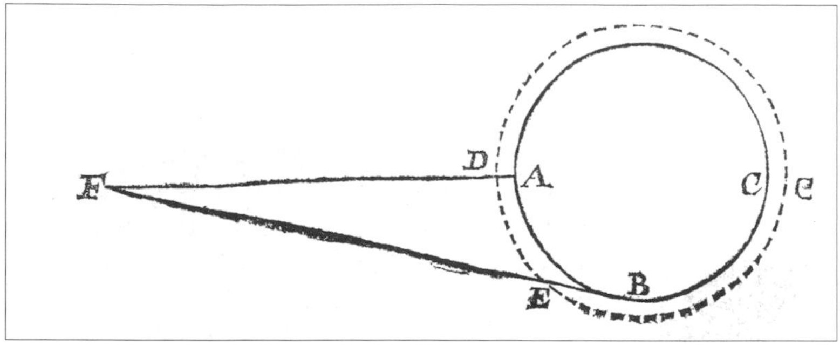

FIG. 73 GALILEO'S DIAGRAM OF LUNAR REFRACTION

Calvino's fiction demonstrates his interest in the devices and experiments of the Oulipo; but his work is also full of wit and compassion, a fundamental interest in human emotion and desire—including, but not limited to, the desire for new ideas. In his work, we see that the "victory of mental order over the chaos of the world" is a humane victory—a celebration, rather than a denial, of humanity.

In his essay on Galileo, Calvino wrote that, for the Renaissance astronomer, "The geometric or mathematical alphabet of the book of Nature will be the weapon which—because of its capacity to be broken down into minimal elements and to represent all forms of movement and change—will abolish the opposition between the unchanging heavens and the elements of the Earth." Half a century before, Gerardus Mercator invoked Atlas, thinking not of the character doomed to bear the weight of the world but of the one in other versions of the myth: a mortal elevated by the gods for deriving the science of astrology, and so discovering the arrangement of the stars. In that version of the story, Atlas is less literal holder of the world than beholder of it; he alone among mortals can contemplate the divine and take measure of the cosmos. Mercator, a religious man, believed careful observation, coupled with divine mathematics, would allow us something approaching the immortals' view of the universe. In a similar way, fiction's geometry is what allows us to build ladders from the world we live in to the worlds we imagine.

FIG. 74 **CHARLES RITCHIE'S *PEGASUS***

PLUS ULTRA

What was infinitely more exhilarating,
I had passed a landmark; I had
finished a tale, and written "The End"
upon my manuscript.

ROBERT LOUIS STEVENSON

What we call the beginning is often the end
And to make an end is to make a beginning.
The end is where we start from.

T. S. ELIOT, "LITTLE GIDDING"

THE FIRST "real" book I read—that's how I thought of it then, and how I think of it now—was Robert Louis Stevenson's *Treasure Island*. According to family lore, I accomplished this feat at age seven, in seven days. The numerical neatness throws the matter into doubt, but there's no question that I read at a young age the copy of Stevenson's novel originally given to my mother when

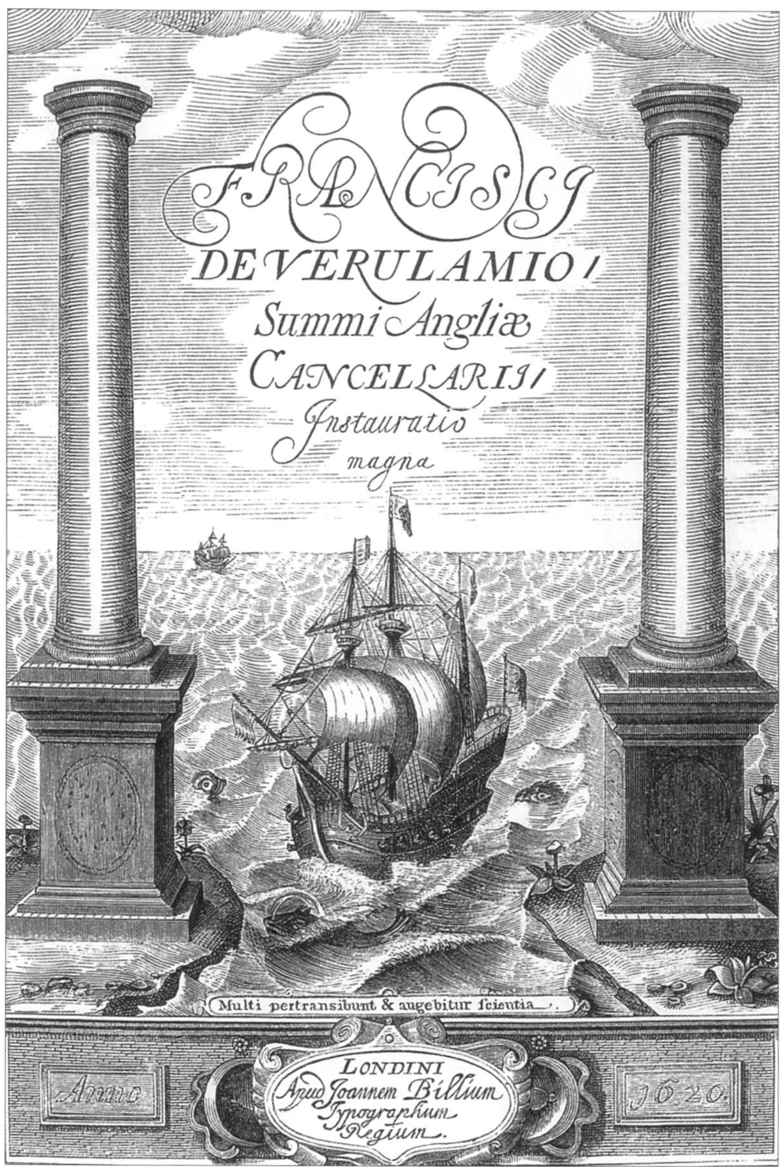

FIG. 75 **THE PILLARS OF HERCULES, FROM FRANCIS BACON'S *NOVUM ORGANUM***

she was a child, from an edition featuring color plates by Frank Godwin. For years I remembered, with real fear, Blind Pew, the Black Spot, and, most of all, the painting used as the frontispiece: Jim Hawkins regarding Mr. Hands, who sits propped up on the deck of the ship, bleeding from what appears to be his freshly severed leg.* Inspiring a very different emotion — an enchanted contemplation that lingers even now—was the book's only original illustration: the map of Treasure Island.

Maps are a common feature of children's books *(Winnie-the-Pooh),* adventure books *(Lord of the Rings),* and books that borrow from the traditions of children's and adventure books (Richard Adams's *Watership Down*, William Goldman's *The Princess Bride*, Michael Chabon's *Summerland*), and they occasionally feature in fiction intended solely for adults (Sherwood Anderson made a map of Winesburg, Ohio, and William Faulkner included his of Yoknapatawpha County ["William Faulkner, Sole Owner & Proprietor"] at the end of *Absalom, Absalom!*). While the map published in *Treasure Island* is not the map Stevenson drew before drafting the novel — that one was lost, either by his publisher or in the mails, forcing him to re-create it—we have his record of how the original map came into being, what it meant to him, and the role it played in the genesis of the novel. Driven indoors by a cool, blustery, wet Scottish summer, Stevenson

> would sometimes . . . pass the afternoon . . . making coloured drawings. On one of these occasions, I made the map of an island; it was elaborately and (I thought) beautifully coloured; the shape of it took my fancy beyond expression; it contained harbours that pleased me like sonnets; and with the unconsciousness of the predestined, I ticketed my performance "Treasure Island." . . . As I paused upon my map . . . the future characters of the book began to appear there visibly among imaginary woods; and their brown faces and bright weapons peeped out upon me from unexpected quarters, as they passed to and fro, fighting and hunting treasure, on these few square

* A mistaken impression, resulting from a small miscalculation of perspective.

inches of a flat projection. The next thing I knew I had some papers before me and was writing out a list of chapters.

A close look at the map reveals indicators of scientific precision: the scale at the top, notations of the water's depth, and the spectacularly elaborated compass rose. But the scale is flanked by mermaids, and while the map includes practical information ("strong tide here," "foul ground"), all of it, including the scale and compass rose, is useless, as a note at the bottom tells us the "latitude and longitude [have been] struck out by Jim Hawkins." The document is a "facsimile" of a fictitious map edited by a fictitious character. But rather than pushing us violently away, the multiple frames around the map create a space between the world of the reader and the world of the novel—a space precisely the size of a boy's imagination.

I am now upon a painful chapter. No doubt the parrot once belonged to Robinson Crusoe. No doubt the skeleton is conveyed from Poe. I think little of these, they are trifles and details; and no man can hope to have a monopoly of skeletons or make a corner in talking birds. The stockade, I am told, is from *Masterman Ready*. It may be, I care not a jot. These useful writers had fulfilled the poet's saying: departing, they had left behind them Footprints on the sands of time, Footprints which perhaps another — and I was the other! It is my debt to Washington Irving that exercises my conscience, and justly so, for I believe plagiarism was rarely carried farther. I chanced to pick up the *Tales of a Traveller* some years ago with a view to an anthology of prose narrative, and the book flew up and struck me: Billy Bones, his chest, the company in the parlour, the whole inner spirit, and a good deal of the material detail of my first chapters — all were there, all were the property of Washington Irving. But I had no guess of it then as I sat writing by the fireside, in what seemed the spring-tides of a somewhat pedestrian inspiration; nor yet day by day, after lunch, as I read aloud my morning's

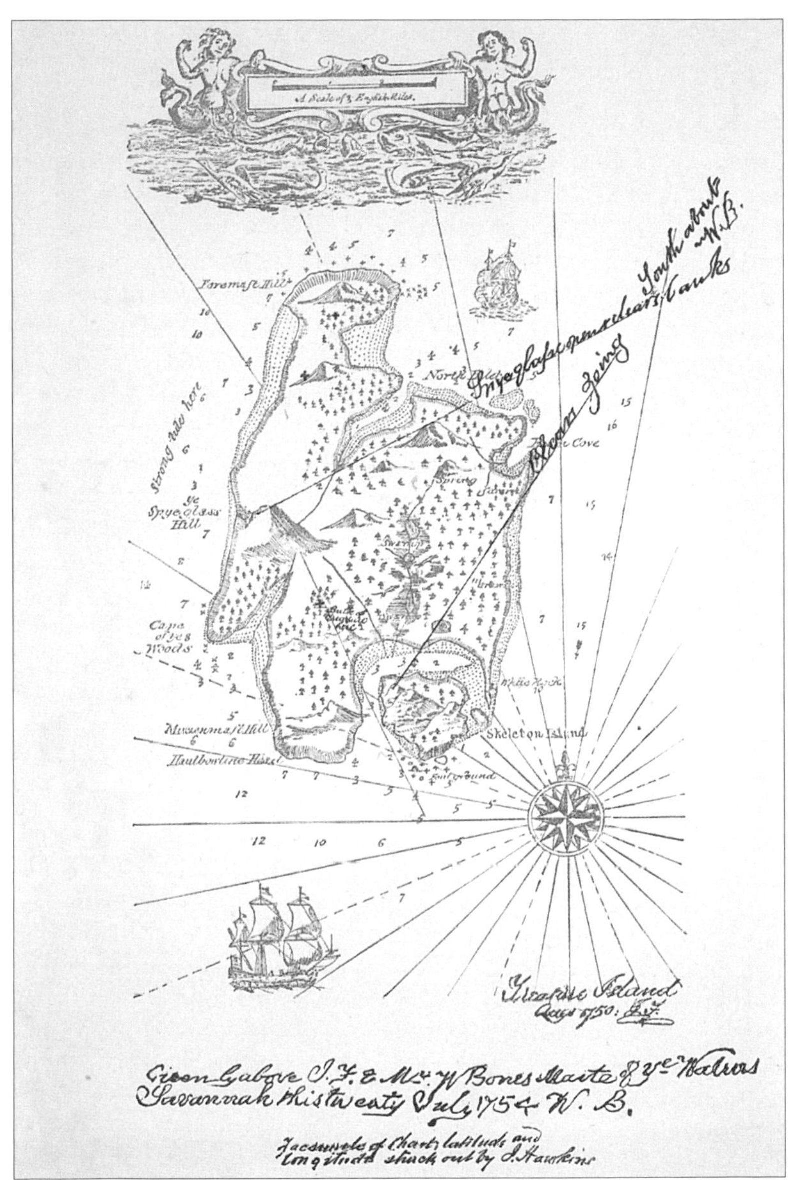

Foremast Hill
North Inlet
Strong tide here
Ye Spye glass Hill
Cape of ye Woods
Mizzenmast Hill
Haulbowline Head
Skeleton Island
Treasure Island
Given by above J. F. & Mr W Bones Maite of ye Walrus
Savannah this twenty July 1754 W. B.

FIG. 76

work to the family. It seemed to me original as sin; it seemed to belong to me like my right eye.

For a very long time, mapmakers have not started at the beginning. Rather, they have started with other maps, sometimes doing as little as adding their own titles and decorations. Eratosthenes relied on the observations of, among others, Pythagoras and Aristotle. Mercator, like Fra Mauro, drew not only on earlier maps but on the published accounts of explorers and conversations with travelers. Reliance on second- and third-hand resources led to countless maps depicting California as an island, and others depicting Terra Australis — mistakes, or fabrications, perpetuated the way urban legends spread over the Internet. John Ogilby's road atlas of Great Britain was quickly pirated, and distorted, most widely under the title *Ogilby Improved*. Today, the expense of map production and the demand for detail are so great that commercial mapmakers struggle simply to revise the previous year's edition, never mind starting from scratch. In the United States, where our first president was a surveyor (who carved his initials, still visible, in a rock wall in Virginia), the federal government got into the business of making maps early and made the information therein freely available. As a result, most United States mapping builds on work in the public domain. For similar reasons, landowners save money on a survey if the metal stakes are still in place, no matter how overgrown or muddy; the surveyors simply check the previous team's marks. They could proceed as if that work hadn't already been done, but why?

We refer to the written work of the past to see what has been done and how it has been done. Reading like cartographers, as opposed to mere map users, we focus on the maker's methods and assumptions. We find tools and ways to use them. We aren't interested in simply rewriting the *Odyssey* or the *Divine Comedy*, or in imitating Chekhov or Raymond Carver. But our work will, inevitably, echo and respond to the work of the past that resonates most strongly for us — just as Carver's "What We Talk About

When We Talk About Love" echoes Chekhov's "About Love" and, more softly, Socrates' speech on the nature of love in Plato's *Symposium*. In the same way that the first place we called home can never be, in our mind, a mere assembly of wood and glass—in the same way that our emotions and recollections are inseparable from that house—the maps we rely on become a part of our landscape. Thoreau said he had the map of his fields engraved in his soul. Dim as my memory has grown, I carry with me Mercator's world as it hung in front of the chalkboard in every Scotts Branch Elementary School classroom; the layout of two golf courses I played, miserably, as a child, on stifling summer weekends; a few crucial exits of the Baltimore Beltway; Tucson's rigid grid of streets; the route my wife and I followed to walk our dog by moonlight twenty years ago; and an actual path in actual woods that served, for several years, as home for a trickster squirrel, an ornery snake, and an entirely reliable fish. While those Hardy Boys books may have been a liability in the expectations they created, the distortions they presented, fifty-some of them, along with the mysteries of Arthur Conan Doyle and Agatha Christie, must have had some influence on the boy who devoured them; though not so much, the adult hopes, as Stevenson's classic adventure, *Huckleberry Finn* and *Roughing It*, *The Great Gatsby* and *Lolita*, "The Blue-Winged Teal" and "Sonny's Blues," "The Open Boat" and *The Sun Also Rises*, *Black Dog*, *Red Dog* and *Cemetery Nights*, "Barn Burning" and "Revelation."

We all have our touchstones.

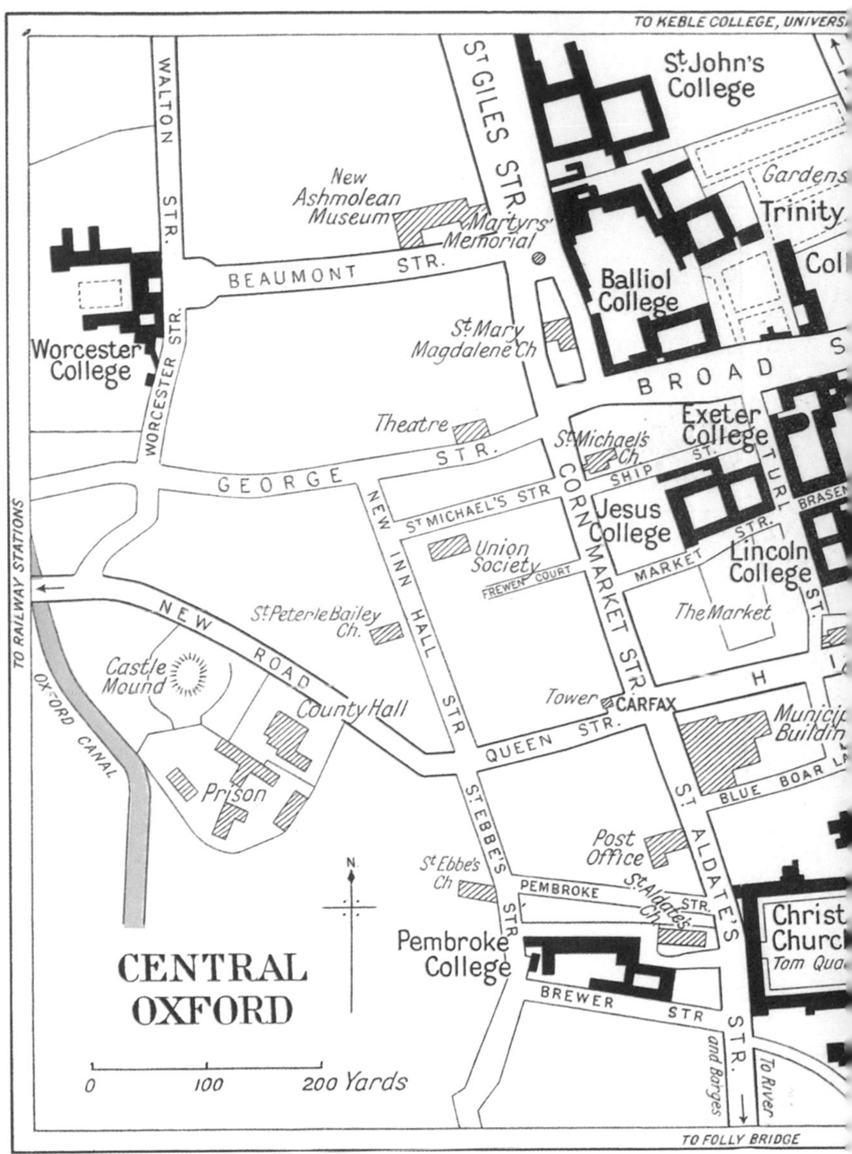
TO KEBLE COLLEGE, UNIVERS
St. John's College
Gardens
Trinity
Col
Balliol College
BROAD
Exeter College
Jesus College
Lincoln College
The Market
Municip Buildin
Christ Church
Tom Qua
WALTON STR.
ST GILES STR.
New Ashmolean Museum
Martyrs' Memorial
BEAUMONT STR.
WORCESTER STR.
Worcester College
St. Mary Magdalene Ch
Theatre
GEORGE STR.
St. Michael's Ch.
SHIP ST.
TURL
CORN MARKET STR.
NEW INN HALL STR.
ST MICHAEL'S STR
Union Society
FREWEN COURT
MARKET STR.
BRASEN
TO RAILWAY STATIONS
NEW ROAD
St. Peter le Bailey Ch.
Castle Mound
County Hall
Tower
CARFAX
QUEEN STR.
H
OXFORD CANAL
Prison
BLUE BOAR
ST. ALDATE'S STR.
ST. EBBE'S STR.
Post Office
St. Ebbe's Ch
PEMBROKE STR.
St. Aldate's Ch.
Pembroke College
BREWER STR
and Barges
To River
TO FOLLY BRIDGE
N.
CENTRAL OXFORD
0 100 200 Yards

FIG. 77 A GLORIOUS INTERSECTION: THE STORIED STREETS WHEREIN THE AUTHOR MET HIS WIFE

> I am told there are people who do not care for maps, and find it hard to believe. The names, the shapes of the woodlands, the courses of the roads and rivers, the prehistoric footsteps of man still distinctly traceable up hill and down dale, the mills and the ruins, the ponds and the ferries, perhaps the standing stone or the druidic circle on the heath; here is an inexhaustible fund of interest for any man with eyes to see or twopence-worth of imagination to understand with!
>
> — ROBERT LOUIS STEVENSON

HERE IN THE early years of the twenty-first century, long after the first reports that the novel is dead; that books printed on paper are headed the way of the phone booth, caboose, and hand-cranked automobile; and over two millennia since Eratosthenes discovered a way to measure something too large for him to see, we can be forgiven for asking if there is, at this late date, anything new to map, or to map anew.

Some believe there isn't. They tell us everything has been said before. "What do the novels and poems of today have to offer," asked Arthur Krystal in *Harper's* magazine a few years ago, "other than implicit commentary on their antecedents?" The suspicion itself rings familiar. "To produce anything new," Byron wrote in 1807, "in an age so fertile in rhyme, would be a Herculean task, as every subject has already been treated to its utmost extent." Nearly 2,300 years before him, Plato proclaimed: "We have learned everything there is to learn. . . . Seeking and learning is all remembrance." Ecclesiastes put it this way: "What has been is what will be, and what has been done is what will be done; there is nothing new under the sun." Even Galileo, in a fit of hubris, boasted, "It was granted to me alone to discover all the new phenomena in the sky, and nothing to anybody else."

> Fifteen days I stuck to it, and turned out fifteen chapters; and then, in the early paragraphs of the sixteenth, ignominiously

> lost hold. My mouth was empty; there was not one word of *Treasure Island* in my bosom; and here were the proofs of the beginning already awaiting me at the "Hand and Spear"! Then I corrected them, living for the most part alone, walking on the heath at Weybridge in dewy autumn mornings, a good deal pleased with what I had done, and more appalled than I can depict to you in words at what remained for me to do. I was thirty-one; I was the head of a family; I had lost my health; I had never yet paid my way, never yet made 200 pounds a year; my father had quite recently bought back and cancelled a book that was judged a failure: was this to be another and last fiasco? I was indeed very close on despair.

According to legend, when Hercules reached the confines of Europe and Libya, he erected two pillars, one on Calpe (the Rock of Gibraltar), the other on Abila. The Pillars of Hercules marked the end of the known world and were traditionally depicted with the inscription "Ne Plus Ultra": Nothing Lies Further.*

And yet . . . something did. In the sixth century B.C., Hanno, having sailed straight through those legendary pillars, turned back from his circumnavigation of Africa, not because he thought he had seen it all, but because his ships were low on provisions. In the fifteenth century A.D., Columbus set off through the pillars determined to find exactly what he expected to find. It seems that no matter how many discoveries we make, we tell ourselves we've reached the end of the knowable world. Maybe some of us are always inclined to claim we've done all we can do, while others of us refuse to rest; or maybe it's that one day we're defiant, the next we're humbled, awed by the scope of the mysteries around us. William Herschel, the eighteenth-century telescope maker and discoverer of Uranus, wrote:

> When, in the course of time, I took up astronomy, I determined to accept nothing on faith, but to see with my own eyes everything which others had seen before me. . . . Seeing is in some

* In the *Odyssey*, they serve as the gate to Hades.

> respects an art which must be learnt. To make a person see with such power is nearly the same as if I were asked to make him play one of Handel's fugues upon the organ. Many a night I have been practicing to see, and it would be strange if one did not acquire a certain dexterity by such constant practice.

While we've probed the psyche for a century, only in recent decades have we begun to map the land under the ice of Antarctica, the ocean floor, and the ozone layer. Satellites revealed new islands in the Canadian Arctic as recently as the early 1980s. Cosmic cartographers, using radio emissions and other sources of radiation, are now mapping parts of the universe more than 13 billion light years away. A probe named for Galileo has sent us evidence of an ocean on a moon of Jupiter, and a modern version of Galileo's tool—the Hubble telescope—has led astronomers to estimate there are a hundred billion galaxies. Hubble himself observed (and Einstein calculated) that the universe is expanding; but even they didn't suspect the visible universe might be as little as 1 percent of the whole. Looking in another direction, scientists recently announced completion of the genetic blueprint of bubonic plague, and the mapping of the 3.1 billion units of DNA of the human genome. According to some, the latter announcement was premature; there are gaps amounting to nearly 1 percent of the total. In their defense, genome mappers say they've reached the limits of current technology.

The genome map and tools like the Hubble telescope don't merely allow us to see what we know more clearly; they give us a new sense of all that we don't know. "Whenever we couldn't conceive of what's out there," writes Richard Panek, "it was because we didn't yet understand what the preconceptions might be that were restricting our view." Which is to say, Seeing is an art which must be learned and relearned.

> In a second tide of delighted industry, and again at a rate of a chapter a day, I finished. . . .
>
> But the adventures of *Treasure Island* are not yet quite at an end. . . . The time came when it was decided to republish, and I sent in my manuscript, and the map along with it, to Messrs. Cassell. The proofs came, they were corrected, but I heard nothing of the map. I wrote and asked; was told it had never been received, and sat aghast. It is one thing to draw a map at random, set a scale in one corner of it at a venture, and write up a story to the measurements. It is quite another to have to examine a whole book, make an inventory of all the allusions contained in it, and with a pair of compasses, painfully design a map to suit the data. I did it; and the map was drawn again in my father's office, with embellishments of blowing whales and sailing ships, and my father himself brought into service a knack he had of various writing, and elaborately forged the signature of Captain Flint, and the sailing directions of Billy Bones. But somehow it was never Treasure Island to me.

AT SOME POINT in the act of exploration — on paper or in our mind — we begin the act of presentation, the creation of a document. The piece we compose is not meant to depict for the reader the path we took. This is what Stephen Dobyns is talking about when he says, "Only after [the writer's discovery of his or her intention] can the work be properly structured, can the selection and organization of the significant moments of time take place. The writer must know what piece of information to put first and why, what to put second and why, so that the whole work is governed by intention." The act of composition challenges us to become conscious of, and to gain control of, something that — through persistence, training, and some combination of talent and happy circumstance — we "found." The alternative to this conscious control — an alternative some successful writers claim as their method—is still more persistence, in the hope that applied intuition will eventually lead to fully realized work. But even this approach relies on the writer's being able to distinguish between a successful move and an unsuccessful one, a good choice and a bad one. This is precisely why, and the extent to which, writing can be taught. Talent is a treasure; yet talent isn't enough.

Stevenson drew and titled his map "with the unconsciousness of the predestined"; the Muse paid a call. We know better than to rely on such good fortune, but we do all we can to welcome it, along with the unplanned, the transcendent, and the magical, hoping that if we stay at our desks long enough — scribble, scribble — we will, eventually, scratch and win. Yet we call writing "work" for good reason: most of our days are spent not receiving gifts but solving the abstract problems we've posed for ourselves, "painfully designing a map to suit the data." When we aren't re-creating lost maps and manuscripts (one century it's lost mail, the next a crashed hard drive), we seek the most reliable and fruitful balance of the rational and the irrational, the known and the unknowable.

Kundera says his mathematical system is both a "formal necessity" and "natural," the product of an "unconscious, incomprehensible drive." This returns us to the question of whether Poe and Nabokov, among others, understood at the time of composition what they later professed to understand about what they had composed. Nabokov was persuasively forthcoming about his process:

> All I know is that at a very early stage of the novel's development I get this urge to garner bits of straw and fluff, to eat pebbles. . . . When I remember afterwards the force that made me jot down the correct names of things, or the inches and tints of things, even before I actually needed the information, I am inclined to assume that what I call, for want of a better term, inspiration, had been already at work, mutely pointing at this or that, having me accumulate the known materials for an unknown structure. . . . There comes a moment when I am informed from within that the entire structure is finished. All I have to do now is take it down in pencil or pen.

We need to be wary of reductive order, the sort of rationalizations that lead to restrictive simplicity. The crucial information isn't *when* the writer became conscious of the appropriateness of an overarching structure, or a metrical scheme, or a particular name for a character, but *that* he did. Kundera, having recognized something true and interesting in what one reader saw, returns to work with a new awareness of his own inclinations and tendencies, a structural design to work with or against. Members of the Oulipo pursue "text generation" with the hope that something marvelous, something unforeseen, will result; they constantly aspire to transcend the sum of their calculated effects. Kundera asks, "How can *uncontrolled* imagination be integrated into the novel, which is supposed to be a *lucid* examination of existence? How can such disparate elements be united?" Nabokov spoke of "the precision of poetry and the excitement of pure science. . . . The greater one's science," he said, "the deeper the sense of mystery."

My son has a gadget called a Levitron. The Levitron consists of a large, thick magnet, which serves as a base; a card of heavy plastic, which rests on the base; and a magnetized top. To set the thing into motion, you spin the top on the plastic; then you carefully raise the plastic, keeping it level. If all goes well, when the top is two inches or so above the base, it bobs into the air, still spinning. You can set the plastic aside and watch the top hover for minutes, in a space defined by the pull of gravity and the push of magnetic repulsion.

Let's say intention is gravity, and intuition is magnetic force. Too much gravity, and our top drops like the proverbial stone. Too much magnetic force, and the top flies off, out of control. But when we strike a balance, the result is just short of miraculous: the product of our effort, and yet beyond us.

FIG. 78 HIGH JUMPING ON THE MOON

> A few reminiscences . . . and the map itself, with its infinite, eloquent suggestion, made up the whole of my materials. It is, perhaps, not often that a map figures so largely in a tale, yet it is always important. The author must know his countryside, whether real or imaginary, like his hand; the distances, the points of the compass, the place of the sun's rising, the behaviour of the moon, should all be beyond cavil. And how troublesome the moon is!
>
> — ROBERT LOUIS STEVENSON

WHEN WE THINK of writers whose work stands out to us, we think of their "countryside": the distinctiveness of their vision and the presentation of their perceptions. One can hardly call Nabokov to mind without hearing, once again, "Lolita, light of my life, fire of my loins. My sin, my soul. Lo-lee-ta: the tip of the tongue taking a trip of three steps down the palate to tap, at three, on the teeth. Lo. Lee. Ta." That quickly, we are swept up by sound, by sense, by rhythm, by logic—by a narrator not quite like any other.

Nabokov's view of the world was shaped by his life as an exile but also, he reveals in his characteristically untraditional autobiography, by the fact that he had synesthesia, or the blending of sense perceptions—what he called

> . . . a fine case of coloured hearing: The long 'aaa' of the English alphabet has for me the tint of weathered wood, but a French 'a' evokes polished ebony. This black group includes hard 'g' (vulcanized rubber); and 'r' (a sooty rag being ripped). Oatmeal 'n,' noodle-limp 'l,' and the ivory-backed handmirror of 'o' take care of the whites. I am puzzled by my French 'on' which I see as the brimming tension-surface of alcohol in a small glass. Passing on to the blue group there is steely 'x,' thundercloud 'z,' and buckle-berry 'k,' while 's' is not the light blue of 'c,' but a curious mixture of azure and mother-of-pearl.

Other artists have enjoyed similar gifts of distortion. After a shell exploded near him during World War II, embedding a splinter of metal in his brain, Dmitri Shostakovich claimed to have come up with several melodies simply by tipping his head to one side. The splinter apparently triggered activity in his auditory cortex. The point isn't that accident or disability creates art, but that for reasons explainable and unexplainable—including culture, historical circumstance, upbringing, the functioning of the senses, formal and informal education, life experience, and even the physical growth of the brain—we each see the world, and think of it, differently. This might begin to explain, among many other things, why some of us are drawn to poetic forms or intricately designed plots, some to the investigation of personality, and others to the music of language.

Originality, that quality some cultures and artists prize so highly, is not without its origins. While we think of Flannery O'Connor as a fierce and outspoken individual, she was deeply engaged with a belief system set in place long before her; and while her fiction is distinctive, she did not reinvent the form of the short story. Dante did invent terza rima, but in the *Divine Comedy*, he explicitly acknowledges his debt to poets who came before him. Psychological realism, inexhaustible as it may be, has been well explored; it seems likely that some change in our use of formal elements, both those we have inherited and those we devise, will lead us from nineteenth- and twentieth-century realism to the realism to come. (Battle lines in poetry have been drawn between versers free and formal, and between those spelunking deep in the caverns and tunnels of language and those who continue to believe in the importance of emotion and meaning.) Milan Kundera calls for the polyphonic novel, Tom Wolfe calls for a return to naturalism, Don DeLillo and Robert Coover and Anne Carson and Thomas Bernhard encourage us in other directions. We have no obligation to follow any of them or to pursue any particular course. Our obligations are to recognize our own impulses and interests, to be aware of the work of the past and present, and to prepare ourselves to fulfill our greatest ambitions. Our goal is stimulation, provocation, invention. Discovery.

Upon assuming the throne in the early sixteenth century, Charles I altered the Spanish coat of arms. A scroll twined around the Pillars of Hercules bore the revised motto, "Plus Ultra," which became the rallying cry of the Age of Discovery. Farther Yet. The title page of Francis Bacon's *Novum Organum*, published in 1620, shows a ship sailing through the Pillars. "Our only remaining hope and salvation," Bacon wrote, "is to begin the whole labor of the mind again, not leaving it to itself but directing it perpetually from the very first." A century later, William Herschel agreed. Herschel, the first man to understand that telescopes penetrate time as well as space, spent the long daylight hours polishing his lenses, listening to his sister read from *Don Quixote* and the *Thousand and One Nights*. When darkness fell, his lenses clear, he discovered a heretofore unknown planet.

> Be rather the Mungo Park, the Lewis and Clark and Frobisher, of your own streams and oceans; explore your own higher latitudes. . . . Be a Columbus to whole new continents and worlds.
>
> — HENRY DAVID THOREAU

IN THE 1980S Beaver Indians in northeastern British Columbia presented officials from the Northern Pipeline Agency with what they called a Dream Map. They explained that the map depicted heaven and its opposite, animals, trails to follow and paths to avoid—all of which had been revealed through dreams. A Dream Map would be buried with the man who made it, to guide his spirit.

Such a document may seem distant from our own experience, but a new generation of cartographers has been mapping cyberspace, a world William Gibson famously described as "a consensus hallucination." Maps of cyberspace attempt to represent visually a world with no physical landscape. While some look like conventional charts, others are three dimensional; while some are dutifully schematic, others are bold interpretations of a "space" that exists only because we need it to exist, so we might understand our technological world. We not only want but insist on depictions of the most abstract aspects of our lives. Not much has changed since the days of those first creation myths. We want to see, and we want to see in ways that make sense to us, enlighten us, and delight us. In stories, poems, and novels, we create worlds of consensus hallucination. While readers suspend disbelief, as writers our job is to sustain belief in a world of the imagination, one as real to us as our computers, as yesterday's bread and tomorrow's news, as our fears and our dreams.

> It is my contention — my superstition, if you like — that who is faithful to his map, and consults it, and draws from it his inspiration, daily and hourly, gains positive support, and not mere negative immunity from accident. The tale has a root there; it grows in that soil; it has a spine of its own behind the words. Better if the country be real, and he has walked every foot of it and knows every milestone. But even with imaginary places, he will do well in the beginning to provide a map; as he studies it, relations will appear that he had not thought upon; he will discover obvious, though unsuspected, short-cuts and footprints for his messengers; and even when a map is not all the plot, as it was in *Treasure Island*, it will be found to be a mine of suggestion.

WE START OFF either with some sense of what we want to find or with curiosity and patience, trusting our imaginations to show us a path that exists, though no one has ever seen it. We remember that a great many of the fruits of exploration were considered,

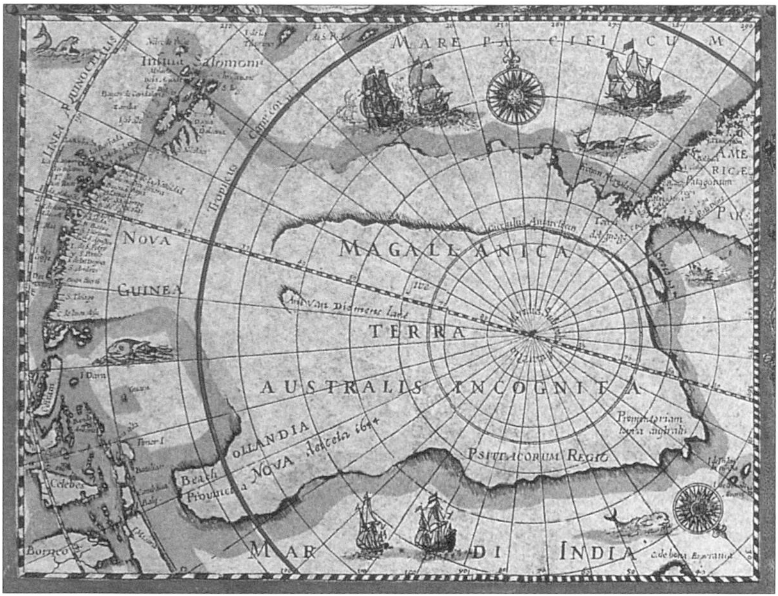

FIG. 79 **DETAIL FROM WILLIAM BLAEU'S *NEW AND ACCURATE MAP OF THE AMERICAS*, 1650**

by some, to be evidence of failure. As one text obligingly puts it, Alexander Dalrymple's "biggest contribution to geography and mapmaking came about because he believed in something that did not exist." Terra Australis, or the Southern Land, appeared on maps for 1,600 years. Much larger than Australia, it was thought to balance the weight of Europe and Asia in the Northern Hemisphere. Dalrymple made such persuasive arguments for the ways this enormous southern continent could benefit Britain that his government sent Captain James Cook on three voyages. Cook never found Terra Australis, but as a by-product of his search he produced the first comprehensive maps of the Pacific, the world's largest ocean.

And then there's the lesson of Christopher Columbus, who died insisting he had reached India, or very nearly so. Never once did he claim he had found a new world—because to say as much would have been to admit failure. Centuries later, T. S. Eliot commiserated:

> And what you thought you came for
> Is only a shell, a husk of meaning. . . .
> Either you had no purpose
> Or the purpose is beyond the end you figured
> And is altered in fulfillment.

We stare at our own backyards, hack trails through the rainforest, paddle through overgrown rivers, wade into swamps even as something pulls thickly at our boots. When we reach what feels like a destination, we turn and map the way for others. But will we show them the trail, or force them to negotiate a muddy slope? Will we label the poison ivy, indicate where the river is shallow enough to cross? Or will we add serpents dangling from the trees? We cannot be trusted. We tell our readers, *Trust me.*

At our best, we don't make road maps so much as chart the territory, creating the stories of Frolicking Green Water Dragons and lost cities, finding order in the very stars—the uncountable but finite bodies that glimmer above us, always in view, always out of reach. In *A Mapmaker's Dream*, Fra Mauro decides the search for the ultimate map ends with the individual. "Wise men contemplate the world," he thinks, "knowing full well that they are contemplating themselves." It may be folly to imagine anything more universal, more objective, more true. Each of us stands at one unique spot in the universe, at one moment in the expanse of time, holding a blank sheet of paper.

This is where we begin.

POINTS OF REFERENCE

Bachelard, Gaston. *The Poetics of Space*. Boston: Beacon, 1994.

Barth, John. *The Friday Book: Essays and Other Nonfiction*. New York: G.P. Putnam's Sons, 1984.

———. *Lost in the Funhouse: Fiction for Print, Tape, Live Voice*. New York: Anchor, 1988.

Bashō. *Back Roads to Far Towns*. Trans. Cid Corman and Kamaike Susumu. Hopewell, N.J.: Ecco, 1996.

Bernhard, Thomas. *The Loser*. Chicago: Univ. of Chicago Press, 1996.

Borges, Jorge Luis. *Ficciones*. New York: Grove Press, 1962.

Calvino, Italo. *Cosmicomics*. New York: Harcourt Brace Jovanovich, 1968.

———. *If on a winter's night a traveler*. New York: Harcourt Brace Jovanovich, 1981.

———. *Six Memos for the Next Millennium*. Cambridge, Mass.: Harvard Univ. Press, 1988.

———. *Why Read the Classics?* New York: Pantheon, 1999.

Carson, Anne. "Beauty Prefers an Edge." Interview by Mary Gannon. *Poets and Writers*, March 2001.

Carter, Rita. *Mapping the Mind*. Berkeley: Univ. of California Press, 1998.

Chekhov, Anton. "Anyuta." In *Anton Chekhov's Short Stories*. Ed. Ralph E. Matlaw. New York: W. W. Norton, 1979.

Chopin, Kate. "The Storm." In *Complete Novels and Stories*. New York: Literary Classics of the United States, 2002.

Costello, Mark. *Big If*. New York: W. W. Norton, 2002.

Cowan, James. *A Mapmaker's Dream: The Meditations of Fra Mauro, Cartographer to the Court of Venice*. Boston: Shambhala, 1996.

Crane, Nicholas. *Mercator: The Man Who Mapped the Planet*. New York: Henry Holt, 2003.

Dante. *The Divine Comedy. Volume I: Inferno*. Trans. Mark Musa. New York: Penguin, 1984.

———. *The Divine Comedy. Volume II: Purgatory*. Trans. Mark Musa. New York: Penguin, 1981.

Davenport, Guy. *Seven Greeks*. New York: New Directions, 1995.

DeLillo, Don. *White Noise*. New York: Viking Penguin, 1985.

Doctorow, E. L. *Ragtime*. New York: Random House, 1974.

Dodge, Martin, and Rob Kitchin. *Atlas of Cyberspace*. London: Addison-Wesley, 2001.

Gould, Peter, and Rodney White. *Mental Maps*. Baltimore: Penguin, 1974.

Glück, Louise. *Ararat*. New York: Ecco, 1990.

———. *Proofs and Theories: Essays on Poetry*. New York: Ecco, 1994.
Gopnik, Adam. "Street Furniture: The Most Complete Map of the City and Everything in It." *New Yorker*, November 6, 2000.

Harley, J. B. *The New Nature of Maps: Essays in the History of Cartography*. Baltimore: Johns Hopkins Univ. Press, 2001.

Hass, Robert, ed. *The Essential Haiku: Versions of Bashō, Busōn, and Issa*. Hopewell, New Jersey: Ecco, 1994.

Hemingway, Ernest. "The Killers." In *The Short Stories of Ernest Hemingway*. New York: Charles Scribner's Sons, 1966.

———. Interview by George Plimpton. *Paris Review* 18 (spring 1958).

Hoffman, Frederick J., ed. *The Great Gatsby: A Study*. New York: Charles Scribner's Sons, 1962.

Homer. *The Odyssey*. Trans. Richard Fagles. New York: Viking Penguin, 1996.

Howells, Carol Ann. *Alice Munro*. Manchester, England: Manchester Univ. Press, 1998.

Jones, Chuck. *Chuck Amuck: The Life and Times of an Animated Cartoonist*. New York: Avon, 1989.

Kenner, Hugh. *Chuck Jones: A Flurry of Drawings*. Berkeley: Univ. of California Press, 1994.

King, Ross. *Brunelleschi's Dome: How a Renaissance Genius Reinvented Architecture*. New York: Walker and Company, 2000.

Krystal, Arthur. "Closing the Books: A Devoted Reader Arrives at the End of the Story." In *Agitations: Essays on Life and Literature*. New Haven: Yale Univ. Press, 2002.

Kundera, Milan. *The Art of the Novel*. New York: Grove, 1988.
Levis, Larry. *The Widening Spell of the Leaves*. Pittsburgh: Univ. of Pittsburgh Press, 1991.
Lewis, G. Malcolm. "The Origin of Cartography." In *The History of Cartography. Vol. 1*. Ed. J. Brian Harley and David Woodward. Chicago: Univ. of Chicago Press, 1987.
Melville, Herman. *Moby Dick*. In *Redburn, White-Jacket, and Moby-Dick*. New York: Literary Classics of the United States, 1983.
Monmonier, Mark. "All Over the Map: Current and Seamless." *Mercator's World*. November/December 2001. 52–54.
———. *Drawing the Line: Tales of Maps and Controversy*. New York: Henry Holt, 1995.
———. *How to Lie with Maps*. 2nd ed. Chicago: Univ. of Chicago Press, 1996.
Motte, Warren F., Jr. *Oulipo: A Primer of Potential Literature*. Normal, Ill.: Dalkey Archive, 1998.
Nabokov, Vladimir. *The Annotated Lolita*. Ed. Alfred Appel Jr. New York: Vintage, 1991.
———. *Strong Opinions*. New York: Vintage, 1990.
Nolan, Christopher, director. *Memento*. Columbia TriStar, 2001.
Ogilby, John. *Britannia*. Facsimile edition. Amsterdam: Theatrum Orbis Terrarum, 1970.
Orr, Gregory, and Ellen Bryant Voigt, eds. *Poets Teaching Poets: Self and the World*. Ann Arbor: Univ. of Michigan Press, 1996.
Panek, Richard. *Seeing and Believing: How the Telescope Opened Our Eyes and Minds to the Heavens*. New York: Penguin, 1999.
Queneau, Raymond, Italo Calvino, et al. *Oulipo Laboratory*. Trans. Harry Mathews and Iain White. London: Atlas, 1995.
Russo, Richard. "The Mysteries of Linwood Hart." In *The Whore's Child and Other Stories*. New York: Alfred A. Knopf, 2002.
Ryan, Michael. *A Difficult Grace: On Poets, Poetry, and Writing*. Athens: Univ. of Georgia Press, 2000.
Salter, James. *Light Years*. New York: Vintage International, 1995.

Sappho. *If Not, Winter: Fragments of Sappho*. Trans. Anne Carson. New York: Alfred A. Knopf, 2002.

———. *Sappho: A New Translation*. Trans. Mary Barnard. Berkeley: Univ. of California Press, 1986.

Schapiro, Mark. "Big Tobacco: Uncovering the Industry's Multibillion-Dollar Global Smuggling Network." *Nation*. May 6, 2002, 11–20.

Stefoff, Rebecca. *The Young Oxford Companion to Maps and Mapmaking*. New York: Oxford Univ. Press, 1995.

Stevenson, Robert Louis. "My First Book: *Treasure Island*." *Idler 6* (August 1894).

Tufte, Edward R. *Envisioning Information*. Cheshire, Conn.: Graphics Press, 1990.

———. *The Visual Display of Quantitative Information*. Cheshire, Conn.: Graphics Press, 1983.

———. *Visual Explanations: Images and Quantities, Evidence and Narrative*. Cheshire, Conn.: Graphics Press, 1997.

Turkov, Andrei, compiler. *Anton Chekhov and His Times*. Fayetteville: Univ. of Arkansas Press, 1995.

Turnbull, David. *Maps Are Territories: Science Is an Atlas*. Chicago: Univ. of Chicago Press, 1993.

Voigt, Ellen Bryant. "A Moment's Thought." In *The Flexible Lyric*. Athens: Univ. of Georgia Press, 1999.

Watelet, Marcel, ed. *The Mercator Atlas of Europe*. Oregon: Walking Tree, 1998.

Wilford, John Noble. *The Mapmakers*. Revised ed. New York: Alfred A. Knopf, 2000.

Wilkinson, Alec. "The Gift." *New Yorker*. November 25, 2002, 64–75.

Williamson, Alan. *Eloquence and Mere Life: Essays on the Art of Poetry*. Ann Arbor: Univ. of Michigan Press, 1994.

Wood, Denis. *The Power of Maps*. New York: Guilford, 1992.

Wood, James. *The Broken Estate: Essays on Literature and Belief*. New York: Random House, 1999.

Woolf, Virginia. *Mrs. Dalloway*. New York: Harcourt, Brace and World, 1925.

LEGEND

THE OCCASION to lecture to a room full of intensely attentive writers not only tolerant of, but receptive to, extended metaphors was provided by the MFA Program for Writers at Warren Wilson College, where this musing took its first form. The seeds of that lecture, "The Writer as Cartographer," had been planted over a decade earlier by John Noble Wilford's introductory and informative *The Mapmakers*, which he has since updated and revised. At about the same time, I stumbled upon Carl I. Wheat's monumental *Mapping of the Transmississippi West*. I was awakened to the discipline of critical cartography and several of its core concerns by Denis Woods's passionate *The Power of Maps*, which led me to Mark Monmonier and J. B. Harley, among many others. Gwen Diehn suggested and then helped create a visual aid called the tetra-tetra-flexagon (which, unfortunately, resists mass reproduction), and Michael Collier extended the invitation to teach at the Bread Loaf Writers Conference, where the delivery of the by-then revised lecture led to a number of other reading suggestions, including the work of Edward Tufte, as well as the opportunity, thanks to the enthusiasm of poet and editor Barbara Ras, to consider this longer form. Along the way, the lecture appeared in the anthology of Warren Wilson MFA faculty essays, *Bringing the Devil to His Knees: The Craft of Fiction and the Writing Life*. My thoughts about intuition, intention, and process have been stimulated and provoked by students as well as colleagues, and especially by contributors to another anthology, *The Story Behind the Story: 26 Stories by Contemporary Writers and How They Work*.

This contemplation of wayfinding comes from a man who is no stranger to disorientation and who, one Christmas shopping season, like a character in some implausible novel, resorted to navigating a particularly labyrinthine mall by making only left turns. Maps no doubt have greatest value to those of us who are most dependent on them. And so this book was written, assembled, and accumulated with substantial assistance provided by all the written work mentioned in the text and bibliography and by a great many people, chief among them Laura, my wife, whose insistence and encouragement are a true and steady compass, and our son, Reed, who more than anyone has trusted my ability to find our way through any number of landscapes. In the late stages, Jasmine Beach-Ferrara provided invaluable assistance in tracking down illustrations and securing permissions. For their inspiration, guidance, suggestions, and support, I also thank Joan Aleshire, Andrea Barrett, Charles Baxter, Marianne Boruch, Robert Boswell, Mary Brown, Sharon Bryan, Richard Chess, Robert Cohen, Bill and Sandy Fallon, Richard Gabriel, Amy Grimm, Judith Grossman, Samantha Hunt, Dorothy Kemp, Kathryn Liebowitz, Margot Livesey, Antonya Nelson, Steve Orlen, Charles Ritchie, Francis Sjoberg, Mary Pat Turchi, Pat Turchi, Ellen Bryant Voigt, and the students, faculty, and alumni of the MFA Program for Writers at Warren Wilson.

ILLUSTRATION CREDITS

3. Courtesy of Harold Warp Pioneer Village.
4. Courtesy of the Walters Art Museum, Baltimore.
5. Courtesy of Edward E. Ayer Collection, the Newberry Library, Chicago.
7. Courtesy of the Library of Congress.
8. Courtesy of Biblioteca Nazionale Marciana, Venice.
9. Reprinted by permission of the Washington Metropolitan Area Transit Authority.
10. From Jean Hugard and Frederick Braué's *The Royal Road to Card Magic* (New York: Harper, 1948), 114, reprinted in Edward Tufte's *Visual Explanations: Images and Quantities, Evidence and Narrative* (Cheshire, Conn.: Graphics Press, 1997).
11. Charles Ritchie's *Draped Chair,* published by Center Street Studio, Milton, Mass. © 1997 Charles Ritchie.
12. © 1999 Charles Ritchie.
15. Cheng-siang Chen's *Birthplaces of the 2,079 Ching Poets, 1644–1911,* in *An Historical and Cultural Atlas of China* (Hong Kong, 1975). Courtesy of Map Division, the New York Public Library, Astor, Lenox, and Tilden Foundations.
17. Courtesy of Universal Studios Licensing LLLP.
22. © 1992 Raven Maps and Images.
23. E. McD. Johnstone's *The Unique Map of California* (San Francisco, 1890). Courtesy of Map Division, the New York Public Library, Astor, Lenox, and Tilden Foundations.
24. Lee Ratcliffe's map from the November 1999 special issue of *Wildlife in North Carolina,* "Rivers of North Carolina." Published by the N.C. Wildlife Resources Commission. Base map © 1997 John Fels.
25. Gwen Diehn's *The Bovine Walk.* Graphite, watercolor, water soluble pastels, 7 in. x 17 in.
26. *Upside Down World* reprinted by permission. © 2003 Hema Maps Pty. Ltd.

29. Courtesy of Performance Education (www.performance-education.com).
30. Map reprinted with permission from S235 *Mountains and Rivers* by Johnson and Browning. © 2000 by Johnson and Browning, Celestial Arts, Berkeley, Calif. Available from your local bookseller, by calling Ten Speed Press at 800-841-2665, or by visiting www.tenspeed.com.
32. Courtesy of the Philadelphia Print Shop, Ltd.
33. Warren Wilson College campus map courtesy of Chris Jayne and Warren Wilson College.
34. Street Luging map © 2003 by Reed Turchi.
35. © The Saul Steinberg Foundation / Artists Rights Society (ARS), New York. Photograph by Ellen Page Wilson, courtesy of PaceWildenstein, New York.
36. Courtesy of Resource Games, Redmond, Wash.
38. From Kathryn Lasky's *The Librarian Who Measured the Earth*. Text © 1994 by Kathryn Lasky; Illustrations © 1994 by Kevin Hawkes. Reprinted by permission of Little, Brown.
40. Charles del Vecchio's *Plan of the City and Suburbs of New Orleans* (New York, 1817). Courtesy of Map Division, the New York Public Library, Astor, Lenox, and Tilden Foundations.
41. From U.S. Geological Survey.
42. Italo Calvino's table of contents from "How I Wrote One of My Books." Courtesy of the Oulipo.
43. RISK ® and © 2003 Hasbro. Used with permission.
44. MONOPOLY ® and © 2003 Hasbro. Used with permission.
46. Limited Edition Cel "Recipes" © 1987 Linda Jones Enterprises. Characters © 2003 Warner Bros.
47. Albrecht Dürer's *Man Drawing a Lute* from *Unterweisung der Messung*. Gedruckt zu Nuremberg: [s.n.], im 1525. Jar. *Institutiones Geometricos*. Spencer Collection, the New York Public Library. Photo: the New York Public Library / Art Resource, N.Y.

48. From Jean Dubreuil's *The Practice of Perspective* (London, 1743). Courtesy of the General Research Division, the New York Public Library, Astor, Lenox, and Tilden Foundations.

65–71. Fractal images courtesy of Paul Bourke.

71–73. From Galileo Galilei's *Sidereus nunciius.* Courtesy Science, Industry, and Business Library, the New York Public Library, Astor, Lenox, and Tilden Foundations.

74. Charles Ritchie's *Pegasus,* published by Center Street Studio, Milton, Mass. © 1999 Charles Ritchie.

75. From De Verulamio, vol. 1 of *Works of Francis Bacon,* 1620 edition. Courtesy of the General Research Division, the New York Public Library, Astor, Lenox, and Tilden Foundations.

76. Courtesy of Thomas Cooper Library, University of South Carolina.

ABOUT THE AUTHOR

Peter Turchi is the author of a novel, *The Girls Next Door,* and a collection of short stories, *Magician.* He has coedited, with Charles Baxter, *Bringing the Devil to His Knees: The Craft of Fiction and the Writing Life,* and with Andrea Barrett, *The Story Behind the Story: 26 Stories by Contemporary Writers and How They Work.* His fiction has appeared in *Ploughshares, Story,* and *Alaska Quarterly Review,* among other magazines. The recipient of North Carolina's Sir Walter Raleigh Award and a National Endowment for the Arts Fellowship Grant, he has taught in and directed the MFA Program for Writers at Warren Wilson College in Asheville, North Carolina, for over a decade.